Confessions from the Jumpseat

Confessions from the Jumpseat

T. Wendy Williams

NIA Publishing

Houston, Texas

Confessions from the Jumpseat

Published by
NIA Publishing
P. O. Box 228
5315-D FM 1960 West
Houston, TX 77069-4410
832-541-4989

ISBN: 0-9727864-0-6
LCCN: 2002096672
Edited by: Melvina Brandley and Eboni Wright
Cover Design by Juan del Fierro
First Edition - Third printing

Printed in the United States of America by Morris Publishing

ALSO BY T. WENDY WILLIAMS

I Laugh to Keep from Crying

Dedicated in memory of my cousin,
Kelwin Rashon Gordon
August 8, 1986 – November 16, 2002
&

The flight crews, families, friends, and
everyone affected by the tragedy of
September 11, 2001.

Once man has experienced flight,
He shall forever walk the earth
Gazing into the sky.
For he has discovered
What makes the birds sing.
---Author unknown

ACKNOWLEDGEMENTS

First and foremost I want to thank God. I want to thank all the inspirations and aspirations behind this novel. I want to thank my beautiful mother, Barbara J. Williams. She taught me how to use my imagination to take me places above and beyond my reach. I want to thank my father, Terry Williams who helped me out when times got tough. I want to thank my sister, Tawanna "Punkin," for getting all her friends to tell their friends about my novels. I want to thank my husband, Derrick Goodwill, for his patience and many words of encouragement. I want to give love and many thanks to my Grandparents, all of my Aunts, Uncles, Cousins, relatives, and friends I neglected to acknowledge in the first novel.

I want to thank my editors Melvina Brandley and Eboni Wright for fine tuning my words. I want to thank the following for promoting and getting me book signings; Dede Boone the young and outstanding publisher of the *Weekly Paramount*, the brothers and sisters at The Shrine Cultural Bookstore, Gwen and Willie Richardson at Cushcity.com, Evelyn Palfrey, Sara Freeman Smith, Tanya Montgomery and Cheryl Black of Beaumont, Texas. Emma Rogers at Black Images Book Bazaar in Dallas. A special thanks to the ladies of My Sister and Me Book Club, the ladies of Coffee, Tea & Read Book Club and Cover to Cover Book Club of Houston, Texas. A special thanks to the ladies and gentlemen at Hastings books for giving me my first book signing.

A special thanks to the following for allowing me to showcase my book at their events: Nicole Campbell of Gathering of Literary Minds, Lori B. Allen of Jack and Jill of America, Inc. (North Houston Chapter), and the Xi Gamma Omega Chapter of Alpha Kappa Alpha Sorority, Inc. (Oakland, CA.) Special thanks to my friend and PR girl Lisa Parker, good friend and future best-selling author, Monica K. Roberts (look out for *Capital Gains*). I want to thank St. Paul United Methodist Church and St. Luke United Methodist church for so much love. Last but not least I want to thank you, the reader, for fueling this muse inside of me and giving your input. If I can inspire, entertain, motivate and cultivate then I have fulfilled my purpose in life. Peace and many blessings.

Jumpseat: a seat where flight attendants sit for take-off and landing. It is on this very seat where some of the most intimate details of personal lives are revealed.

TABLE OF CONTENTS

Whitney's Time

First of all, let me tell you my definition of hell. Those of you in the airline industry will know what I'm talking about. Hell is a four-day trip on a hot, musty airplane. Hell is listening to a screaming baby cry from New York to Orlando. Hell is spending three nights in a strange hotel room, and staying a night in one overlooking a cemetery. Hell is having a passenger write you up after you refused to serve him his eighth miniature bottle of gin. Do I need to go on? Okay, hell is getting off an employee bus and seeing the front tire of your car on flat. Finally, hell is having this happen to you all in the same week. Now when I arrive home, the last thing I want to hear is the phone ringing.

"Yeah," I answer, obviously annoyed.

"Yeah?" It's my co-worker and fellow flight attendant, Roxy. "My, aren't we in a very talkative mood tonight."

"Roxy, didn't I just spend four days with you?"

"Yeah? And?"

"And, what could you possibly say to me now that you didn't say to me on the plane?" I ask.

"I am having a basement moment."

I find this very amusing, "Roxy Figueroa, I love you like a sister but do you know what time it is?"

"Yes."

"What time is it?"

"Oooh, listen at you."

"Roxy, what time is it?"

"It's Whitney's time."

"That's right. Every time I come home from a horrific four-day trip, I need at least one hour to myself. Right?"

"Right, but..."

"But. Here's what I suggest you do. Take a deep breath, count to ten, write down ten good things about yourself, and maybe just maybe, you will move out of the basement and on to the first floor. Get my purnt! I love you, adios and night, night."

I hang up and unplug the phone. My girl, Roxy, has a serious low self-esteem issue that she's dealing with at the moment. So forgive me, there are times when you just have to get a backbone and deal with it. Right now, I am looking for my D'Angelo CD and thirsting for a Calgon moment. After I undress, I turn on the faucet and adjust the temperature of the water. I then sit back and watch as it cascades like Niagara Falls into my huge garden-sized tub. The temperature is hot, but not scorching. I reach up and turn off the lights. I need no candles because I am very comfortable being in total darkness. I don't have to close my eyes, because the darkness allows me to clearly envision D'Angelo standing in front of me performing *How Does it Feel?* I am getting a bit carried away because I see all of him and not just the half that's shown on the music video. I laugh to myself and stop. Then I picture Dewayne. It's been eight years since I had an intimate moment with him. I will never forget that humid spring night. I was supposed to be at my Senior Prom. Instead, I ended up 45 miles away at a hotel in Galveston, overlooking the Gulf. I was 17 and Dewayne was 22. The Isley Brothers were playing and I remember the exact moment when my daughter, Déjà was conceived. It was precious, second only to the day she was born. Dewayne was not as fortunate as I was to be a part of it. A month before she was born, he was sentenced to ten years on drug possession charges. Because of a good discipline record, not to mention, a good lawyer, Dewayne is getting out in two weeks. To tell you the truth, I don't know how I feel about it. On the one hand, I am delighted because my daughter will have her father back. On the other hand, I am nervous because as soon as he gets out, I know he'll resume his lifestyle. Instantly, I stop thinking about Dewayne.

A smile emerges from my lips as I picture my daughter, Déjà. She is so precious, angelic, smart, and my greatest inspiration. One look at her sun kissed face and her almond-shaped eyes and I melt all over with love. I am so proud of myself. In spite of my rough childhood, I managed to become the mother I never had. I am consistent. I am dependable. I don't use drugs and I don't bed hop. My mother was only fifteen when she had me. And without missing a beat, she gave me away to my grandmother. Now, Grandma Nana was an alcoholic. She was unfit to keep a dog let along me. So I was shipped to my aunt Lola's house.

When she got tired of me, I went to Aunt Maxine's house. When she got tired of me, I went to Aunt Nita's house. Life looked good there, until Aunt Nita started bringing home a steady boyfriend. At 13 years old, I was tall, slender, and passed for a girl of 18. Males often took notice of me, and one evening when Aunt Nita wasn't around, her boyfriend took it upon himself to make a move on me. He didn't know that I could fight the way I did and I gave him a swift kick in the nuts. I knew that was it for me so I packed my things without confronting Nita and moved into my friend Nicolette's house. Nikki, as I prefer to call her, lived in the hood, and the hood was crawling with drug addicts. My mother was among them. I was ashamed to show my face at school because everybody knew my mother was a well-known addict. Mentally, I tried to distance myself from the situation, yet I put myself in a compromising position when I started dating Dewayne. Some days it got hard for me to look at myself in the mirror because I would ask myself, *"Whitney, how could you love a drug dealer? The same man who could have possibly sold your mother a crack rock?" Then I would answer, " Unlike your mother, Dewayne has been consistent and he has shown you true love. He took you off the streets and gave you a stable home, something you never had with your own mother."*

Every thing I learned about life I learned from Dewayne. He initially took on the role of a big brother to me. I was 16 when we met and I was impressed with his fast-paced lifestyle. If I needed anything all I had to do was page him.

At last, I get out of the tub feeling like a 120-pound prune. My hair is all wet but that's alright, I'll call my friend and hairdresser, Byron, first thing in the morning. As I plug up my phone and check my caller ID, I see the last call was from Edward Kelly, my co-worker and fellow flight attendant. He just called to see if I made it home safely. Eddie is very sweet like that. The second call was from Roxy. I already knew her situation. The third call was from Byron. I wonder what he wants? I pick up my phone and dial my call notes. I skip my other messages and go straight to Byron's message.

"Wanda Jean." I laugh when I hear the lisp of his baritone voice, and *Wanda Jean* is our nickname for each other. "Girl, Mama is tore up from the floor up, I am not feeling well, I must have that flu that's going around. Anyway, when you get my message, call me. Bye."

I immediately dial Byron's number and he answers the phone by the second ring.

"Hey Wanda Jean," he says. He makes it known he has caller ID. "I take it you got Mama's message."

"Yes Wanda Jean you picked a really good time to get sick. I need my hair done tomorrow."

"Slap a wig on it."

"See? You didn't have to go there."

I hear Byron cough.

"You hear how I sound and honey you ought to see how I look."

"Do you need me to bring you soup and crackers?"

"No, all I need is rest. Girl, I got so sick I had to turn away my clients. Nikki had to take up my slack."

"For real? Damn Wanda, I hope you don't have that virus."

"I just got the flu bitch, not HIV."

"Don't get snappy with me I can't help it if you're buck wild."

"Let's squash this conversation, okay?"

I laugh, "What am I going to do with you?"

"Honey just send a prayer up for Mama to get over this."

"Okay. I love you Boo. Get well."

"Before you go, have you talked to Dewayne?"

"Not since Sunday."

"When is he getting out?"

"On the 21st."

"That's two weeks away. Why haven't you told me? I could've gotten reservations at the Sky Bar."

"For what? A party?"

"No, for church," he says, facetiously, "Yes, I'm talking about a partay."

"I'll do something that's more on an intimate scale."

"I see what you have in mind."

"I'm talking about having a small gathering at his parent's house with just a few friends involved."

"Don't count me out. Anyway, how is your flight schedule for next week?"

"I work Monday through Thursday."

"Shit. Well for your hair's sake, let's hope I get over my illness before this Saturday."

"Will you squeeze me in?"

"Of course."

"Thank you Boo, I love you."

"Sure you do."

I laugh as I hang up the phone. I take a good look at myself in the mirror and let out a huge smile. It's now Whitney's bedtime.

In A Perfect World

As I stare at my wife's angelic face, I keep reminding myself; here is my college sweetheart and for the last five years, my backbone. In my mind, I am not feeling her. I am not feeling her at all. I am numb to her touch, and what's so f-ed up about it? You notice, I didn't use the curse word because I don't curse. I am the only son of a minister. But, anyway, as I was saying, my numbness with my wife has been an ongoing thing since day one of our relationship. I love my wife. I love her very much and in a "perfect world" a man is supposed to have feelings of intimacy for a woman. That's what I've been telling myself for the last 11 years. My life is a complicated one.

Since age 16, I always knew my fantasizing about hard and sweaty bodies would define my sexual preference. But I dared not give even the slightest indication that I had homosexual tendencies. I wanted to live up to everybody's expectations, especially my father's. I love him, I admire him, and the last thing I want to do is disappoint him. So, as a teenager, I played the role of dutiful son and ladies man. Although it shouldn't come as a big surprise, I even participated in sports. I was quarterback of my high school varsity football team and a member of the high school varsity track team.

It was after a track meet, in my 11th grade year that I got my world turned inside out. I will never forget Broderick Hines for as long as I live. That night after the track meet, I gave him a ride home. I really don't remember how the conversation began but we arrived at the topics of girls and oral sex. Then, out of the blue, he asked if I ever had a girl give me oral sex. I lied and told him yes, but he could see through me like glass. He asked me how did it feel? I didn't know what to tell him other than, it felt good. I remember, during the conversation, feeling myself rise at the thought of having oral sex performed on me. I looked at Broderick and he looked at me. The next thing I know, he's taking me to a whole different level. It was a level unmatched by any person. You see, Broderick was my first.

Since that night in my car, Broderick and I had a rendezvous seemingly every other week. I couldn't get enough of him and he definitely couldn't get enough of me. I was six months into the relationship with Broderick before I had my first encounter with a female. It just wasn't the same. To tell you the truth, I don't even remember the girl's name. Then, I meet my wife, and I put those feelings for other men on the back burner. I convinced myself, and everyone else, that I loved women. It worked for nine years. And boy did my mind and body pay the price for it. I was so depressed that I sought therapy from a shrink. I had to because during my freshman year in college I witnessed some "associates" of mine beat a gay guy to a bloody pulp. That could've been me. I knew immediately, I didn't want that to be my reality. To me, being gay is a never-ending battle. If you are gay, and black, you are constantly on the frontline. So, to keep my mind off my sorrows, I took medication, mainly antidepressants. Then Scottie comes along.

I met Scottie Van Buren on a Super Bowl Sunday about two years ago in the men's restroom of a popular sports bar. We were both standing at the urinals and I noticed him glancing at my penis. He didn't try to hide it. We didn't say anything to each other. But, I noticed, inside the bar, I couldn't keep my eyes off his exotic looking features. He had a nice, chiseled, honey-bronzed face and dark, confrontational eyes like that popular wrestler, *The Rock*. And he had nice, succulent, kissable lips like the rapper, LL Cool J. He was wearing a fitted, deep forest green shirt that outlined huge, upright, pectorals and not to mention the ripples of his abs. He must have been from the tropics or heaven itself because he was absolutely gorgeous.

Those feelings that were once put on the back burner began to resurface. After the game, I watched him like a hawk as he made his way to the billiards. Shortly afterwards, I joined him. We talked about the game while he racked the balls. I found out his name and what he did for a living. I got an adrenaline rush when he told me he worked as a 737 pilot with Worldwide Airlines. I ended up spending the night with him and I remember waking up the next morning in his arms. My God! That felt like the most natural thing in the world. I belonged with Scottie. He allowed me to get back in touch with myself. I wanted to be with him so much that I quit my job and became a flight attendant. Everyone thought I was crazy for leaving a nice, masculine job and settling for a job as a flight attendant, a job dominated by women and known to attract its fair share of gay men. My father more than the rest of the family, went through the roof. He didn't speak to me for a week. After I told him about all the perks he'd receive, his attitude did a 360° and it was "Welcome home, my long lost son."

My wife never expresses it verbally, but her actions indicate to me she is still not happy with my decision to become a flight attendant. She doesn't understand how desperately I needed a drastic change in scenery. My job as assistant coach of the junior varsity football team was wearing me thin. Besides, if I continued teaching, I would have ran the risk of seriously harming someone's child. Kids nowadays don't play with the same heart or intensity as kids did back in my day. So my transition from football coach to flight attendant was the best decision I ever made. And besides, when your nose is wide open the way mine is behind Scottie, you would make a transition as well.

As my wife and I lie in bed, I stare at her face once more. She is awake now and staring at the ceiling. I can tell something is bothering her. So, I give her a kiss.

"Brooke, is every thing okay?" I ask.

"Yes, every thing's fine," she sighs.

I listen to the tone of her voice. Her voice is anything but okay.

"Are you sure?"

"Edward, when are you going to find a real job?"

Here we go with this again. "What are you talking about baby? I have a real job."

She sighs again, "I'm tired of making all the money in this house."

"Brooke, baby, you talk as if we are falling on hard times. My job pays quite a few bills in this house, and if I'm not mistaken, there's enough left over to buy the groceries too."

"Eddie, there is no stability in the airline industry. Baby, can you honestly see yourself doing this in ten years?"

I think about Scottie and all the great times we have.

"Yes, I can."

She shakes her head and gets out of bed to put on her silk, turquoise Victoria's Secret robe

"I can't believe it. My being a flight attendant still bothers you?"

"And honey it's not only the money but every time I turn on the television I hear about a plane crash. Eddie, I'm just afraid for you, that's all."

"Trust me, if anything happens, you will be well endowed."

Brooke disappears into the bathroom. I close my eyes and think about Scottie. I'm wondering what he's doing at this moment. He and I usually bid our flight schedules to have the same days off. Today is Friday and we are supposed to have lunch.

Since it is my day off, I am the designated chauffeur for my wife. Brooke and I ride comfortably in silence to her job at Shell, where she works as a marketing executive.

"So what are your plans?" she asks.

"After a much deserved rest, I may do a little yard

work. You know with a real job you don't have that luxury."

She smiles slightly. Her dewy skin is a radiant perfection of caramel and milk chocolate.

"I'll call you, and if I'm not too busy we'll have lunch or something," she says before giving me a kiss.

"You do that and if I don't answer I'm probably still outside working on the lawn."

"Just put your pager on."

"Brooke you know I can't work in the yard with the pager hooked to me."

"Yes you can. I'll call you." She shuts the door.

"Okay honey." I respond in defeat.

I watch as she struts her 5 feet 5 inch frame into the building. I feel myself rising. It's strange, but at the same time, it's supposed to be a natural reaction.

***

Scottie opens the door and greets me in a pair of silk boxers, "What's up?" I ask, before I walk inside.

"I just woke up," Scottie replies as he turns and swaggers through his large, spacious living room and into the den. I watch and my mouth waters. *Lord give me strength.*

Inside the den, the channel is on *BET* of all stations, and on the television is D'Angelo of all people. Every time I watch that video I have to relieve myself. D'Angelo's body is like a work of art, a sculpture to be exact.

I sit down and watch as Scottie nonchalantly flips through the channels, "Today just might turn out to be a good day. I sold 1,000 shares of my tech stock at 55 dollars each."

"Not bad, so what toy are you planning on buying today?"

"I'm going to use some of it for a down payment on a Harley."

I've known Scottie long enough to know that money leaves his hands as quickly as it comes into them. He's a big spender. His home is a testament to the fact. His fetish for vintage cars is another testament. In his garage, as I speak, is a cobalt blue 1965 Jaguar, a black 1969 Lincoln sedan with suicide doors, and a charcoal gray 1982 Corvette Stingray.

"A Harley as in Harley-Davidson?"

"Yeah, I always wanted one."

Scottie reminds me so much of a 33 year-old kid, whose background mirrors my own. Scottie grew up in a biracial home with a Caucasian father who was strong and demanding and who took pride in his only son's well being. His mother was Polynesian and the object of her son's affection. As a teenager, Scottie hid his sexuality from himself and everybody else. Unlike myself, he dealt with it on a different emotional level. Hiding it didn't affect him one bit. Not even as an officer in the military. He told me he had a field day in the military. He told me he was amazed at the number of gay men he came across who were in the closet. Then, like myself, he tried his hand at marriage, only to see it fall apart one year later.

"Scottie, why don't you take the money and invest it in another area of your portfolio?"

"Eddie, my portfolio is heavily invested as it is. If every thing goes right I expect to sell my 1,000 shares in Worldwide tomorrow. Our stock is at $40 and that's the highest it's ever been."

"That's quite a leap." I said, "I may sell my shares and start a scholarship at my old high school."

"Maybe later. Right now all I can see is you, me, and my Harley."

"What is the deal with pilots and Harleys?"

"To me, a Harley symbolizes adventure. An untamed wildness, so to speak."

"Wildness is right." I respond.

"Once you mount a Harley, you feel like the *king of the road*. Everything around you is obsolete. It's just you, your Harley and the golden sunset."

I picture Scottie riding down the freeway in black

leather pants, rusty cowboy boots, a white muscle shirt, and black leather gloves. I smile to myself.

"What are you smiling about?" He asked.

Without saying a word, I stand up and make myself at home as I have done countless times before. I take off my shoes and my shirt and expose my own chiseled down physique. I'm no D'Angelo but I'm pretty darn close. Besides, it's good enough to get Scottie's mind off the Harley.

"Scottie go jump in the shower. I can smell your butt way over here," I said jokingly. Actually, the house smells like a garden of fresh potpourri. Scottie turns off the T.V. and sniffs under his arms.

"I thought you liked the smell of musk." He replied, and with another remote he turned on the stereo. My ears are in tuned with the opening chords of Frankie Beverly and Maze's *Happy Feelings*. The surround sound gives the room a lively feel and the bass line from the music is radiating all through my body.

Scottie and I come together for a soft, sweet and gentle kiss. I must tell Brooke the truth. My two-way pager goes off, while vibrating furiously against my right hip. Scottie releases me from his strong embracing arms. I lift the pager to view my message. It's Brooke paging me for lunch.

Stuck In the Basement Blues

I always know when I am beginning to reach my lowest point. First, things don't go the way I plan. I lose control of the situation and my roller coaster of emotions plummets. My friend, Whitney, tells me I need an hour to myself. To do what? To think more in-depth of how screwed up my life really is? Pa-lease, what I really need right now is a .38 to locate that no-good, poor excuse of a man I call Walter Nunnley. I priority paged him 15 times this morning. Now what could he possibly be doing at 10:00 am on a Saturday morning? I pick up the phone and page him again. At that moment I hear no dial tone, only silence.

"Hello?" I ask in a semi-sexy voice.

"Are you okay?"

I smile like Miss America at the sound of Walter's sexy voice on the other end.

"Hi baby. I was just about to page you again. Where have you been this week?"

"You don't listen, do you?"

"Yes, I listen. The question is, do you listen? I told you before you left to page me as soon as you get to wherever it was you were going."

"I did."

I hold my cellular phone to my face and scroll my incoming calls. I see no recent calls from Walter.

"When, Walter?"

"I called you Monday night."

I scrolled again. I see nothing from Walter. "Are you sure?" I asked.

"I'm positive."

"Where are you now?" I looked at my caller ID and

saw *Unknown caller, unknown number*.

"I'm in Miami."

"When are you coming home?"

"Tomorrow. I'll call you as soon as I get in."

"Are you rushing me?" I asked

"Yes, I have a meeting."

"On a Saturday morning, Walter?"

"Of course. Today is the last day."

"And you can't hop on the plane and come home tonight?'

"No, I'm having dinner with the VP of Royal Airlines."

"Can you talk about it?"

"I'll tell you when I get in tomorrow."

"Stop by and see me before you go home."

"I'll call you."

"Bye, Walter."

He hung up without saying goodbye. I hate it when he does that. I almost pick up the phone and page him again, but he's had enough pages in one day to last him through the rest of the month.

I open my bedroom window and it's pouring down rain outside. I hate days like this when Walter isn't around. Houston can be the loneliest place in the world when you don't have a man beside you. The only reason I moved to this God-forsaken place is because Walter helped me land a job with Worldwide Airlines. Before this gig, I worked for a charter airline based out of Atlanta called Georgian Airways. It catered to corporations throughout the U.S., and I was on a flight from New York City when I met Walter. My first impression when I saw him? Wicked, and I mean that in the best way. Walter stepped onboard with a Louis Vuitton garment bag draped over his shoulder, and a navy Giorgio Armani suit covering his tall, masculine frame. His skin was chocolate, in the purest form. His salt and pepper goatee was trimmed neatly around his full lips. The minute our eyes met, I knew he and I were going places. During the flight, he didn't hesitate to come into my galley. Usually I don't allow that to happen, but ask me if I minded this time? Hell no! He told me to forgive him for being unprofessional, but he could not live with himself if he didn't get my number. I checked out his wedding finger to see if any ring was present. Yes, there was but I didn't let it stop me. Shit, I never do! Walter was good as mine. We didn't beat around the bush. After dinner at the Palm Restaurant, he invited me back to his room. I made no qualms regarding how I felt about him and how he made my body feel. I didn't hold back. We mated exquisitely.

During moments like this, when he's giving me the cold shoulder, I look back on that night and say, *Roxy, chick, you should have waited.* But Walter still gave me his pager and cell phone numbers. And, for a week, he still called to see how I was doing. He invited me to spend a couple of days with him in Houston. He even went as far as getting me a job at the airline where he works and an apartment. That's not something you do for just anybody. I don't know. Somewhere along the way, he lost interest. Nowadays, if I don't do most of the calling, and if I don't make the plans, nothing gets done. I hate that! So what if he has a wife!

My phone rings. I glance at the ID box and see it's Whitney calling me from her cell phone.

"Oh! Now after two days you feel like talking," I said, after I pick up the phone.

"You know the routine."

"Where are you?"

"I just left my hairdresser and I'm on my way to the mall. I was calling to see if you wanted to go."

"I'm still in bed."

"Get your little behind out of the bed. What's the matter? You still have that stuck in the basement blues?"

"I did earlier. But, I feel better now."

"Why? Walter called?"

"Yes, Chick. He's coming home tomorrow."

"Say what? Where is he?"

"In Miami. He said he paged me Monday."

"Ummm, hmmm," I hear her respond, skeptically.

"Anyway, it's raining outside. Why are you going to the mall in all this?"

"I have to allow myself enough time to find something for Dewayne's welcome home party."

"Get out of here, he's getting out?"

"Yes, next Friday."

"It's on now girlfriend," I say, picturing Whitney's wide smile.

"You and I need to piece together a unit to wear."

"I'm down. Just give me enough time to get dressed."

"I'm going to drop off Déjà at Dewayne's parent's house, I'll be there in one hour."

"I need more than a hour."

"Oops, excuse me! I lost my head! What was I thinking?" Whitney shouts.

"It's evident you don't know who you're speaking to."

"My bad, Ms. Jennifer Lopez."

"Don't get it twisted."

"Call me on my cell after you've finished."

I hang up and immediately dial the automated number to my checking account. The operator tells me that I only have a balance of $50.56. What in the hell can I get with $50.56? Immediately I get depressed. I need money in the worst way. My credit cards are all maxed out, Walter is tripping and life couldn't get any worse for me. I just hope, wherever we go, I can open a new account. Yeah, I'll do that.

***

When Whitney and I walk into Saks Fifth Avenue, I see a pair of Prada shoes available for $425.00.

"Omigosh, those are so cute!" I say, as I try on the display shoe and examine it in the mirror. Whitney picks up a

Prada shoe in another style. She drops it to the floor and puts her slender foot inside.

"Just because I'm digging the Prada doesn't mean you can," I say.

"I don't like it anyway," she says, before putting it back on the shelf.

I take a second look at the shoe on my left foot, it's too square and boxed in. It's more a winter shoe than a spring shoe. I place the shoe back on the display shelf and pick up a pair of Fendi mules.

"Whitney, do you have any idea what you're wearing for Dewayne's welcome home party?"

"Not really."

"You have to wear something sexy. That man hasn't touched you in almost ten years."

"Yes he has," she says, through a smile.

"When? Where?"

"He touched my thighs once during visitation."

I laugh, "just once?"

"Yeah?"

"That's really tender," I say, "and what did the guards say?"

"Dewayne was smooth. Whenever they had their backs turned, he'd put his hand on my thigh. Anyway, stop talking about it."

"You are getting hot chick, I see you blushing."

As we stroll through the store, I notice quite a few heads turn. Not because of our conversation, but because of the way we look. Whitney, as always, is dressed from head to toe in the latest designer fashions. Her shoulder length, silky, black hair bounces carelessly when she walks. Her toasted-almond complexion is radiant in M.A.C. She's about 5 feet 10, 125 pounds soaking wet, and slightly bow-legged. Her behind is not too big and she's shaped like a supermodel. Myself, on the other hand, I'm 5 feet 6, I weigh about 130 pounds, and most of it is ass. A lot of people mistake me for

Jennifer Lopez, which is why they do a double take when they see me. To tell you the truth, Jennifer Lopez and I have some things in common. We are both from South Bronx, except I relocated to Connecticut when I was adopted at age five. We are both Puerto Rican, and like Jennifer once was, I am involved in a relationship with a flashy, arrogant (mistaking for confident) black man. I just wish I had her funds right now.

After three hours, Whitney and I leave the mall. I am broke, yet I am in good spirits. I just put $600.00 on a brand new Saks card.

"All that shopping has me hungry," Whitney says once we get inside the car.

"I don't have any money," I say. "So take my broke ass home."

"I'll treat this time," she starts up the car and puts in her latest Mary J. Blige CD. "Lets go to Wings-n-Things."

Good. I say to myself, *I'd rather have Buffalo wings than a peanut butter and jelly sandwich any day.*

Desperate People...Desperate Things

Roxy and I stroll through the airport terminal like runway models in our charcoal gray uniforms with the single, platinum stripe. For me, this is the glamorous part of the job. I always make sure my uniforms are dry-cleaned for every trip and my shoes are polished. I make sure my nail polish is either clear or garnet, and my dress is cut just a little below the knee. I remember one of my elementary teachers say that a woman should not show the back of her knees. I always take her words to heed, not that my knees look bad, but because it presents a classier look. Now Roxy, on the other hand, bends the dress code over backwards. To her, the shorter the better. I'm surprised a supervisor hasn't brought it to her attention.

Today she's quiet. I wonder what happened between her and Walter so I ask, "Did you see Walter last night?"

"I don't want to talk about him."

"He didn't show up," I respond.

"I hate a liar," she says, "I paged him ten times and put sixty-nine in it, and he still didn't call."

"Roxy, that man has a wife he's not worried about you."

"That's lame."

"Roxy, may I suggest something to you?"

"What?"

"Get your own man."

We walk in silence for a few steps.

"I've tried but nobody even comes close to Walter."

"That's nonsense. What about the attorney fellow you met on the plane last month who had the roses sent to the hotel?"

"I went out on one date with the man and guess what

he picked me up in?"

I flash my eyes to prepare for Roxy's outrageous response, "What?"

"A Chevy Cavalier."

"What's wrong with a Chevy Cavalier, Roxy?"

"He's too damn cheap and he thought that just because I ordered lobster and a bottle of Dom Perignon I'm supposed to give him something. Not no, but helll no!"

"You know what your problem is...you're too superficial."

"And I've got a right to be. Whitney, this skirt doesn't come up for any man who thinks he can get by with a little coochie and a smile. A brother has to come correct and Walter is the only one who can."

"I don't see how you do it, somebody else's man is not my idea of a healthy relationship."

"Oh, and your man being in prison for eight years is?"

"At least he's mine."

"I don't know, he could be Big Rob's man in cell block four."

I can do nothing but laugh at that last remark. "You go to hell and send Walter with you. Anyway, as I mentioned earlier, you meet too many men in this industry. Find somebody else."

"But I can't find anyone else."

"Come on Roxy, as beautiful as you are."

"But Walter makes me feel good."

"In what way besides sexually?" I ask.

Roxy couldn't think of a quick answer.

"That's what I thought."

"He provides for me emotionally."

"In a negative way."

"Sometimes, but not all the time."

When Roxy and I board the plane, we notice Eddie sitting in the first row of first class. He's reading a newspaper and sipping on coffee.

"Good morning Eddie, I hope you had a pleasant weekend?" I ask, as I place my suitcase in the overhead bin.

"It was okay."

"How's Brooke?"

"She's fine."

I notice Eddie's uniform is starch-ironed. His black, winged-tip shoes are so shiny that I can almost see my reflection in them. Eddie is very clean-cut too. His complexion reminds me of rich, creamy, peanut butter. He has no sign of facial hairs and his skin is as smooth as a baby's bottom. He has large doe-like eyes and thick eyebrows, not to mention long eyelashes. He kind of reminds me of a light-skinned Tupac Shakur.

The Captain and first-officer arrive at the same time. They tell me their names but I forget. I had flown with the Captain before and he was very nice. Initially, the first-officer comes across as cool. The Captain gathers us together in the forward galley of the 737 for a crew briefing. In the crew briefing, we discuss everything from evacuation signals to how many knocks you use before you're allowed to enter the cockpit. I take every safety-related issue to heart and since I always fly the lead position, I'm left in charge. After the briefing we take our posts. Roxy sets up the first class galley, I am the door greeter, and Eddie works the aft galley. Together, we try to be quite professional. But, sometimes a flight can get incredibly boring after three-and-a-half hours. So, we usually gather in the aft galley, shut the curtains, and try to talk as quietly as possible.

The first five passengers board and I greet each one. The first is a Caucasian man who appears to be in his mid to late 50's. He's dressed in Hugo Boss and only carries a leather briefcase. I love business travelers. That's why I prefer working weekdays instead of weekends. Business travelers know the routine and they don't bring a lot of luggage. Now don't get me wrong, you may have a few business travelers that pack every thing from the house into the overhead bins, but the majority of the passengers are alright in my book.

I pick up my hand-held microphone and begin sharing travel instructions with our passengers.

"Good morning ladies and gentlemen and welcome onboard Worldwide Airlines flight 411 with non-stop service to New York City's LaGuardia Airport. For those passengers just arriving, all carry-on bags must be stowed either underneath the seat in front of you or in the overhead bins."

I give the passengers a moment to let my announcement sink in. Sometimes I say something humorous just to make sure they're listening.

"To those passengers seated at the exit rows, please take a moment to review the safety information card in the seat pocket in front of you. You will be tested on the material just prior to take-off. The passenger with the highest score will receive a complimentary, round-trip coach ticket to any destination Worldwide Airlines flies within the continental United States."

I hear Roxy laugh. "You are so crazy," she says, before pouring a can of Bloody Mary mix into a cup filled with ice. She then garnishes the drink with a stick of celery. "You better stop it."

"That's the only way they'll pay attention."

I give the tomato-smelling drink to the gentleman wearing the Hugo Boss suit. Next to him sits another Caucasian gentleman in his late 50's. He's dressed more casual and he's not wearing a tie.

"May I get you something to drink, sir?" I ask, in a pleasant voice.

He takes a look at the gentleman's drink sitting next to him. "I'll have a Bloody Mary, and will you let me mix my vodka?" He replies, in a dialect typical of New Yorkers.

"Sure," I smile in his face. My smile disappears quickly when I turn my face to the first class galley, "Roxy, I'll take a Bloody Mary and don't mix in the vodka."

"Vodka at 9:30 in the morning?" Roxy whispers.

"I think we have a potential alcoholic on our hands," I whisper back.

Prior to taking him a drink, I check on the pilots to make sure they're all right.

"Hi guys, you need anything to drink?" I ask.

"I'll take a cup of black coffee," replies the Captain.

"And I'll take an orange juice, with no ice," says the first-officer.

"Great. Did you hear that Roxy?"

"Loud and clear," she says as she pours the coffee.

Boarding is the hardest part of the process. Our company expects us to serve pre-departure drinks to our first-class passengers. They expect us to hang up their coats. We are expected to double-check with catering to make sure they provide us an adequate amount of meals. We have to make sure there are no duplicate seats. We have to make sure there are no children sitting at the exit rows. We have to assist passengers with bags. We have to get an accurate count of passengers. Wait, there's more. We have to try to get the main-cabin door closed at least five minutes before departure. Glamorous isn't it?

Before the main-cabin door is closed, Eddie and I double-check our passenger count. The Airport Service Agent awaits an okay from the Captain. The Captain turns and looks at me.

"Whitney, are you ready?" He asks.

"Yes, I am." I reply.

The Captain then gives the thumbs up and the agent shuts the door. I pick up the microphone. "Okay flight attendants, prepare your doors for departure and cross check."

Roxy and I cross check our doors to make sure the floor brackets are in place and the doors are properly sealed. Eddie joins us in the forward galley with his safety demonstration seat belt in hand.

"It's showtime!" he says.

"Eddie give me a few minutes, I'm trying to clean up my galley." Roxy says. She's putting away the remainder of her soft drinks. We don't offer to help because Roxy won't allow you to. Her galley is totally off-limits and if you find yourself crossing that boundary, she'll let you know in a heartbeat.

Eddie glances at his Gucci watch, and glances at me with his large light-brown eyes. He doesn't know it, but he looks so sexy.

"One minute to showtime," he says to Roxy.

With that Roxy deliberately takes her time. They constantly bicker back and forth to each other, but its all done out of love.

"Thirty seconds," he says.

"All right! All right!" Roxy secures her galley and grabs her demonstration equipment. She then gives Eddie a playful nudge and stands in front of her first-class passengers. For a morning crowd, they are a rowdy bunch and I can hardly hear myself speak. I stop in mid-sentence and wait until they stop. I hear Roxy shush them.

"Thank you," I say before I proceed with my safety demonstration monologue. Any time we go to New York City, I can always count on a rowdy, aggravated, fast-paced, needy crowd. I want this! I want that! There is almost never a quiet moment. After I do my safety demonstration monologue I do what they call in the airline industry a "compliance check". I take a good look at each passenger and make sure he or she has his or her seatbelt fastened, tray table up, seatback up, and bag pushed completely underneath the seat. What makes me angry is that I make an announcement for everyone to do this, but you still find those few who either don't listen or they're just too stubborn to do what you tell them to do.

About two hours into the flight, during one of our breaks, Roxy comes to our back galley as her usual bitchy self.

"What's wrong now?" I ask. This was the third time for her.

"I am about to go crazy up there!" she says, before helping herself to a couple of miniature vodkas.

"You're a native New Yorker. You can handle it," Eddie says.

She gives Eddie the finger.

"What do you want me to do about it?" I ask.

"Nothing!" she snaps, as she searches for another miniature bottle.

"Nothing?" I ask.

"Again Whitney, read my lips…Absofuckinglutely nothing!" she throws back the curtain and charges down the aisle.

"It's evident, Walter isn't showing the girl any love," Eddie says, before he sits back down on the flight attendant jumpseat. Whatever Roxy says or does, doesn't surprise us any more. Eddie and I have come to the realization that she is a "drama queen," but we still love her nonetheless.

"The girl has low self esteem."

"I agree."

"She's a beautiful girl and she's smart. Her problem is that she doesn't even know it."

"Whitney, I came up with this conclusion in training," Eddie says.

"What?"

"Roxy wishes she were you."

"Get out of here."

"Don't act like you don't know," he says.

"How did you arrive at that conclusion?"

"By observation," he says.

"I'd like to hear this observation," I say, as I turn sideways and fold my arms.

"Number one, she tries to dress like you, and we both know the girl can barely pay her rent."

"Tell me about it."

"She tries to have your demeanor, but come on, we know she can't help the way she is, although she tries so hard."

"Go on," I say.

"Number three, she'd rather have your man instead."

I laugh, "Now you've gone out in left field."

"I'm serious so trust me. Whenever Dewayne gets out, you watch her."

"Roxy wouldn't go that far."

"Never underestimate her. She's a desperate case and desperate people do desperate things."

"She ain't crazy," I say, while at the same time I picture her trying to flirt with Dewayne.

"She's a little bit of that too," Eddie says, through a chuckle.

Later that evening, after we arrive at our hotel near the theater district, we change clothes and catch the number three subway uptown to Harlem. Eddie and I had been talking about Sylvia's on the jumpseat, and I couldn't wait to sink my teeth into a smoking hot, tender, juicy, piece of fried chicken. Of course, Roxy tags along for dramatic purposes. She claims she's on a diet, I don't know what for. If it's her behind she's trying to lose, she's only fooling herself. The rest of her *outer* appearance is flawless.

We arrive to a packed house and the hostess informs us of our fifteen-minute wait. Eddie and I don't mind the wait but Roxy impatiently sucks her teeth.

"Don't get me wrong, I have much love for Sylvia, but she ain't worth the wait."

"Bye." Eddie waves her off, "I thought you were on a diet anyway."

"I am," Roxy says, before she retrieves her cell phone to punch in Walter's number. I assume it's Walter's number because I don't know if she has any more friends besides Eddie and myself.

"Hi, this is Jennifer Rice from Royal Airlines. Is Walter Nunnley there? May I speak to him?"

Jennifer Rice? I know she doesn't have to lie and say she's someone else just so she can speak to Walter. That is so pathetic. Just down right pathetic! I steal a glance at Eddie to see if he's paying attention but he's busy staring at a large collage of famous faces. I glance back at Roxy and watch as she shifts her weight to one side in anticipation of talking to Walter.

"Walter, this is Roxy. What happened last night? No, I will not hold. The last time I did, your secretary answered and said you were gone to lunch."

Eddie and I wanted to laugh so badly. Poor thing.

"I don't know what your problem is but you better get it together."

I'm sorry, if Walter hadn't gotten it together by now, chances are he never will.

"Walter, I don't ask for very much, all I ask is that you spend a little more time with me…but you tell me the same thing…I'm tired of you talking about it, hell, just do it!"

"Hey, hey, please spare me and the rest of Harlem all the gory details," Eddie says.

But Roxy's not hearing it. She goes on and on for the next fifteen minutes, telling Walter things I'm sure he already knows and really wouldn't care to hear from her. By now she's built an audience and Eddie and I are trying to pretend she doesn't exist.

"Don't tell me you're having to use an alias in order to communicate with your man now," Eddie says, once we're seated.

"Eddie stay out of my business, I am really not in the mood for your sarcastic shit okay?"

Eddie, in a calm and aloof manner, holds up his hands, "I'm sorry Jennifer, I mean Roxy."

I try not to laugh but it's getting harder by the minute.

"I'm not taking any more of his shit."

"What? Are you're leaving?" I ask.

"Yes."

"That's the smartest thing I've heard you say all day." I respond and hold up my hand to give her a high five, but she wasn't in the mood to return it.

"So how long is this going to last?" Eddie asks, "You said you were leaving three months ago and you didn't."

"This time I mean it, I'm moving the hell away from Houston."

"Really?" I ask. My facial expression reveals how I truly feel.

"Yes, and don't look at me like that." Roxy picks up on it.

"Like what?" I ask.

"Like you don't believe me."

"Because I don't."

"Some friend you are."

"That's right, and only a true friend will tell you the truth," I say, as I watch the waitress approach the table asking us for our drink orders. I order a Diet-Coke, Eddie orders a Sprite, and Roxy a Diet-Coke.

"Walter thinks he has it all figured out but I got a few tricks up my sleeves as well," Roxy says, playing with the keys on her phone pad. I think back to what Eddie says about desperate people doing desperate things.

"Roxy, as my father used to say, don't let your mouth write a check that your butt can't cash," Eddie says while eyeing the glass of Sprite the waitress places before him.

"And what is that corny shit supposed to mean?"

"Don't set yourself up for failure," Eddie says, in a serious tone.

"I don't have to worry about that," Roxy says with an air of confidence that convinces even the most skeptical of skeptics.

"Rock on with your bad self," Eddie says, "I want to propose a toast to my dear friend, Roxy and her quick recovery over Walter."

"Cheers." I respond before sipping my Diet-Coke. In my mind, I'm wondering just how long she'll last.

No Sign of A Cure

In the midst of packing my things I hear my doorbell ring. I glance at my watch and it's 9:30 in the evening.

"Who is it?" I ask, aggravated and pissed.

"It's me!"

"Your key doesn't work?"

Damn. Quickly, I glance at myself in the mirror, I wasn't expecting Walter to show up and that's another thing I hate about our relationship. It's always on his terms. When I want to see him, I go through great lengths to make sure I look and smell good for him. Most of the time I end up spending the night alone. Now when I'm hot and sweaty, like now and when I least expect it, he shows up. I untie the ribbon from my hair and let my golden brown hair fall just below my shoulders. I take one last look at myself in the mirror, and before I open the door I say to my reflection, *Roxy, chick this is it. Leave him alone and move on.* I open the door to find Walter standing before me dressed to the nines in a short-sleeved, white linen shirt and navy polo slacks. His sexy and hairy chest is exposed, and he is armed with a single red rose and a sexy smirk.

"Don't just stand there, give your man a kiss," he says. His teeth are gleaming like a new set of ivory piano keys.

"Walter, take your tired, little trifling rose and go somewhere else with that, okay?"

I notice a look of shock flashing across his middle-aged chocolate face, "I apologize, I must have the wrong address. I'm going to walk out this door," he turns and swaggers out the door, "and when I return, the lady I see before me now better not open it, or it's going to be hell to pay. Now close the door and let's try this again."

"Come in Walter." I mumble.

"I can't hear you. What did you say?" he asks, trying to sound serious.

"I said, Come in, dammit."

"That's what I'm talking about." He walks in and gives me a kiss on the neck. It's one of those kisses that stops you dead in your tracks and you can't help but shed your panties afterwards. Which is exactly what I find myself doing. Not even three minutes after he walks in, he tosses the rose in the air, grabs me like I'm an inanimate object, and spreads me like jam on top of the kitchen counter.

"Walter stop. I need to take a shower."

"No you don't. I like it when it's sweaty like this." He huffs as he's breathing, panting, and lapping between my thighs like a thirsty dog who hadn't anything to drink in five days. I try to lay there and pretend like I'm not enjoying it, but next to rocky road ice cream, there's nothing better to me than Walter's tongue. It has a mind of its own. I try to reach over and turn on the faucet, with Walter's face still buried in the valley, and make an attempt to douse myself with cold water. I can no longer muffle the excitement built up inside of me and I suddenly hear myself scream out Walter's name. Like a steamy love scene, our bodies move in salsa-like motions until we find ourselves lying on the cold ceramic tile floor. Walter removes his shirt, slacks, and briefs in one swift motion, and exposes me to his rich, dark chocolate temple of a body. The very sight of it renders me speechless.

"You like it when I fuck you don't you...yeah, you talk all that shit about leaving me, now look at you...you can't leave this dick...you love this dick, don't you! DON'T YOU!"

"Yes!" I scream.

"I know damn well you do! I got your ass dick-whipped!"

As I look into Walter's face and see him glaring down at me. I say to myself, he's right; I do have a bad case of the she's gotta have it syndrome, and there is no sign of a cure in sight. As we wallow around the floor in the throngs of passion for some strange reason a song by Diana Ross comes to mind... *If there's a cure for this, I don't want it.*

"Is this what you've been paging me for?" he asks, with a thrust so powerful that it causes my body to arch with intensity. I am so entranced in our escapade of pleasure that I can no longer answer him.

"I can't hear you, what!" He shouts, towering over me in male domineering fashion.

"YES! YES!" I force myself to scream out.

"Girl that's what I want to hear!" He says, with a slight smile in his voice.

When we climax, and I come to my senses I am so disgusted with myself that I go into my bathroom, shut the door, and curse quietly at my reflection in the mirror. At times like these I wished I weren't born into the life I've come to know as my own. I never really knew my real parents, but I sometimes wonder if my mother was promiscuous. Or, if my daddy was a playboy or a philanderer, who left a string of babymama's everywhere. Since I was a little girl I have seen and felt dicks and pricks of all colors, shapes, and sizes. I've had two abortions and I even had a case of chlamydia. I am fine as long as I don't see the dick staring me in the face. But as soon as there's a handsome, tall, muscular frame attached to it, I go crazy and if the brother ain't funny with his money, then it's on. I have done so many things in my young life to rival women twice my age. But, it's a part of my life that I cannot change, no matter how hard I try. I am a freak, a whore, a slut, whatever you want to call it that's what I am and what amazes me is how tolerant I am of it. It doesn't bother me in the least bit. Some people call it an illness. I just call it a year, a month, a day in the life of one, Roxanna Maria Figueroa.

***

I should be immune to disappointments. Walter had

plenty to dish out at me. I remember the month after we met he promised to treat me to a day at the spa and dinner at Morton's. I got the spa treatment but when it came time for dinner Walter was a no-show. Another time he promised to pin on my flight attendant wings during the graduation ceremonies. When he didn't show up I was devastated. Whitney knew someone who worked for the airlines who pinned on her wings. Why didn't Walter show up to do something as simple and as meaningful as that for me?

"So are you going to unpack? Or, are you going through with your plans to leave?" Walter asks.

I take a minute before I answer, "What do you want me to do?" I ask.

"You do whatever you want. You're an adult capable of making your own decisions."

I hate it when he turns it around and I always end up answering my own questions. I want to hear what he has to say sometimes. "I don't know what I want to do, I want to hear what you think."

"You are always indecisive, you need to make up your own mind, I can't think for you Roxy."

I take one of the pillow shams and hit him across the head. "You don't ever just come out and say it do you?"

"Say what?" he asks.

"Just say whatever it is you want to say to me."

"Roxy, if you want to leave fine. If you want to stay I'd be more than willing to help with the rent."

"So it doesn't matter one way or the other to you if I leave or stay?"

"I didn't say it, you did."

"See, you're doing it again."

"Doing what?"

He knows damn well what he's doing and it frustrates the hell out of me.

"Just leave it alone, okay?" There's no sense in arguing with you."

"You are the one who's blowing everything out of proportion. I just asked you a question, Roxy." He leans over and proceeds to check the temperature of my forehead with the back of his hand. I quickly remove my face.

"It must be close to that time of the month," he says. "I can always tell because you're always temperamental."

"You make me so sick."

"Whoa, time out." Walter forms the time out "t" with his hands. I think I struck a nerve because he stops watching television to give me his undivided attention. I've had my fair share of black men to know that when they have to stop watching television to give you their attention, then you've messed up. Prepare for a drilling. Prepare to get your feelings hurt. That Ivy-League education way of reasoning that Walter uses so eloquently goes straight out the window and is quickly replaced with street-urban vernacular; attitude and all.

"I make you sick? Apparently not, because your funky ass is still here."

"I like being with you, Walter. What part of that don't you understand?"

"Didn't I tell you I'm a busy man? I am Vice President of Worldwide Airlines. I sit on five different boards and I travel forty-two weeks a year. I don't have time to devote to my marriage, let alone a relationship."

"So you have time to devote to sex?" I ask.

"I can get sex anywhere," he says with a smirk. "But remember, you and I came to an agreement, that whenever I had the time we could spend it here together. So stop complaining and start cherishing the moments I spend with you."

I didn't want to argue any more with him and I quickly change the tempo of the conversation.

"So how long are you in town?"

"Long enough for you to enjoy another round of me." He takes my hand to kiss it.

"Wow, I must feel like the luckiest girl in the world." I reply, sounding like a programmed robot.

"You got your man here to make love to you, just relax and enjoy the moment, baby."

He takes me into his arms and I try to embrace him in a nice, loving fashion, but it is so hard. It is so, so, hard.

It's All Coming Together Now...

Tears are on the brink of falling from my eyes as I watch my oldest sister, Countess, belt out the old gospel hymn, "I Surrender All." She grips the tune effortlessly over her plus sized frame with a powerhouse presence and an amazing range that gives Patti LaBelle and Aretha Franklin a run for their money.

As I sit there quietly taking in her sweet, angelic voice, I think back over my life and how I've deceived myself and everyone else. I want to come out and tell the world, especially my wife and father, that I'm not the man they think I am. Every day I think about it. The moment when I reveal to the world that Edward Mitchell Kelly, Jr. is a homosexual, living in the closet. I know a lot of people won't understand and I am willing to accept that. I am even more willing now to accept that my father will turn his back on me. Brooke will be angry, hurt, and will divorce me. I know a lot of harm will be done, but that's a situation I am willing to accept. I have to set myself free, because I feel like a bird, trapped in a cage. As tears fall freely down my cheeks, I try my hardest to pat them dry with my handkerchief. I look at the altar and see my father standing there with his right hand stretched out.

"Is there anyone here who feels burdened?" he asks, "You feel like the weight of the world is on your shoulders? God is the answer, surrender all to him."

I stand to my feet and raise both of my hands in praise. I want to go to the altar and confess, but a little voice inside of me is saying now is not the time. As my father continues to name all the reasons why you should surrender all to God, I hear that voice inside of me fading away and before I know it, I am joining my father at the altar. The expression on his face is that of a million questions. But, nonetheless, he reaches out to embrace me. Meanwhile, I hear Countess, my mother, and Brooke's high-pitched screams of praise. Then like wild fire the entire congregation erupts into a series of high pitch screams.

"Hallelujah, praise the Lord!" My father shouts, "The angels in heaven are rejoicing!"

I am too because as soon as Countess finishes singing and the congregation settles down, I take the microphone in my trembling hands and proceed to speak.

"First, giving honor to my Lord and Savior Jesus Christ, my father, Pastor Edward Kelly, Sr., the congregation, visitors, and friends. I'd like to share with you my reason for coming to the altar this morning. For the past 11 years I have been keeping a secret from my family, from my friends, from my wife and from myself."

Silence finally finds its way over the once noisy and rambunctious sanctuary. It is so quiet that I feel as if I am speaking to an empty room, but the congregation is far from empty. There are approximately 1,100 people present and all eyes are on me. I hear the pulsating sound of my heart beating three times louder than usual and a sudden ringing in my ears.

"I'd like to make a confession." I glance at Brooke and she is practically sitting on the edge of her seat, her tear stained face is lingering on my every word.

"Ladies and gentlemen, I am gay." I allow the words to flow from my lips with ease.

My father smiles nervously at me and then at the congregation. It is the first time I see my father speechless. He is silent for quite some time.

"Daddy, I'm sorry. I've kept this secret away from you for so long. I never, ever wanted to disappoint you. I always wanted you to be proud of your only son, but-" I pause and listen as Brooke screams out my name, "Eddie! Eddie! Wake up baby! Wake up!"

I become disoriented and I look up and see Brooke staring down at me, "Baby wake up. You're having a bad dream."

"A dream?" I hear myself speak. I am saturated in a pool of my own sweat.

"Yes, baby. Do you want to talk about it?"

I take my hand to wipe away the sweat from my forehead, "It just seemed so real."

"Here, drink this." I take a glass of ice cold water from her hands. It is so chilling and refreshing that it cools my wet body. "Thank you, baby," I say before giving her a tender kiss on her beautiful, lightly-glossed lips.

"I've never seen you this worked up over a dream before, Eddie."

"Did I say anything?" I ask, remembering when she told me of the times I talked in my sleep.

"It depends," she says. "Were you dreaming about us being alone on a deserted isle?"

"No, baby."

"All that sweating and you weren't thinking about us?" she asks.

"No baby. Was I talking in my sleep?"

"No, you didn't say anything this time."

Thank goodness. I look at the clock. Today is Sunday, and unlike the dream, I don't know if I can make it to church and have the same nerve to get up and confess my secret to the world.

"I'll have to catch daddy's sermon next Sunday."

"Edward, you know what that means?" Brooke asks, as she rubs my chest.

I know all too well what kisses on the neck and chest rubs mean. For about six months Brooke has entertained the thought of having children. She's been trying everything from sexy lingerie, to porno videos, to going below the waist to get me in the mood. I don't want a child but I'm too afraid to let her know. I try to change the subject whenever it comes up knowing there are only so many times you can do that. To be honest with you, I don't know just how much longer I can go on with this charade. It is so unfair to Brooke. I have to increase my dosage of antidepressants because I constantly find myself up against the wall. About six months ago, I got a vasectomy without Brooke's knowledge. How did I pull that off? I lied and told her I was on a four-day trip. I always knew sooner or later the issue would come up. I know it's wrong and trifling of me but I just can't bring myself to come to grips with my reality. I witnessed so much animosity and turmoil towards gays during my years at Texas A & M that I'm apprehensive and too afraid to deal with it straight up.

As Brooke kisses and caresses every angle of my body with her sweet, gentle lips, I close my eyes and Scottie's chiseled rock hard body comes to mind.

"Brooke, stop." She is on her way downtown and I stop her just before she gets there.

"Edward, what is it now? Look," she pauses, "I want a baby so bad that I can literally taste it, no pun intended!"

I laugh. Before I can say anything, she stops me.

"I don't see what's so damn funny. I am ovulating. This is the right time and the right moment, Edward. You are leaving tomorrow and that makes me have to wait three days. Dammit, I can't wait. I want you here and I want you right now!"

"Honey, looks like you mean business."

"I want this more than anything Edward and you're playing around with me." I gaze into my wife's eyes and see the pleading eyes of a child.

"I'm sorry, Brooke." I take her pleading face into my hands and begin to kiss her lips. When I close my eyes Scottie pops into my head. I'm trying to shake off his face but it's taking over every essence of my soul.

***

"Son, what happened to you today?" Daddy asks, before he takes a swing at the ball. We both watch as it goes sailing over one hundred yards of rolling St. Augustine green only to land in a shallow pond.

"Even good Christian folk like myself need to take a break every now and then." I respond as I "t-up" in position to take my shot.

"You're back sliding son," Daddy says. He's surveying my test swing, "just a little more to the left," he adds. I swing my Big Bertha golf club over the ball and watch closely as it sails near the 18th hole.

"Pops, while we're on the subject, why are you out here today? It's 3:45 in the afternoon. Shouldn't you be preaching at somebody's Pastor and Wife's Anniversary Program?"

Daddy and I tease each other back and forth. Sunday evenings on the golf course are usually rare, so when the opportunity presents itself we take advantage of it.

"That's next Sunday." he says.

"Tell me the truth Pops, don't you get just a little tired of the anniversaries?"

"Son, I'd be lying to you if I said I didn't."

I chuckle at his frankness. It is that same type of honesty that I've come to love and respect over the years. As a kid growing up, I remember when members of the church would call the house with their problems. From time to time I would eavesdrop and I remember my father telling a member, flat out, that he didn't want to hear her complain about so-and-so doing this or so-and-so doing that. He told her to work it out and call him back when she got it together. That same honesty translates into his sermons. My father doesn't hold back and all who can't say "amen" oftentimes say "ouch."

I am dying to ask him how'd he react if he found out his only son is a closet homosexual? I remember his nervous smile in my dream because it seemed so real.

"Pops I had a terrible dream this morning."

"Oh yeah, what about?"

"Wow, I don't know how to say this." All of a sudden my palms began to sweat and my heartbeat increased. "I had a dream I was gay, and I stood up in church to confess it."

"You did what?" Daddy stopped concentrating on his form and stood erect.

"I had a dream that I was gay."

Daddy studies me for a moment. Just like the dream, he is speechless.

"I know it's overwhelming…"

"Hold up," he says, cutting me off. "Why would you dream something like that?"

"I don't know. It disturbed me, it still disturbs me." I study Daddy's reaction once more, and he's shaking his head.

"Yes, it's very disturbing," he adds.

"Hypothetically Daddy, how would you react if your only son told you he was gay?"

"God help me." He replies and takes out a handkerchief to wipe away a few beads of perspiration from his forehead and mouth, "I would be hurt, I would be devastated."

I try not to react to his last statement, but my facial expression gives away my darkest secret. A secret I swore I would never tell.

"Edward, look at me." I hear the preacher-like authoritative tone in his voice and I force myself to give him eye-to-eye contact.

"It's all coming together now. First the flight attendant job, now the dream." Daddy looks as if he's been hit with a two-ton crane, "Edward Mitchell Kelly, you are not telling me that you are…"

I feel tears rush to the brim of my eyes. I try to bite my lip in hopes they don't fall but they do.

"My Lord," Daddy says, softly, "You are gay?" He looks upward to the sky for a moment.

"Yes Daddy." I pinch myself but this isn't a dream. I've just told my father, the only man I respect and fear, second to God, that I am gay.

"How long have you known?"

"Since I was 16 years old." As I respond, I somehow feel myself getting lighter and lighter.

"That's 11 years."

"I know," I say.

"You've been hiding it all these years from me, from your mother, and from Brooke?"

"I've been hiding it from myself, too."

Daddy takes his $150.00 golf club and tosses it angrily to the ground. "My Lord, my God! Eddie, you got a lot of explaining to do!"

Daddy's peanut butter complexion is now bright crimson and his nostrils are flaring like a raging bull. I almost want to run because I know that any minute he will charge after me. He takes out his handkerchief once more to wipe the small beads of perspiration forming around the corners of his forehead.

"Pops, I just want to know one thing?" I ask, in an almost pleading fashion.

"What is it?"

"I just want to know if you will still accept me as your son?"

I see my father struggling, almost stuttering, "Edward, you're gay?" He laughs nervously, "you've been lying all these years."

"I know, but Pops you haven't answered my question?"

"I don't have an answer to it. You want me to accept a way of life that's not appealing in the eyes of God."

"I don't want you to accept my lifestyle, I want you to accept me, your son."

"I can't." He picks up his bag of golf clubs and places it in the empty seat next to him, "I just can't." He starts up the motor to the golf cart.

"I'm still your son!" I shout, as he drives off leaving

me standing at the ninth hole. As the cart moves further out of sight I feel somewhat relieved, relieved that I've come true to myself and opened up. I'm also scared and hurt. All I can think about is Brooke and how she'll react when I tell her. I don't want to go home just yet.

***

After two minutes, Scottie finally opens the door wearing only a pair of white Calvin Klein boxers. I'm trying so hard to concentrate on his eyes but I'm finding myself lusting hungrily like a predator ready to strike its prey.

"What's up?" he asks, staring closely at me as I walk inside.

"I fucked up," I surprise myself when I say it.

"How?"

"I told my Pops I was gay."

"You did what?" he shouts.

"I came out!" I say, feeling somewhat proud yet empty.

"You didn't."

"Yes I did."

"Damn, Eddie."

"I know. Now I got to tell Brooke," I say, with tears in my eyes.

"If you don't, your father will."

I find my size 12's pacing the floor, trying to figure out a way to approach Brooke.

"What am I going to do Scottie?"

"You were going to tell her sooner or later; weren't you?"

Instantly, I feel my legs getting weak. My heart feels as though a million pins are piercing at it. I can almost feel it leaking inside my body.

"I can't go home. I can't do it Scottie."

"Yes, you can," he says.

"No, I can't."

"Of course, you can. She deserves to know, Eddie.

You owe her that, man."

I wish the clock would stop, but not even the hands of time could stop long enough to comfort me through my dilemma.

***

Brooke is bound and determined to make it difficult for me to tell her. When I arrive home she is sitting in bed reading a book containing names of babies. There are scented candles burning and Kenny G. playing softly from the speakers.

"Hi honey," she says, greeting me with a pleasant smile. As I stare into her eyes, I realize that it won't be long before her smile disappears.

"What are you reading?" I ask, trying to stall with small talk.

She lifts the book so I can see it, "The perfect name for the perfect baby."

Beads of perspiration are surfacing on the corners of my forehead and underarms.

"Eddie, how does Amilcar sound? You think that's a good name for a boy?"

I take a deep breath, I'm afraid to exhale for fear my heart might jump out of my mouth.

"That's a nice name." I respond, as I sit on the corner of the bed fully dressed.

"What do you think about Desiree? You think that's a good name for a girl?"

"It's beautiful."

"My Grandmother's name was Desiree. I think it might sound a little too old."

"Brooke put down the book, there's something I want to tell you."

Immediately, Brooke's mood shifts from jubilant to anxious. "Eddie what's wrong?" she asks.

I close my eyes and allow the salty tears to fall down my cheeks.

"Eddie." She removes the covers and rushes to the foot of the bed where I sit. "Eddie what's wrong? Are my parents okay?"

"Yes."

"Are your parents okay?"

I only nod my head.

"Countess, Kenny and the boys, are they alright?"

"Everybody is okay." I close my eyes.

She takes my tear stained face into her soft delicate hands and kisses my lips gently, "What is it baby?"

"Brooke, I am gay." I open my eyes to study her reaction.

"You're what?" she replies. Her eyes are dancing a mile a minute, "W-w-wait a minute, I don't understand Eddie."

"Brooke I'm gay, I like to be with men."

Brooke pauses for a moment to take in my information. I can tell she's trying to search for answers. Slowly, she stands to her feet. "I don't believe this! I really don't believe this!" She laughs nervously.

"I'm sorry."

"Oh my God! Oh my God! No, this can't be happening. God, no!" She falls to her knees and cries in agony. I try to reach out to console her, but she flinches.

"I'm so sorry, Brooke." The sight of her crying is unbearable for me to watch. I try closing my eyes again and looking in the other direction, but I still hear her.

"Eddie, how long have you been this way?"

I turn to look at her face, "Before we met?"

"Oh God!" she cries, and quickly shakes her head. "Oh God, no! Eddie why did you wait so long to tell me?"

"Because I feared seeing you like this." I reply, "Brooke, I'm so sorry honey."

"Eddie I want to know one thing. Have you had sex with other men since we married?"

"Yes." If I'm coming clean I might as well come correct.

She grabs her head and shakes it in disbelief and looks to the ceiling with her tear-stained and swollen eyes. She lets out a loud ear-piercing scream. "Oh God, what have I done to deserve this?"

I stand to my feet and try to help her up from the floor.

"Eddie, don't touch me!"

I obey and watch helplessly as she cries in a loud agonizing, almost in a mournful-like moan.

"God, I really wanted a baby so bad! I can't believe this is happening to me. Oh God!"

"Brooke."

"Eddie, leave me alone!"

"But Brooke."

"What part of that don't you understand?" she asks. "As far as I am concerned, you are a stranger to me, and if you don't leave I'm going to call the police!"

"Brooke let me at least explain."

"Explain what Eddie? You've said enough! You have ruined my life. If I contract HIV from you, your ass is going down for murder."

"That's what I want to tell you, I've always used protection."

"Eddie, why are you still here? Get out!" She quickly stands to her feet, picks up a shoe, and points to the door. "The very sight of you makes me sick."

As I make my way through the living room to the door, I pause and take one last look at my house. Although it's spotless, it feels as though a tornado has ravished the foundation. I open the door and without looking back I walk outside to the darkness that awaits me. Then like a rock out of nowhere it hits me. The truth is out. The very persons that I didn't want to know are the first to know. The lifestyle that I secretly stashed away in a closet for 11 years is out. At last, I am set free. However, this freedom has many costs.

T. Wendy Williams

Welcome Home

I can kiss my supervisor, Julian, for being so kind and understanding. I called and asked for a personal drop from my flight schedule. I told him in my best damsel-in-distress voice, that I was having major family issues and without question he told me to take the week off. I really needed this week to plan for Dewayne's welcome home party. He's getting out on Friday morning. And, that night his family and close friends are giving him a celebration to top all celebrations.

I immediately get on the phone to call my best friend, Nikki. She and I, along with Byron, plan to spend the day shopping for the party.

" It's on now, Nikki "Alizé" Robinson!" I say, once she picks up the phone. I know she's smiling on the other end, I can hear it in her voice.

"You are just showing out because your man is coming home."

"That's right, and you are responsible for throwing out the red carpet, because after all, it was you who got us together in the first place."

"Remind me not to play match maker ever again."

"You are so silly. So what time are you going to be ready?" I pick up an emery board to file my nails.

"Ummm, give me until noon-thirty," she replies.

I glance at the clock on my wall and it reads 10:15 am. At the same time, the call waiting beep chirps in. "Hold on."

"That's probably Dewayne." Nikki says.

"You're probably right, but hold on." I click over, "Hello?"

"Pee Weeee," Dewayne says, in a slow sexy voice,

"How's my baby girl?"

Although it's been eight years, I still blush like a teenager.

"I'm waiting for you to come home." I say, as I stop shaping my nails and curl up like a cat on my white leather sofa.

"Yeah? I'm ready to come home, too."

"Friday can't get here fast enough."

"It'll be Friday before you know it."

I realize I have Nikki on the other line. "Hold on, let me get Nikki off the phone."

"Tell her I said hello."

"Okay." I click over. "Nikki, it's Dewayne, I'll see you at 12:30."

"Tell Dewayne to burn his commissary wardrobe. I'm sending him an outfit through his brother, Derek, so he'll leave the penitentiary in style."

"I'll be sure to tell him." I click over to Dewayne, "Nikki says she's getting you an outfit and sending it by Derek."

"Shit, if it were left up to me, I would leave here buck-ass naked."

"We got a lot planned for you baby." I say with my eyes closed. I'm picturing Dewayne walking through my living room door in slow motion.

"I can't thank you enough for being down with me all these years. You could've dumped me and found you somebody else but you didn't. I can't tell you how many times your voice and your letters kept me going."

I smile like a Cheshire cat. Dewayne can be very sentimental. He shares true sentiment in his letters. That's where his real feelings emerge. I am forever amazed at his ability to capture raw, sensitive, and philosophical prose. He's an artist, too. He's forever drawing pictures of Déjà and me. Dewayne missed out on a lot of Déjà's growing up years but that's all going to change. We exchange more pleasant conversation before his 15 minutes are up.

"I'll see you on Friday, okay?"

"I love you Pee Wee and don't forget to tell our daughter how much Daddy loves her."

"She loves her Daddy right back."

The phone clicks and there's total silence on the other end. Dewayne's face is still fresh in my mind as I hold the phone in my hand. Like a hyper child, I jump up and run into my bedroom and open the door to my walk-in closet. I'm staring at the outfit I think I'm going to wear but my attitude with clothes changes just like the weather. And let's not get started on shoes. After I finally decide on an outfit. I take a Calgon bath, do my hair, put on my makeup, and before I know it, it's noon.

As I stroll down Main Street blaring Whitney Houston's latest CD, a sight too painful to behold interrupts my thoughts. I see my mother pushing a grocery cart loaded with old blankets and sacks. I know it's her because she's bow-legged and pigeon-toed and if I don't remember anything else about her, I'll always remember her walk. She always walks like she's in a hurry. I slow down to get a good look at her face. She notices the car and proceeds to walk even faster. The look on her face let's me know she is pissed off. I push my button to let down the passenger's window.

"Mama!"

She slows down a little. Her face doesn't look like that of a forty year-old but that of someone much older. Years of drugs and prostitution have taken their toll on her. As I drive closer to where she's walking I see that her eyes are sunken into her head and like every crack head, she appears to be in a daze.

"Whitney, is that you girl?"

"Yes, it's me."

She abandons her cart and approaches my car. She's wearing an old Houston Rockets t-shirt, and brown double knit pants with black pointed church shoes. "Girl, you looking good," she says, with a smile revealing teeth stained by years of drugs and neglect. "Where you going wit' your pretty self?"

"Nikki and I are going out. Where are you going?"

"Girl I'm just walking. You know, getting my daily exercise," she says, with a cackle.

"Mama, where do you live now?"

"Huh?" she asks, like she didn't hear me the first time.

"I asked where are you laying your head nowadays?"

"Here, there, anywhere I can baby. Why, you got a place for me?"

"Yes."

I want so much to reach out and help my mother. I think that's why God spared her this long. He left her around for me to help her. He may have great things in store for her. I pray each night before I go to bed for God to watch over her and direct her into a path clear of drugs. I ask the same of my grandmother. At sixty-five, she still drinks and spends her Fridays and Saturdays at the "hole in the wall café."

"Mama, will you get in the car with me?" I ask.

"What?" she asks, in a surprised manner. I think I caught her totally off guard. "You want me to do what?"

"Get in the car."

"I can't leave my buggy on the side of the road, somebody might steal it," she says in agony. I suspect she has a stash underneath.

"Leave it there, nobody's going to steal it." I unlock the door so she can get in. But she refuses to move.

"Mama do you have drugs stashed underneath that blanket?"

She takes a moment to answer, "As a matter of fact I do."

I am not in the least bit surprised. "Why don't you leave all that behind and get in the car with me?"

"You know I can't baby, I'll die from the withdrawal."

"I'll get you back into rehab."

"It ain't going to do me any good, I'll get high when I get out."

"Not if you're living with me."

"Are you still with that boyfriend of yours?" she asks.

"Yes."

"Where is he nowadays, I haven't seen him in a while?"

"He's in jail."

"Oh, it finally caught up to him."

"I guess."

"Well Whitney baby, your mother don't want to change, I love to get high and I'll probably keep getting high until the day the good Lord comes and takes me away, if the devil doesn't get me first."

By now I'm hurting, "All right, Mama."

"You take care girl, don't worry about your Mama. I've been a ho and a dope fiend off and on for a lot of years, I know how to take good care of myself."

I drive off leaving her standing by the curb looking like a bag lady. I fight back tears as I look in my rear view mirror and watch her staring back at me.

"Whitney, Whitney," Byron waves his hand over my face, "Earth to Wanda Jean."

I can't shake my mother from my head and although Nikki and Byron are like a modern day Fred Sanford and Aunt Esther, my heart is still bitter.

"You've been drifting off and on all afternoon. What's wrong?" Nikki asks.

"I saw my mother today," I say, before I sip my glass of Chardonnay.

Nikki and Byron are silent for the first time in a long time. I glance at Nikki and she proceeds to eat her salad. Byron, feeling sorry for me, covers my hand with his. "Whitney, how is she doing?" he asks softly and sincerely.

"The same, nothing's changed." I pick at my salad

with my free hand. I feel tears rush to my eyes.

"So did you get a chance to talk to her?" Byron asks, before he takes a napkin to dab at my eyes.

"Yes. I asked her where was she staying nowadays. She didn't tell me exactly where, but God, she looked a sight."

""Don't they all," Nikki responds, "What was she wearing?"

"An old Houston Rockets shirt, brown double knit pants, and black church shoes."

"Oh stop," Byron says as he glances at Nikki to get her reaction. Nikki is so nonchalant when it comes to my mother. They have a terrible history. One Christmas, when I lived with Nikki, I allowed my mother to come over because it was cold outside and I felt so sorry for her. Plus she seemed like she got her act together. She had been working at Popeyes chicken when I saw her leave late one night. All she had to keep her warm was a plaid flannel jacket. Her Popeyes cap and shoes were so worn down the bottoms had to be pieced together with duct tape. I told her she could spend the night so we could wake up at least one Christmas together. I made the mistake of falling asleep. The next morning there wasn't a single present underneath the tree. Mama took everything, including the wrapping paper.

"Aside from the obvious, Whitney, I don't understand why you continue to reach out to her," Nikki says.

"Because I feel in my heart that one day she'll come to her senses again."

"Honey I don't see anything wrong with keeping hope alive," Byron says.

"Whitney for as long as I've known you, I've known your mother to be off and on drugs, if she hasn't stopped by now..."

"I'm going to see if I can get her into rehab again." I hear myself respond, out of the blue. "This time I'm going to put her into the same program Natalie Cole was in."

The waitress approaches our table with the entrees. I have angel-hair pasta with shrimp and marinara sauce, Byron has baked ziti, and Nikki has a stuffed eggplant.

"You're going to do what?" Byron asks. I allow the waitress to shred fresh parmesan over my pasta and leave before I answer.

"I'm going to find my mother and put her into rehab."

"Whitney, I'm not going to sit here and let you spend your precious time and hard earned money. Now, your mother has to make up her mind if she wants to change, and there's no rehab out there that'll do it for it for her," Nikki says, sounding more like she's my mother.

"If only you could see what I saw today, and what I've been seeing everyday since I was a little girl. I have to help her, she needs me." Byron and Nikki look into my eyes and see that I am dead serious. I could easily turn my back and pretend my mother doesn't exist. After all the pain and embarrassment she caused in my life as a kid growing up, I could've easily passed her up on the side of the road today. But I didn't. I truly feel there's hope for her.

We spend the next half hour at the restaurant before the three of us call it a day. After I pick up Déjà from Dewayne's parents and settle in, I can't help thinking about my mother. I think more about her than I do Dewayne for the rest of the night.

***

I look at myself in the mirror for the tenth time. I wanted everything about my outfit to be perfect for Dewayne's eyes. I'm wearing a sexy black cocktail dress that shows off my long slender legs, and black, strappy, three-inch heels revealing my cute pedicured toes. In less than an hour he'll be showing up and I'm getting butterflies just thinking about it. I hear the doorbell ring and my heart is pounding like a bass drum in my chest. I open the door to the bathroom and walk down the hall to where I see a hand full of Dewayne's relatives standing with their cocktails in hand.

On the speakers, which are strategically placed in each room of the condo, I hear the sounds of Marvin Gaye's, *Got to Give It Up*. By now there are five couples dancing like they're trapped in the 70's, and my palms are sweating profusely as I make my way to the door. I look through the peephole and see its Roxy. I open the door.

"Hey, Chick," we say to each other and proceed to do the diva's cheek-to-cheek greeting.

"I'm glad you showed up," I say to Roxy. She's stunning in the silky white Donna Karan halter-top with the boot cut pants she purchased at Saks.

"I got you and Dewayne a welcome home gift," she says, referring to the pink and white rectangular box in her hands.

"Thank you. Come in. Where's Eddie?"

"I don't know. He was acting a little strange this week, like he was ill or something."

"I'm glad you made it. Come here, I'd like you to meet some people."

I take time out to introduce Roxy to Dewayne's mother, Donna. I also introduce her to his oldest brother, Dwight, Jr., who volunteered his spacious, 25th floor condo to house the party, and reintroduce her to Nikki and Byron.

The doorbell rings again and all eyes seem to fix themselves on me. Donna, Dewayne's mother walks to the door and opens it.

"My baby!" I hear her scream and I see her and Dewayne embrace. I feel tears rush to my eyes as I watch them rock each other from side to side.

"Daddy!" Déjà screams out behind me, and she rushes up to Dewayne and leaps into his arms. She knows who her father is from the visits.

I smooth the wrinkles in my dress before I approach him. The moment our eyes meet, I rush up to put my arms around him. He smells so good and feels so good in my embrace that I don't want to let him go. We kiss and hug for the next five minutes, totally oblivious to everything around us.

"Break open the champagne bottle, our man of the hour has finally arrived!" Dwight, Jr., who's doubling up as host as well as the d.j. announced, "Welcome home baby brother!" Dwight rushes off the mic to give Dewayne one of those hugs where they slap and lean into each other with a black power fist.

Dewayne, not letting go of Déjà and me, walks around the room to greet the mid-size crowd of people. He thanks them for coming and thanks them for staying "down" with him.

"What took you so long to get here?" I ask him before planting another round of kisses on his lips.

"I had to stop by the barber to get a haircut," he says, rubbing his hand over his fade. His face is clean shaven and if I'm not mistaken, I must have grown taller or he must have gotten shorter, because we are eye-to-eye with each other. Dewayne notices it too.

"What happened? Did you grow taller on me?"

"I think I have," I respond, while staring into his ebony eyes. I can't help myself and we kiss each other once more.

"So, this is Dewayne?" Dewayne and I open our eyes when we hear Roxy's voice.

"I'm sorry Roxy, if I haven't introduced you two. Dewayne, Roxy. Roxy, Dewayne."

Roxy extends her hand to Dewayne.

"Nice to meet you." Dewayne replies, before he shakes her hand.

"Has anybody ever told you you look a lot like Ice Cube?" she asks. "I like Ice Cube, I think he's cute." *No she's not trying to flirt.*

Dewayne gives Roxy a look like why are you telling me all this?

"I'm excited for you, Dewayne. Whitney talks about

you all the time."

"Likewise," he says, then excuses himself.

"Where are you going?" I ask.

"To dance with my little girl," he says. I watch closely as he takes Déjà by the hand and leads her out to the dance floor.

"How sweet," Roxy coos behind me.

"He loves his daughter so much," I respond, before I rush over to grab Donna's hand. "Donna, where's your camera?"

"Look in my purse."

When I retrieve the Kodak disposable camera from her purse I get in perfect position to take the perfect shot. Through the lens I see an eight-year-old girl having the time of her life with her father. She wasn't bashful in the least bit. She was showing Dewayne a thing or two to the amusement of everybody.

"Who taught you how to dance like this?" Dewayne asks.

"I taught myself," Déjà replies.

Dewayne is astonished. I notice Nikki with a video camera not missing a beat. Her daughter, Diamond, joins her father, Derek, Dewayne's older brother and together the brothers serenade their daughters like the princesses they are.

Byron takes my hand, "You want to dance?"

"Not with you," I respond.

"Come dance with me 'cause I want to ask you something."

I roll my eyes to the ceiling. Byron not only wants to dance, he wants the low down on everybody at the party.

"Come on Ginger Rogers," he says jokingly as he takes my hand into his. "Now your friend Roxy, I notice she's checking out all the men at this party, including your man."

"She was flirting with Dewayne earlier."

"Oh, no she didn't."

"Yes, but Dewayne just blew her off."

"Now she's getting real acquainted with Dwight, Jr. Isn't that his girlfriend over there by the bar?"

I glance over my shoulder at a honey-colored sister about my height, wearing a green Gigi Hunter number, and sipping on a Martini.

"I don't know. He changes girlfriends like he changes underwear."

"Girl hush."

Dewayne taps Byron on the shoulder.

"No you cannot!" Byron replies before Dewayne can utter the question.

Dewayne takes my hand, "You had plenty of time when I was on lock down. Now it's my turn."

"I'm just joking, man," Byron says before he gives Dewayne a big hug, "Only because you're my cousin." Byron departs and sashays his Armani-dressed body to the bar where the honey-colored sister is standing.

"Let's say you and me slip away from here and find somewhere to celebrate our own private party."

"Sounds good to me," I respond. I am feeling the same as I did on my prom night.

I let Donna and Dewayne's father, Dwight, Sr., know that Dewayne and I are leaving and that I packed Déjà's clothes for the weekend. They don't mind keeping Déjà, as a matter of fact they get angry when I don't let her spend more time with them.

Dewayne and I make a quiet exit without anyone noticing us. Once outside in the car, we continue to kiss and hug each other.

"You feel so good," he whispers in my ear.

"You do too," I respond, holding Dewayne in my arms and stroking the soft waves of his low-cut fade.

"I'm finally out of the pen," he says.

"Yes you are, and you know what?"

"What?"

"You better stay out this time!"

"I shouldn't have gotten in to begin with, I don't have to tell you again how it went down."

"No you don't have to explain."

I didn't want to hear it for the millionth time how his homeboy, Marco, snitched on him and Dewayne turned himself in. His homeboy has since vanished without a trace. I don't know if Dewayne had gotten rid of him or he just up and left the country. I really don't want to know.

"Dewayne, are you staying out of the game?"

"For you and Déjà, yes."

"Are you serious?" I ask, not believing what I'm hearing.

"Of course. You see how much I lost out on Déjà's life, I don't want to lose out on anymore."

I try not to smile so much but I can't help it, "Dewayne you really mean it, you've given it all up?"

"I promise I have. Derek and I were talking on the way here about going into real estate and me possibly getting my license."

"How are you going to get a license with your felony?"

"I may have given up selling drugs, but I haven't given up hustling."

"I forgot. I lost my head."

"I know people, you know I haven't lost contact."

"I know."

"But I promise you and Déjà, I've quit the drug dealing hustle."

I feel my prayers have been answered. I prayed daily for Dewayne to stop. Now if only my mother could stop.

"I saw my mother earlier this week and it's been on my mind to get her into rehab."

"Whitney I'm just going to be real with you. Your mother is too far gone to get help."

"No she isn't."

"You never cease to amaze me," he says, with a chuckle.

"People said I would end up leaving you after the first year but I proved them wrong. I always thought that when you got out you would go back to dealing, but I was wrong. Maybe my mother can prove us wrong, and kick her habit."

"It just might happen. But not anytime soon."

I sigh and lean my head against the window.

"Come here." Dewayne takes my hand and pulls me closer to him.

"You know what really took me so long today?" he asks.

"What?"

He held up a diamond ring. "This," he replies. "Derek and I spent all day looking for it."

"No," I reply.

"You deserve it and a whole lot more."

I try to act like a tough girl and hold back the tears.

"Will you marry me?" he asks.

Literally, I get so choked up that I cannot answer.

"I'm sorry." Dewayne gently pats my back, "I didn't mean to make you choke."

"It's okay." I reply, "Yes."

"Yes, you will marry me?" he asks.

"Yes, I will marry you." I reply, though my voice is scratchy.

"I'll accept that," he replies before he gives me another hug. As we embrace, I breathe a sigh of relief. Instead of making love, we spend the rest of the night inside the car, in each other's arms.

If It Were Not For Me

I pop open my bottle of antidepressants and throw two tiny white pills into my mouth. I tilt my head back and swallow them dry, without water. The way I feel now, I could possibly take the whole bottle. I replay this week's episodes with Daddy and Brooke over and over inside my head. Sometimes I wish I hadn't done it. Then there are other times I feel that it was the best thing I had ever done. I mean, no more hiding in the closet. Though looking back, I wish I had come out sooner. I wouldn't have put Brooke through this travesty. I know she's crying her eyes out and I want so badly to tell her that although I am gay that doesn't mean we can't be friends. But she ain't hearing it. I know it for a fact.

I feel my pager vibrating against my hip. I pick it up to examine the text message. It's showing my parent's number. I pick up the phone to dial the number and it's up by the second ring. My heart is pounding like African Congo drums.

"Hello?" It's my mother's voice.

"Mom?"

"Eddie honey," she says. I can hear the sigh of relief in her voice. "Thank God. Are you all right, son?"

"Yes, I'm okay."

I hear Countess's voice in the background asking of my whereabouts.

"Where are you son?" my mother asks.

In spite of the circumstances, it sure feels good to know my mother still refers to me as her son.

"I moved out of the house Mom, I'm staying with a friend."

"Eddie honey, why don't you come back home?"

"I can't come home. Pop still doesn't want to own up to the fact that I'm gay and I'm still his son."

"Eddie, let the Lord handle him. Right now what I want you to do is get your things and come home."

"I can't, Mom."

"Countess and I want to see you. We are worried sick about you."

"Can you and Countess meet me at a restaurant?"

"Yes Eddie, just tell us where you want us to meet you?"

I give her directions and within an hour she and Countess show up. I embrace them and I'm trying so hard to fight back the tears but they consume me.

"It's all right son," my mother says to me. She and my sister both console me like a child, relieved to find a loved one after being lost in the wilderness. We order and the three of us sit and pour our hearts out. I love my mother so much. I don't know what I'd do without her. In my opinion, I think Mothers are in this world to love us. Fathers are in this world to judge us. Mothers will love their children unconditionally. Fathers will love their children under certain conditions.

"Eddie," Mother says before taking my hand, "have you gotten checked?"

"Yes Mother, I'm fine."

"Eddie, I don't want to sound too naive," Countess begins. She is radiant in red and although she is often jolly and full of laughter, I can tell that the news of my sexuality is somewhat shocking to her. But unlike my father, she understands that this is how I am and this is the way it's going to be. She can accept it or reject it. I think she chooses to accept it.

"How do you really feel?" she asks. Like she has nothing else to say.

I take a deep breath and release, "Overwhelmed."

"You had me fooled and I'm your mother."

"Mother, I tell you, it's terrible." I reach in my pocket and reveal my bottle of antidepressants, "I'm taking these."

Mother retrieves the bottle from me, "Oh son."

"My psychiatrist suggested it."

"Your psychiatrist?"

"Yes."

"How do you feel now that this is out in the open?" Countess asks.

"I feel like a new person. Though I did it at the expense of two very important people."

"I will talk to your father so don't you worry about him. Brooke is who I'm worried about. Poor child, I called several times to check on her but she isn't answering the phone," mother says before tapping my hand.

"I know she hasn't done anything foolish."

"I don't know. News like this could really do damage to a person's mind."

"I need to go and check on her, Mother. Countess may I use your cell phone?" I ask. "I'm sure she won't recognize your number on the caller ID."

I dial the number, hold my breath and listen. Brooke is still not answering the phone.

"No answer," I reply as I give the phone back to Countess.

Instantly, I lose my appetite, "Mama if you and Countess will excuse me, I have to go and check on Brooke."

"We'll follow you."

After I pay the tab, I drive like a bat out of hell to my old house.

When I jump out of the car, I immediately see smoke coming from the garage.

"Oh no," I feel my heart fluttering. I glance back at my mother and Countess. My mother's face is crimson and she grabs her chest, "Eddie, I hear the car in the garage!"

When I stick my key inside to unlock the front door, it no longer fits. Frantically, I run from window to window, banging on the glass and screaming out Brooke's name.

I screamed and with the strength of 10,000 men I charged the garage door with a karate type kick.

"Brooke!" I yelled and continue to kick the garage.

By now the neighbors are walking out of their homes with questionable stares.

"Brooke!" I yelled once again. I find a rock heavy enough to smash out the large bay window in the living room.

"Eddie, be careful honey!" my mother screams.

I ignored the sharp edges and leaped through the window like Superman.

"Brooke!" I yelled once again as I made my way through the kitchen and to the door leading out to the garage. When I opened the door I was overwhelmed with shock. I flip on the garage lights and sitting in the car in front of me is Brooke. When I try to open the door, it's locked. I try to open the passenger's door and it is locked as well.

"Brooke!" I screamed again before taking a baseball bat and pounding the passenger's window a few times before shattering it into a million pieces. I finally unlocked the door, turned off the ignition, and retrieved her body from the car. I also noticed a letter written in blue ink. With the knowledge I received from my flight attendant training, I administer C.P.R. on her. I give her two breaths and proceed to use compressions to her chest.

"Brooke, don't die on me! Please!"

I administered two more breaths to her body. I refuse to accept that she could be dead. I hear policemen shouting behind me but I refuse to let her body go.

"Mr. Kelly, could you please step aside!"

"Hurry up and get her some help!" I yell.

I watch teary-eyed as a couple of paramedics lift her lifeless body onto the stretcher.

My mother and Countess are standing nearby crying. I am too hurt and angry with myself to cry. If she is dead, and I pray to God that she isn't, I won't be able to live with myself. She would still be alive if it were not for me.

The Latina Mamacita

I am so happy for Whitney; I'm even a bit envious. She has her man back and she seems so happy and content. I noticed by the end of the evening, neither she nor Dewayne was any where in sight. They retreated like two thieves in the night, but I don't blame her. I don't blame her in the least bit because Dewayne is fine. I may be a bit sick for thinking like this but the brother has it going on. He's my type, 24/7. You know, a roughneck; take no-nonsense, will-beat-a-sucker-down type of man. When he walks he oozes respect and a woman feels very protected whenever he's around.

I imagine he makes love with the utmost intensity, and having been locked down, I know Whitney was fed three times over that night. I get on the phone and call her immediately.

"Hello?"

"What's up Chick?"

"Nothing."

"Just nothing?"

"Yes."

"How is Dewayne?" I ask.

"He's fine."

I know damn well he is.

"What's wrong with you?" I ask.

"Nothing, why?"

"You're not saying much."

"Because I'm not hearing much."

"Did Dewayne make love to you all this weekend?"

"Aren't we a little nosey?"

"Don't try to act like little-Miss-Innocent, I know you

were screaming in five different octaves."

"Enough about me, what about you and Walter?"

"Walter who? We're not talking about Walter today, we're talking about you and Dewayne."

"All right, since you're just dying to know; Dewayne asked me to marry him."

"No way!"

"He proposed Friday night."

"I'm so happy for you Whitney, you deserve it. Hell, you stuck by him for eight years."

"Anyway, let me call you back, I'm getting ready to take Déjà to school."

"Are you keeping your trip today?" I ask.

"Yes, I'm keeping it."

"Okay, bye."

Wow, now I'm really envious. Whitney's got it going on. I just know now that Dewayne is out of prison I'm going to lose that friendship I have with her. When people get married, they usually hang around other married people. Single people like myself are cast away like swine at a Nation of Islam rally. Besides Whitney, I have no other friends. Eddie is okay, but lately, Eddie's been acting funny. Last week, he hardly said ten words to me. I asked him was he okay? He just replied with one-liners, just like Whitney did today. I wonder what's the deal with the one-liners? What have I done? I noticed at the party, people kind of held me back at arm's length. Even Whitney and her friends, Byron and Nikki, acted a little funny. Am I a threat? In some ways I'd like to think so, but when it comes down to Whitney and Eddie, I don't like feeling like an outsider or a threat.

***

When I strut inside the flight attendant lounge I immediately spot my supervisor, whom I hate. I call her a mini-Hitler because she loves to dictate. She could see you on the employee bus and ask you about a scratch on your shoe, or ask you dumb questions about the four business cornerstones of Worldwide Airlines. Who cares? All I want to know is are they paying her extra to hound people the way she does? I notice her checking me out when I sign my name to my trip pairing. I know my skirt is too short for regulations, but I don't care. I'd like to give the supervisors something to talk about so I can give them a piece of my mind. I want to tell them that my boyfriend Walter, who's Vice-President of the airline, couldn't give a fat rat's ass about these flight attendants and how they're dressed. As long as these girls and guys are bringing in the dollars, not to mention the awards, they don't care.

I spot Whitney strolling through the crew lounge to check in. She appears to be glowing. I wished I had some of it. I could really use it about now.

"Hello future Mrs." Whitney shushes me before I can say more.

"I don't want the whole world to know," she replies.

"I'm sorry. I'm just excited for you."

"Good, let's keep the excitement between us."

"Listen at you. Let me take a look at this ring."

I feast my light brown eyes on the platinum marquis cut solitaire ring. What a beautiful jewel. I am so jealous. "Whitney, if I were you, Chick I would flaunt this pretty piece and get it insured. If it gets lost, just get another one."

"I don't want my ring all banged up."

"Yeah, I know what you mean. But God, it is so pretty Whitney."

"Thank you."

"Have you talked to Eddie today?" I ask, still staring at her ring.

"No. He should've been here by now."

"He's probably sick."

"So what do we have, a reserve?"

"Yes, unfortunately. I'm glad I'm working first class and not coach. I cannot stand working with reserves."

"Refresh my memory if you will. In fact, it wasn't very

long ago that you were a re-serve."

"At least I had a clue about the job."

"Let's go girl," she says, before the two of us do our usual catwalk through the terminal, turning the heads of both men and women.

I'm sharing a jumpseat with Margeaux, the reserve. She's talkative and she's getting on my last nerve. In this industry you come in contact with all sorts of flight attendants. I'm going to narrow my list down to the five most common types. Now first of all you have the top-of-the-line high maintenance flight attendants like my friend, Whitney, who gets spoiled and who never has to worry about where they're going to get the money to pay their bills. They dress nice and live very comfortably. And, they're usually involved with pilots, aircraft mechanics, professional ball players or entertainers. Secondly, you have the talkers like Margeaux, who do nothing but talk about nothing and who will volunteer information about themselves. Third in line are the "Drama Queens." They are the flight attendants who can't stand the passengers. They can't stand the job, but they are here for two reasons; the flight benefits and they have to get their bills paid. The fourth group includes members of the Mile-High Club; they are those flight attendants who are infamous for getting laid on the plane and anywhere else. Finally, you have the welfare recipients. Welfare recipients are those flight attendants who can barely afford to buy a decent meal on layovers. They're scraping the bottom of the jar for pennies and they are the first in line to tip the van driver when they know they need that extra dollar.

I want to tell Margeaux to shut up, but I listen as she rambles on and on about how difficult it is to be a reserve flight attendant in Houston.

"Why don't you transfer to Newark?" I suggest.

"I don't like Newark, it's too cold in the winter."

"Is that the only problem you have with Newark?" I ask.

"That and the people on the East Coast, especially New Yorkers, are so rude."

"Hey, I'm from New York." I respond. However, she does have a point.

"So do you live in Houston now?" she asks.

"Yes." I respond.

"What part of town?"

I want to be rude and say none of your business, you talking-Tina rag doll.

"I live in River Oaks." I respond.

"That's a nice area."

"I'm minutes from downtown and the Galleria." I say.

"How nice." She gives me this far-off look that says, how can you afford to live in that area on your salary?

When the fasten seatbelt sign turns off I am relieved. I am also the first to run to first class where I assume my position.

I scope my first class cabin and notice a couple of cute guys sitting together in the last row. Now that's one thing you don't see too often; two young and attractive African-American men sitting together in first class. I rush back to the galley to check out the manifest and their status as far as their frequent flier miles. I see the names Carlton Ogilvie and Walter Nunnley. I rub my eyes to see if I read the name correctly and sure enough it says, Walter Nunnley. Damn, I know Walter doesn't have a son. Maybe it's just a coincidence. I steal a glance around the corner to get a good look at him. He's Hershey chocolate just like the Walter Nunnley I know. And, he has the same sly grin just like Walter. As I take my orders, I am constantly distracted by the idea of Walter possibly having a son and not telling me about it. When I finally make my way to their row I start first with Carlton. He's trying to flirt with his eyes. He is cute, but he's not my type. I don't dig light-skinned guys. They seldom have that fierce-like quality that the smooth dark chocolate brothers always seem to capture. I am convinced that this is Walter's son, the moment we lock stares. He has that same sexy and magnetic quality that attracted me to Walter.

"So, Mr. Nunnley?"

"That's correct," he replies, undressing me with his eyes.

"You wouldn't by chance be related to Walter Nunnley, the Vice President of the company would you?" I ask.

"How'd you guess?"

"That's not a common name and besides, you look just like him."

"That's funny, a lot of people say I look like my mother," he says.

"Is that so?" I ask.

"Very much so."

We stare at each other a moment before I pull myself back to reality, "So Mr. Nunnley, are you having lunch today?"

"What I want isn't on the menu."

I think that it is rather bold of him to flirt so openly with me, so I quickly add my reply. "I can get you a cold sandwich and a bag of carrots from coach."

"Or you can give me your name and your phone number?"

I want to tell him so bad that his father already beat him to it, but then again, he could be a great substitute, a big chip off the old block.

"I'll think about it."

"You do that."

As I turn and walk away I can feel his and Carlton's eyes gazing at my back side. I take advantage of the attention and give them an eyeful of the Latina Mamacita.

***

"So, Walter's got a son?" Whitney asks before she takes a bite out of her salad.

"Yes and he's sitting in first class." I reply.

"Who's Walter?" Margeaux asks with a mouth full of food.

"Margeaux, this is an A and B conversation, would you mind?" I ask.

I notice her face turning a fire engine red.

"Anyway, why am I talking about it? Come and see for yourself."

"I will after I finish my salad."

"Don't forget." I shut the aft galley curtain behind me and make my way through the repulsive domain of "Coach." I don't see why anybody would want to travel for four hours to Seattle in anything but first class. When the call button from a coach passenger lights up, I pretend I don't see or hear it and resume my duties in first class. When I step on the other side of the curtain that separates first class from coach, I look straight ahead and see "Little Walter" standing in my first class galley. I'll be damned, déjà vu all over again. I walk seductively in his direction and look him over.

"What are you doing in my galley?" I ask, trying to sound serious.

"I'm sorry." He holds up his large hands and I inconspicuously check him out. He's about his father's height, and he has the same athletic build. Hell, I should be with him instead of his father. While staring at his son, I'm wondering just how old is Walter Sr.?

"How old are you, if you don't mind me asking?" I ask.

"Guess?"

"I asked you the question."

"Just guess."

"Okay you're 32."

"Damn," he replies like I offended him or something, "I look 32?"

"Well if you told me initially I wouldn't have guessed such a high number."

"I'm 28," he replies.

Perfect. He's just a couple of years older than me.

"You seem much older than 28." I reply, and I try to do my calculations to see how old Walter Sr. must be. It's funny, in the two years that I've known Walter he and I never went through that getting-to-know-you phase like most people. That's why our relationship is so screwed up. Our relationship is built solely around unforgettable sex. As I gaze into Walter Jr.'s face, I am toying with the thought of sleeping with him. Two is better than one. When one lacks, I will definitely turn to the other in my time of need. How did I get so lucky?

"So why are you going to Seattle?" I ask.

"I work for Boeing."

"What exactly do you do?"

"I'm an engineer."

Ummm, he's sexy and smart. I'm going to have so much fun with him.

A Special Prayer

When I finally settled down in my room I picked up my cell phone to check my voice messages. My adorable daughter left me one telling me that she made all A's on her report card. I promised I'd take her to Disney World if she did, so it looks like I have to make reservations. I get a second message from Byron about a party he's giving for some ball player. The third message is from Nikki, talking about her customers at the beauty shop. The fourth message comes from Eddie.

"Whitney, I was hoping you'd answer the phone. I desperately need someone to talk to." Eddie ended his message so abruptly that I became alarmed. I immediately dialed his number only to get his answering machine.

"Hello Eddie, I'll have my phone on if you need me, please call. Bye."

20 seconds after I hang up, the phone rings. It's Eddie.

"Hello Eddie, honey what's wrong?" I ask.

"Everything."

I didn't like the sound of his voice, "You sound like you've been crying?"

"I have."

"Eddie, what happened?"

I listen as he sobs. All kinds of thoughts are running through my mind, "It's all right."

"Whitney, she's gone."

"Who?" I ask as my heart races a mile a minute.

"Brooke."

"Gone where, what do you mean she's gone?"

"She killed herself."

"Oh no Eddie, you're lying! Why did she kill herself?"

"I told her I was gay."

I am rendered speechless and my heart is on the verge of exploding. I try to pinch myself to see if I am dreaming. I know I didn't hear him right.

"Eddie, you're kidding me right? I look at the calendar to make sure it's not April Fool's Day and Eddie isn't playing a joke. I just can't picture him being gay.

"Eddie, you're not gay."

"Yes I am, Whitney."

"Oh Eddie." My eyes water with tears, "I'm so sorry Eddie, is there anything you need me to do?"

"Just pray for me." His voice trails off, "Not only have I lost Brooke, but my own father won't accept me."

"God Eddie, your father knows too?" I sniff. I know how much Eddie cares about his father and how his father's love and acceptance means the world to him.

"I wish I had opened up much sooner. Brooke would still be alive."

"Eddie, how long have you been gay?"

"Since I was 16 years old."

I am baffled, I can't believe I didn't know and I usually know these things.

"Eddie, let me know if there is anything you want me to do, just anything, you name it."

"If you could just give me Brooke back, I would be the happiest guy in the world."

I provide no comfort to Eddie because I find myself crying, weeping loudly over the phone, "Eddie, do you feel like praying?"

"I should be mad at God, but at the same time I'm useless without Him or Her."

"Eddie close your eyes and listen to me," I say before I begin to pray. *"Dear God, we come before you today with heavy hearts. My friend Eddie has just lost his best friend, his wife. Dear*

God I know we should never question why. But, sometimes Lord that's all we have to go on. However, you said in your word that you will wipe all tears from our eyes. There's no burden too hard, and no prayer unanswered, because you are the same God who delivered Daniel from the Lion's Den, you are the same God who delivered Shadrach, Mechach and Abenego from the fiery furnace. You cast miracles then and You are still casting miracles now. All I ask is that you cast a miracle in my dear friend Eddie's life. Send your Angels of mercy to guide him and his family and his wife's family. Lord, we pray for her soul. Lord, we also ask that you heal the wound between Eddie and his father. Mend the tie that binds their beautiful relationship together. God, through you, all things are possible if we only believe. I believe you will work a miracle in Eddie's life. And, in turn, he will be a miracle to someone else. I ask these and all other blessings in your son Jesus' name
I pray, Amen."

"Thank you Whitney."

Eddie and I cry like babies. I'm crying because I can't believe I have all that bottled up inside of me. I can't remember the last time I prayed like that. Where I actually felt the words and believed them to someday come true. I know tonight before I go to bed I'm going to say a special prayer for my mother.

I got on the phone and called Dewayne on his cellular phone to tell him the awful news.

"You just never know," he replies.

"Dewayne, I thought he was kidding."

"You'd be surprised how many guys are walking around like that. They pretend they're all hard and butch, knowing very well they'll toss a salad on the down low."

"It's scary," I reply.

"Are you going to be okay?" Dewayne asks.

I smile quietly to myself, "Yes."

"Do you need me to wire you some money?"

"I think I have enough to last me to the end of the trip."

"You're in Seattle, right?"

"Yes."

"Are you near the Pike's Market?"

"How do you know about Pike's Market?"

"Remember you told me about it once before."

"Okay, I did."

"Would you mail some salmon, lobster, and snow crabs home?"

"Yes, what's the occasion?"

"You'll see when you get here."

Damn

After my much-needed conversation with Whitney, I sit for a moment and reflect back on Brooke's suicide note. Tears are falling from my face as I recant bits and pieces of her words. In her letter she expressed how much she looked forward to having my children and how the news of my sexuality crushed her like a diesel. She said, and these were her exact words, *"Eddie, I don't expect you to change. You must move on and reach your level of happiness, just as I must move on. However, let me assure you this... I can't go on living...because life without my husband, Eddie is not a life worth living at all...I'm terribly sorry, but this is too much for me to handle."*

My thoughts rewind to the look in her mother's eyes when she opened the door and saw me standing there. I couldn't blame her one bit when she screamed and charged after me, pounding furiously at my chest.

"You killed my baby! You killed my baby!" Her voice echoes on and on inside of my head. I close my eyes and picture Brooke's father, slumped over on the couch. The minute he sees me, he's furious and upright like a cobra and it takes Brooke's aunt, her mother, and her two male cousins to restrain him. I can't blame him one bit. His only daughter is dead and it's my fault. Although I didn't physically do anything to her, my coming out was equally as devastating, almost as if I forced her to sit in the car.

I grab my bottle of antidepressants and gulp down three dry pills. Right now I'm contemplating suicide and my palms and forehead are sweating like crazy. On the radio, a Donny Hathaway song is playing. He's singing about giving up and how his light of hope is burning dim. I get out a piece of paper and a pen and begin to write my letter.

Dear Family and Friends. Since the age of 16, my life has been nothing but a lie. I've hurt so many people. I can't even begin to explain. I just know that I can never live what some consider a normal life. So, I must do what I consider best for me and end this big ball of confusion...

The phone rings, startling me to death. I stare at it for about 15 seconds before I pick up.

"Eddie... this is your Pops."

I close my eyes and allow the tears to roll down my cheeks, "Pops, how are you? I didn't expect to hear from you."

"I called to check on you. I figured you might want someone to talk to right now."

I burst out into a sob. This is so unexpected, and that alone moves me. For a minute I let out everything inside me.

"It's all right." I hear Pops consoling me.

"Pops, how long are you going to be up?"

"For as long as you want to stay up."

"I need to talk to you and I need to see you in person."

"Come on over, Son."

"What?" I reply, not believing he just called me Son.

"I said come on over, my son." He said it again loud and clear.

"I'll be over in ten minutes," I reply. Quickly, I slip on a pair of old sweats, an old smelly t-shirt and slide my feet into a pair of Nike flip-flops. When I open my door, Scottie is standing in the doorway.

"Scottie, what's up?"

"I just thought about you, you probably need someone to talk to." He looks at me closely.

"Scottie, you'll never believe who just called."

"Who?"

"My Pops, I'm going over to see him right now. Do you want to ride with me?"

"I do. But, I don't think your old man would go for that and besides, it's your moment."

"I'm so glad he called, Scottie." I try not to think about the suicide letter and to look on the bright side instead. My father, the man who I least expected, calls me just when I'm three sentences into my suicide note. This is surely a sign from God that I need to change my life. I owe it to Him to do just that.

***

Pops says he's sorry for reacting the way he did on the golf course that day. He says that although it's going to be difficult and it's something he's prayed over countless times, he's going to accept my lifestyle. It seems too good to be true. I pinch myself just to see if it's real. When I see the tears of happiness in my mother's eyes I am reminded of the times in school when I received merits and praise for a job well done. I remember how happy it made my mother feel and how she cries so easily.

"I've been praying for this day to come, Edward, God knows I have," she says to me.

"I have too, Mother." I give her a kiss and when she leaves I continue my conversation with Pops.

"Pops, what made you call me tonight?" I ask.

Pops looks me directly in the eye and says, "That could've been you, Son, and I wouldn't have been able to live with myself if I'd known that you needed my support and I wasn't there to help you through your situation."

"It's funny you mention that because right now, I'm feeling the same way about Brooke."

I can't talk about Brooke without crying, "I wanted to live a normal life but Pops, deep down inside I tortured myself and I was deceiving Brooke."

"Son, why do you want to be gay?"

"Pops, it's just what I am, and it's a situation I can't change."

Pops gives me a long tired sigh. "Like I said earlier, I've prayed about you many times and I ask the Lord to change my heart and give me a clear understanding…Are you happy?"

"Sometimes."

"I see young menfolk like you prancing all around the Church, you're not going to start prancing around like that are you, Son?" he asked as if he would be embarrassed again to claim me as his son if I did that.

"No, Pops," I said.

He responds with a sigh of relief.

We go on talking for about three hours until my eyelids grow heavy and when I look up, Pops is asleep and roaring like a lawnmower in his easy chair.

***

I am so happy to see Whitney. She, along with my parents and my sister Countess, seem like a ray of sunshine appearing through a dark cloud. Everybody else is giving me the cold shoulder at Brooke's funeral. All of her girlfriends are rolling their eyes at me while their husbands won't even acknowledge me. The obituary doesn't mention my name, saying only that she leaves behind cherished memories with her loved ones, her mother, Mrs. Althea Randall and her father, Mr. Theodore Randall, and a host of other relatives and dear friends. My mother takes me aside and to my surprise she's furious.

"Honey, I know the family is hurt but couldn't they at least acknowledge the fact that she was married?"

Jules, Brooke's cousin, overhears mother and makes a nasty comment, "I don't blame the Randalls for not mentioning him."

Mother's head almost snaps as she whirls around to catch a glimpse of the person. He gives my mother a look that says, Yes, I said it. And what are you going to do about it?

"Look Mother, I don't want any trouble. I'm going to leave."

"Eddie, you don't have to go anywhere. Brooke was your wife and you should stay also."

"To tell you the truth Mother, I'd rather just say good-bye and leave."

"Don't leave Son, please stay," Mother says while holding my hand in hers.

Whitney takes my other hand. She's breathtaking in a black mini-skirt that caresses her long, smooth legs and ankle-strapped heels showing off her cute, clear-polished toes. My mother excuses us so we can talk.

"Thank you for coming," I say, before I give her a hug.

"That's what friends are for. Roxy sent you this," she gives me a card, "and she says to give her a call sometimes." Whitney and I give each other a look that says, please.

"Roxy and I can't have a decent conversation without arguing," I say before opening the card.

"We all miss you Eddie, but we want you to be okay."

"I'm going to take a month of leave and go somewhere."

"Where?" Whitney asks.

"Hawaii, since I've never been."

"I think Hawaii will be just fabulous for you."

"Yeah…I'll spend most of the time sipping on pineapples and trying to get this madness behind me."

"I noticed," Whitney says underneath her breath.

"I'm ready to leave, but my mom insists on me staying."

Whitney shrugs her shoulders, "I don't know, just tell her you don't feel good, you ate something that made you sick."

"I'm just going to tell the truth. It's time for me to go."

I excuse myself from Whitney and make my way through a crowd of more nasty looks until I spot the Randalls. When I approach them, Mr. Randall's onyx-colored eyes narrow in at me in disgust.

"Mr. Randall, Mrs. Randall I know…"

"You don't know nothing about nothing!" Mr. Randall roars at me, "You don't know pain and suffering and what it's like to lose your only child!"

"What do you mean? Brooke was my wife, I have to live daily with the ugly reality that if I had only kept my mouth shut, that maybe she wouldn't have done this."

"You know she worshipped the ground you walked on, Eddie. You were her first love, her college sweetheart."

"But hear me out Mr. Randall, I had one of two choices. Either live with the secret or be honest and tell her. God knows if I had known she was going to do this, I would've taken this secret to my grave."

"You would've been better off killing yourself!" Jules strolls by me sucking his teeth, "The world would've been a better place...one less faggot we have to worry about!"

Before I realize it, I punch him square between the eyes, startling me and everyone around me. I hear Mother's voice and Mrs. Randall's voice scream in unison. I tower over him like Ali over Liston and dared him to get back up because this *faggot* was prepared to lay him flat on his back *again*. People seem to forget that underneath there's still a man with raw emotions. I am so wired up that I don't even feel the swelling in my knuckles. My mother rushes to my side. I remember how he had given her an ugly stare and responded so nasty to her comment that I'm glad I decked him, he had it coming.

"I'm sorry," I hear myself apologizing to no one in particular and I make a dash out of the funeral home.

"Eddie!" My mother's voice cries out behind me, "Eddie, stop and listen to me!" I stop and turn around. Elegantly dressed from head to toe in black, she walks up to me with a pleading look in her eyes and says, "Now I know that the comments he made to me and to you were wrong, but Eddie, your father and I raised you better than this. Don't walk away from the family."

My father, Whitney, and seems like everyone else from the funeral home rushes outside, "Mama, I already apologized, no one wants me here, and if Brooke could speak she wouldn't want me here either."

"Edward Kelly, Jr. have you lost your mind?" My father asks.

"Yes, I have," I reply.

Pops wasn't expecting me to answer "yes" but I did. The whole funeral, with the exception of my few moments with Whitney, was mad chaos. That funeral home was colder than a Chicago blizzard with a -50° wind chill factor. I had no choice but to leave and face whatever consequences occur as a result of this. I'm sure old "sore nose" will press charges but at this point in my life, I didn't give a damn. Did I say damn?

The Mile-High Club

You know when you get a rude and obnoxious passenger who thinks he's king of the world and he's treating you like you're the shit on the bottom of his shoe? You know when he asks me for something to drink, he gets a little something extra in it and I'm not saying what. All of this madness brings me to Roxy's list of rules for the unruly passenger:

1. Never attack, verbally nor physically, a flight attendant who is preparing your food or drink. I don't need to say anything else.

2. Never yell out "Oh, Stewardess!" That alone drives me insane; it makes me think you haven't been on a plane since 1975.

3. Never touch or tug on a flight attendants' dress. If she wants you to tug or touch on her, she'll let you know on a company napkin.

4. Never press a flight attendant call button when the flight attendant is standing next to you. If you have kids who constantly press the button, I will personally tell them that the next time they press the button it will eject their little asses right out of the plane.

5. Never ask a flight attendant to put your heavy bag in the overhead bin. When they ask me; I tell them I'm four months pregnant or I just had back surgery.

6. I know this is so unoriginal but I must say it anyway, I am here to save your ass not kiss it.

Now give me my paycheck so I can buy myself a new pair of those cute Manolo Blahnik shoes I saw in Saks. I'm not worrying about my bills because Walter, Sr. pays my

$1,100 rent, he pays $537.00 for my BMW 525, and on occasion, he pays for my cell phone. I could ask Walter, Jr. for $1,100 and get myself a new Louis Vuitton garment bag and a red Gigi Hunter dress. I can say it's for my rent. After all, he spent a couple of nights at my place. The second night was a close call because 20 minutes after Walter, Jr. left, Walter, Sr. showed up. But let me back up to the first night. It was beautiful. Walter, Jr. and I made music and, if I'm not mistaking, we sang all night long. The next morning Walter, Jr. opened my front door and found a note that said, *"As a courtesy to your neighbors, use a muzzle on your mouth the next time."*

I think Walter, Jr. is whipped; he calls me every day. I make comparisons to him and his father. Walter, Jr. is better in the screwing department and Walter, Sr. is better in the oral department. During orgasms they both shake like they've been electrocuted and their eyes roll around in their head. Walter, Jr. likes to talk right after sex. Walter, Sr. likes to sleep right after sex. Walter, Jr. has a longer penis. Walter, Sr. has a fatter penis. My phone rings and I glance at my caller ID. It's Walter, Jr., again. I don't say 'hello' anymore.

"How much do you miss me?" is how I answer the phone.

"So much I want you to meet me in Miami."

My ears perk up, Miami is one of my favorite places. "When?" I ask, looking at my schedule.

"Tomorrow."

"I don't like to fly stand-by so have it arranged where I can get first class positive space or buy my ticket."

He pauses for a second, "You act like you've done this before."

"Don't worry about that, just do what I tell you and get me to you on the first thing smoking."

"What are you wearing?" he asks, seductively.

"I'm naked, why?" I'm lying. I'm fully clothed.

"Touch yourself."

I pretend I'm touching myself but he doesn't know

that.

"Okay, baby." I breathe, "I'm touching myself, now what do you want me to do next?"

"I want you to taste it."

I make a loud noise like I'm licking my finger, "Okay, now what?"

"Now touch yourself again and I don't want you to stop until you have an orgasm."

"Okay, baby." I remove the phone from my ear and stare at it in disgust, I'm moaning and groaning and trying not to laugh and pretend I've had the best orgasm since sliced bread. Walter, Jr. doesn't know but I'm ready to get off the phone and get to the Galleria before it closes. I hear Walter, Jr. moaning and groaning. I have the suspicion that he's probably relieving himself for real. Men, they're so stupid and gullible. The only thing they're good for is money and sex. Love is nowhere in the picture. No matter how much I want it to be, it just never is.

The advantage of being involved with the Vice-President of the company or knowing someone in a high place is that you get so many perks. You also take into account that, when you're as gorgeous as I am, you can write your own ticket. I'm sitting in first class wearing a tan and silky dress, a sheer headscarf, two-and-a-half inch Gucci pumps, and a pair of my brown tinted Gucci Girl sunglasses. The flight attendants are staring at me with their noses in the air and the guy beside me just can't stop smiling at me. I check him out. He's a bit on the handsome side with a nice chiseled Hawaiian copper-toned face and body. I smile back and glance at his finger. There are no rings present so I began to flirt.

"Has anybody ever told you you look a lot like The Rock?"

"Yes, I hear it all the time."

"Are you his brother?" I ask, before I cross my legs. I notice his dark, elliptical eyes travel a bit to my legs.

"No."

"Then what do you do?" I ask.

"I'm a first officer on the 7-3."

My eyes and ears perk up, "With Worldwide?"

"Yes."

"How long have you been flying?"

"Ten years."

"Wow. Tell the truth now, are you married?"

"Divorced."

"Oh really, I see you didn't get stuck with a lot of alimony or child support payments, you still look good." I reply checking out his white linen jacket and linen pants. He had on a nice pair of leather Kenneth Cole sandals and an eye-catching Rolex watch on his wrist.

"We didn't have children."

"That was smart. So you have a girlfriend?" I ask.

"No, I don't."

"A fine ass man like yourself doesn't have a girl-friend?"

"I'm single as they come, baby."

"Oooo, I like the way your lips say baby." I reply staring at them.

He finds my remark very amusing, "You're straight forward, aren't you?"

"Yes, I think so."

"Well let me ask you a question. What is your name?"

"Roxy." I respond, "Is that your question?"

"Not exactly, I'm curious as to what an attractive woman like yourself is doing traveling all alone to Miami?"

"I like to go shopping in Miami." I smile, "Can't you look at me and tell I like to shop?"

Studying his expression, I'm sure he had other things on his mind. Guys can't help it around me.

"Yes," he replies looking directly into my eyes.

The flight attendant approaches us and asks for our drink orders but I decline. If I don't make it myself, nine times out of ten, I don't ask for it, especially in first class. I usually bring my own small bottle of Evian. The pilot, on the other hand, orders a gin and tonic with a lime.

"You sure you don't want anything to drink?" he asks.

"I'm positive," I respond. After the flight attendant leaves I ask the gentleman for his name.

"Scottie," he replies.

"Typical pilot name," I respond. "If your name isn't Scottie, it's usually Bill, Bob, or Jim."

"Well Roxy isn't a typical flight attendant name, and you're certainly not an ordinary flight attendant."

"What do you mean?"

"There's something special about you. You have an aura. It's almost like you're regal."

"Almost! Scottie, I am a princess! Fall down and worship me!"

We both laugh.

"What are your plans, other than shopping in Miami? I'd like to take you out for dinner."

"Would you really?" I ask.

"I sure would," he says, before he retrieves the drink from the flight attendant.

"I'm meeting with a few friends and we're flying down to the Bahamas for a day," I say with a straight face. To be quite honest I don't know what plans Walter, Jr. has in Miami.

"I'm on my way to the Bahamas. I have a condo there and if you and your friends need a place to crash, you can crash out there."

"How nice of you." I respond, twirling my fingers in my hair like a little girl, "We might take you up on that offer."

"I'd love to have you guys over to keep me company, especially you."

"Me? Why?" I ask, already knowing why, but I just like hearing the different reasons.

"Forgive me for being so straight forward, but I think you have the sexiest body I've ever seen."

"Tell me something I don't already know."

"Really, I want to ask you something…are you a member of the mile-high club?"

"Hell no," I respond looking at him like he had just lost his mind.

"I apologize, Roxy…it's just you're so beautiful, and so honest and straight forward, I got carried away."

"Apology accepted." I respond, "Why would you ask me a question like that?"

"I'm just curious."

"Why? You think I'm a slut?" I ask, trying to sound like I'm offended.

"No, no, no, it's not like that at all and I'm sorry I offended you."

"May I ask if you're a member of the mile-high club?"

He appears to be blushing, "What do you think?"

"I'm asking the question."

"You would be the first to induct me?"

"I could. Let me think on it."

An hour into the flight, I feel a certain urge to act on Scottie's question. We talked about everything from the pilot's union, stocks and bonds, to his last marriage. I look inside my pocket book for a condom before I get up to go to the restroom. I notice everyone with the exception of one person is asleep. The first class flight attendant is nowhere around and I feel a certain little tingle easing it's way up my spine. I make eye contact with Scottie and motion with my index finger for him to come here. He eases up slowly with a wicked-like grin on his face like he's about to hit the jackpot. The both of us try to squeeze inside the lavoratory and luckily we're on a 757. If it were anything smaller, we would be SOL.

We look at each other as if it were the first time. Scottie leans closer and kisses me. Ummm, he's a magnificent kisser.

I try to ease my panties down in the easiest way, but when you're in a two by three feet box , you do it the best way you can. Scottie reaches behind me to close the lid on the toilet, he maneuvers by me, pulls down his pants and sits on top of the lid, losing all cool points with me. I wish I had a video camera to capture this moment. I'm trying not to laugh but it's so funny as we try to figure out the best way possible to do it. Finally, he gets up and turns me directly towards the mirror and he positions himself inside me.

"You have the condom on, right?" I ask, looking at his reflection in the mirror.

"Yes," he responds. I notice small beads of perspiration on his forehead.

I close my eyes and grunt softly as he pushes himself as far as he can go inside of me. Now, I usually don't mess around like this but this was a chance I just couldn't pass up. If you appear to have a lucrative cash flow and you're interested in getting down with the Latina Mamacita, you may be able to sample some, which is just what I give Scottie, a sample. He looks at me with a confused look on his face.

"What's wrong, why are you stopping me?" he asks.

"You'll get more when I see you in the Bahamas." I say before pulling down my dress.

"Roxy, don't leave me hanging like this."

I glance at the condom covering up his limp penis.

"What did I tell you?"

"You won't see me in the Bahamas."

"Why not?" I ask.

"What do you think?"

If he was mad because I stopped him short of his glory, it was just too damn bad. I took a damp napkin and manage to wipe myself before I pulled up my panties and opened the door. The first class flight attendant was in the galley, luckily she had her curtain closed so she couldn't see us coming out. I went back to my seat, picked up my Essence magazine and didn't even acknowledge Scottie when he sat down.

"You shouldn't have stopped me like that," he says with a disgusted look on his face.

"You men always think you can get something for nothing."

"You sound just like a slut," he replies. His copper-bronzed face is now red.

"Call it whatever you want," I reply nonchalantly, "I'm not your ordinary flight attendant. You're so used to those girls who have sex with you just so they can brag about sleeping with a pilot, and most of you are so damn cheap you won't even treat them to a nice dinner."

The first class flight attendant approaches us. She immediately asks Scottie for his order and glares at me.

"Excuse me," I raise my finger.

She just stares at me without answering.

"Is there a problem?" I ask.

"No, why would you ask?"

"Because you've been looking at me like you've lost your fucking mind."

I feel the passengers sitting in the seat in front of me staring back at me.

"Miss Figueroa, I only stared at you because throughout the flight you haven't chosen anything to drink nor eat. I was merely making eye contact or at least acknowledging you in case you changed your mind and wanted something to drink. Is that a problem?"

"Just do your job," I reply.

She looks at me and rolls her eyes. I'm sure she's calling me every kind of derogatory name in her head, but she knows better than to get into a confrontation with me.

"You are vicious," Scottie says to me.

"I'm a Princess. You said it yourself," I say, before I continue reading my magazine.

***

Walter, Jr. meets me at the gate adorned in a designer

suit I didn't recognize. When we embrace it seems the whole world stops and gets caught up in this beautiful moment.

"Hello, beautiful," he stares at me in amazement.

"Hello, handsome," I say, before I wipe part of my lipstick from his succulent lips.

His assistant, DC, retrieves my bag and trails us as we walk hand in hand through the terminal.

"So what are we doing today?" I ask. "Oh I know, let's go to South Beach. I want to get a cute bikini."

"And what else do you want to do?"

"I want to go jet skiing, and I want to go to dinner and I want to go to a club."

"And what else?" he asks, swinging my hand and smiling into my face.

"You horny devil, why do you always want sex?"

"Because you're sexy."

"You know you have to put a ring on my finger."

"Could be something worth thinking about."

I look up at him, "Don't think. Act on it." I respond.

"Don't doubt me."

He seems so bashful yet he has a layer of confidence lingering underneath. I notice Scottie strolling by us. Before we landed he wrote the number to his condo on a business card. He wanted to walk me to the car, but as soon as he spotted me hugging Walter he changed his mind.

***

When you're the Son of the Vice President of a major airline, you don't have to park where everyone else parks. You get a special all access pass and you don't have to pay. DC chauffeurs us around in a white Lincoln Navigator.

"Where do you want to go first, love?" he asks.

"Take me to the Fashion District, I want to go shopping."

"You hear that DC?" Walter, Jr. asks.

DC, who is a black man about 60 years-old nods. "Can you guys feel the air?" he asks.

"Yes DC. Please turn on the radio. You know what station I like."

DC pushes button number one and a radio station that showcases rap and hip-hop comes through the speakers.

"You like Luther Campbell and the 2 Live Crew?" Walter asks.

"I like some of their music. I'm from the Bronx and I'm not really into that booty music."

"Oh, you like that House and Vogue type of music."

"I like Big Pun and Fat Joe," I say, showing much love to my fellow Puertorricaños.

"They're alright," he says nonchalantly.

His cell phone rings and he excuses himself to use it. I glance out the window at the lovely Miami scenery. I certainly appreciate the turquoise water, the oceanfront high rises in the distance, the palm trees leaning against the wind, and Little Havana.

DC cruises along Washington Blvd., which has its share of boutiques, nightclubs, and restaurants. We pull up to a boutique and DC opens the door for me. Then he walks around to the other side to open the door for Walter, Jr., who's still on the phone discussing the wingspan on the Boeing 777.

Once inside the posh boutique, I survey the plethora of bikinis and one-piece swimsuits. I see one that immediately grabs my attention. It's a goldenrod, one-shoulder wrap bikini. Only my breasts and lower part of my body are covered, giving me a chance to show off my killer abs. I look at Walter to see if he's paying attention. But, just like his daddy, he's busy talking away on the phone.

A saleslady approaches me. She's a tall, slender Pamela Anderson look-a-like, with a bronze- tan complexion, bouncy blonde hair, and real perky breasts. She probably got her boobs done at the Miami Institute of Plastic Surgery in Miami, "just one look is worth a thousand words," but you didn't hear that from me.

"Hi," she says, in a highly animated voice.

"You're just too happy aren't you?" I ask, checking out her black strap sandals, denim Guess skirt and red spandex shirt. She gives me a questionable look as if she doesn't have a clue in the world as to what I'm talking about.

"I beg your pardon?" she asks before swinging her golden locks over her shoulders. She has huge Mick Jagger lips.

"I want to try this on," I say, holding up my stunning one-piece.

"Okay, would you like to try it on now or do you want to take a few minutes to look around?"

"I'll look around, but I definitely want this one."

"That's a real popular one this year."

"Oh yeah?"

I hope she's only making small talk, because the one thing I hate most is buying something someone else is wearing.

"That cute, little actress Jada Pinkett-Smith came in here last week and purchased one just like it."

"Suddenly, I'm not interested in this piece."

"What are your chances of running into her wearing it?"

I see another swimsuit on a chocolate covered mannequin. It's more a swim dress with a bikini bottom.

"Excuse me," I say to my perky, plastic surgery, Mick Jagger-lipped saleslady, "I want to try this one as well."

"Sure," she excuses herself and escorts me across the Pergo floor to the dressing room. "My name is Samantha if you need me."

Moments later, Walter appears in my dressing room. I model the first bikini for him.

"Do you like it?" I ask.

"I love it," he says before walking up and giving me a huge, comforting hug. "You are the finest woman on this planet and I want to make love to you right here, and right now."

"You are terrible, let's wait," I say before easing my way out of his embrace. I then turn to look in the mirror at my gorgeous body in the bikini.

"What if I don't want to wait?" He wraps his long muscular arms around me.

I laugh to myself thinking about the incident that occurred earlier between Scottie and I. I always find myself getting caught in confined spaces.

"It wouldn't hurt you to wait ten more minutes. Now, leave so I can try on my other swimsuit."

"Let me help you get undressed first," he says while removing the strap from my left shoulder.

"Stop tripping."

"I'm not." He replies with a wicked grin on his face, reminding me of his father. He then plants a sweet gentle, kiss along my left shoulder blade. Then looks me in the face before planting a sweet gentle kiss along my right shoulder.

"Stop," I hear myself telling him, before I realize it we're kissing away and off comes my bikini. I close my eyes and allow myself to drift into an exotic place, not too far from here. Walter and I are so caught up in each other that I don't hear Samantha knocking on the door. I'm thinking it's the beating of my heart, but I hear her ask, "Is everything all right in there?" to which I reply, "Yes, now go away!" I'm sure she hears the heavy breathing, the sounds you make when you're not just screwing, but making love, which is what I'm doing now to Walter, Jr. I'm making love to him. He knows it, I know it and Samantha knows it, too.

***

Walter, Jr. and I are relaxing in a hammock in the back yard of, check this out, his family's vacation home. Come to find out, this is where Walter, Sr. spends his weekends. No wonder I hardly see him anymore. This place is immaculate with its ocean side view of the Atlantic. It has pink marble floors, huge granite columns, and an infinity pool that appears to go on and on into the deep turquoise. I can honestly see why Walter, Sr. would spend his quality time here. The place is peaceful, tranquil and beautiful. The yards are sprawling with palm trees, St. Augustine greens, and pink flamingoes. The shit is a trip!!

"So, are you and your father really close?" I ask.

"Yes, we are."

"Have you told your father about me?" I ask.

"No, not yet."

I was glad, yet somewhat offended. Why? I'm probably the best thing that's happened to Walter, Jr. Why hasn't he told him about me? Am I a best kept secret?

"Why haven't you told your father about me?" I asked, really wanting to know the answer.

"To be quite honest with you Roxy, I initially thought of you as a quick lay, something that couldn't develop into anything serious, but things have changed."

"A quick lay?" I roll my eyes at him.

"Things have changed and I really like you. You're more than just a pretty face, you're honest, you're funny, you're adventurous, you have all the qualities I look for in a woman."

If Walter, Sr. came out here right now and saw us, I wonder what he'd say?

"So when am I going to meet your parents?"

"Soon."

I can't wait to see the look on Walter's, Sr.'s face when Walter, Jr. parades me on his arm. He will never guess in a million years that I am having relations with his only Son. I'm going to give Walter, Jr. a big passionate kiss and act all mushy and affectionate in front of his father. I want to make him so furious, as he has made me. I really love Walter, Sr. because he's a good guy and an astute businessman. But on a personal level, he stinks. I know all three of our paths are going to cross. Why else would Walter, Jr. happen to pop into my life?

Jumpseat Confessions

Why do flight attendants feel they must share their innermost secrets with other flight attendants on the jumpseat? Roxy and I had this conversation before about flight attendants who volunteer information about themselves. It's enough to make you wonder, are we all dysfunctional? Why is the divorce rate in the airline industry so high? Why are there so many gay men flying? Why would a flight attendant brag to another flight attendant about sleeping with a pilot only to find out that pilot is the other flight attendant's husband? These things happen all too often in our line of work, and the passengers wonder why we're so hostile at times.

I put the microphone to my lips and make my greeting to the 155 passengers aboard our plane, "Good evening ladies and gentlemen, my name is Whitney and I'll be your flight service coordinator. Working this flight with me in first class is Roxy. In the main cabin, you have April and Cameron. If there is anything the four of us can do to make your flight more enjoyable, please feel free to ask. I would like to take this opportunity to welcome onboard our Superb Flyer Club members. If you are a Superb Flyer Club member, you will be earning valuable sky mileage for your flight to San Francisco. As a reminder, once the Captain turns off the fasten seat belt sign, this will be the only indication that it is safe for you to get up and move about the cabin. Until then, please remain seated with your seat belts fastened. Once this 737-800 series aircraft has reached a safe and comfortable cruising altitude, the flight attendants will come through the main cabin with a beverage and dinner service. If you chose to have a cocktail, beer, glass of wine or a margarita with your meal, you may do so at a cost of four dollars. The flight attendants do not carry change so when you order make sure you have the exact change. We also have a variety of complimentary soft drinks including; Coke, Diet-Coke, 7-Up, Diet 7-Up, Dr. Pepper, Diet Dr. Pepper, and Ginger Ale. Our other variety of drinks include orange, apple, cranberry and tomato juices, coffee, tea, sparkling water, club soda, tonic water, and bloody mary mix. For your convenience, there are four lavoratories on this plane; two in the rear of the plane, one near the mid-galley and one in first class. Presently, we ask that you sit back, relax, and enjoy your flight to San Francisco."

I put down the microphone and continue conversing with Cameron, one of my classmates from inflight training. She's telling me about the bitter divorce she's going through with a pilot she met two years ago, right after we completed training. Cameron says that she came back early from a trip to find another woman, who turned out to be another flight attendant, walking around naked in her house like she owned it.

"What did you do?" I ask.

"At first I was speechless, I was like *what in the hell are you doing in my house?* She gives me this explanation about some big misunderstanding and I made her leave my house, naked."

"No!" I covered my mouth.

"Yes I did!"

"Where was your husband?"

"Turns out he had made a run to Spec's to get some champagne, when he came back he was shocked to find me sitting on the bed."

"Didn't he know better than to bring another woman to your house, and in your bed?"

"Bill was stupid, and I hate myself for falling for him so soon."

"How long did you two date before you married him?"

"Six months."

"Cameron, didn't you have a child?"

"I'm pregnant now."

"No."

"Yes."

"Your first?"

"Yes."

Cameron sighs and her hazel eyes become blurred with tears, "I always had this picture of the three of us being a happy family, but that's not the case anymore."

"Are you keeping your baby?" I ask.

Fidgeting nervously with her hands, she shakes her head.

"Oh, Cameron." I give her a hug.

"I'll be fine," she says, before wiping a tear from her eye.

"Are you sure you're going to be able to fly the rest of your trip?"

She nods, "I'm a big girl. I can handle it."

Roxy struts into the first class galley to prepare it for her service. She notices Cameron wiping a tear from her eye and she looks at me with an expression like, *what's going on with her?*

"Roxy, how are you these days?" Cameron asks, trying to make small talk.

"I'm fine." Roxy replies as she unwraps a tray of terry-clothed oshiboris.

Cameron stares momentarily as if she wants to say something else to Roxy but changes her mind and proceeds to make her way to the back.

"What's wrong with her?" Roxy asks once Cameron is on the other side of the first class curtain.

"Trouble on the home front."

"Isn't she married to a pilot?"

"They're getting a divorce."

"What else is new?"

"She's pregnant with his baby."

"She ought to have it and stick him with child support," Roxy says so nonchalantly.

"Listen to you."

"What? There's nothing wrong with that. I'd rather get paid $1,000 a month in child support than to get an abortion and receive nothing."

I roll my eyes at her and get the first class manifest with the names of her passengers and begin to take their orders. Today's menu features a choice of prime rib with garlic-mashed potatoes, steamed green beans and carrots. This is a popular choice because the first twelve people request it along with a glass of Cabernet. The other choice; spinach and lasagna Florentine with marinara sauce didn't set too well with a couple of passengers.

"You have anything else besides lasagna?" A prim and proper Caucasian lady asks.

"I'm sorry, lasagna is my only choice." I respond in a calm and soothing manner.

"I'll just take a salad instead."

I write her request down in writing. Another gentleman wasn't as polite.

"I'm a Superb Flyer Club member. I should have gotten asked first."

"Sir, everyone here is a Superb Flyer Club member. Now, I'm sorry you didn't get your choice. If you have any problems with the service, please call our 1-800 hotline and voice your complaint."

He rolls his eyes at me, "I guess I have no choice but to take the lasagna."

"Yes, sir, you do have a choice; you eat it or you don't eat it," I say and walk off before I give him a chance to respond. I don't understand it when you offer passengers a choice and when they don't like it they assume you have something else. If I had another choice don't you think I would have mentioned it? I go over the orders with Roxy, who already has her white wine chilled and red wine opened to room temperature. She has her glasses iced-down and mixed nuts ready to be served.

"I'm all done and it's all yours," I tell her.

"Whitney, when you finish I want to talk to you."

"Uh-oh, what is it now?"

"I'll tell you after you finish."

"Is it about Walter?" I ask.

"Sort of," she says.

"Your life is one big soap opera," I tell her.

***

April, the galley flight attendant, sets up the cart just the way Eddie would if he were here. Speaking of Eddie, he's taken a month of leave and right now he's on a flight to Hawaii for a little R and R. I can't blame him for wanting to do so after what went down at the funeral. It was horrible. I felt so bad for Eddie and my heart goes out to him and to Brooke's family. I still can't believe a man as fine as Eddie is gay. He's so masculine, he's the last person you would suspect of having sexual feelings for another man.

Cameron, the load flight attendant, and I are ready to push the bar cart up the narrow aisle of the 737-800 airplane.

"I'll make an announcement to let everyone know you're coming up the aisle," April insists and she gets on the PA system to address the passengers.

Although an announcement was made warning everyone that a 300-pound bar cart would soon make its way through the aisle, you still have a few passengers with their feet and shoulders sticking out who try to get an attitude when you bump into them. Cameron and I get to the first three rows of the main cabin. In my usual way I grab a napkin and start with the passenger at the window first.

"Hi, would you like something to drink?" I ask.

"What do you have?" she asks.

Obviously she didn't listen to my announcement.

"Would you like a soda or juice?" I ask.

"Juice."

"I have orange, apple, tomato, or cranberry."

"Cranberry is fine."

I scoop some ice into a glass and begin to pour the cranberry juice. As I hand the juice to the girl she says, "Oh I forgot, I don't want ice in it."

The expression on my face is anything but courteous. She notices and says with a sheepish grin, "I'm sorry."

"It's not cold," I assure her.

"I'll take it." An older lady who must have been her mother reaches out to retrieve it.

I make another one for the girl by the window. I'm surprised at how calm I am. By now, April has made her way with the dinner portion of the service. Tonight's choice is turkey or tuna on a sourdough bun.

"Turkey or tuna?" I ask the girl by the window.

It takes her forever to respond, "I'll take the turkey."

On to the next row, "turkey or tuna?"

"I should have a vegetarian meal," the gentleman says in a loud, resonating voice.

"What is your name?"

"Harris. Bob Harris."

"Cameron, ask April if she has a special meal for Bob Harris?"

Cameron asks and April goes over her list of special meals. Now in order for one to get a special meal, for example, if you are vegetarian, diabetic, Hindu, Jewish, etcetera, you must call Worldwide's catering hotline at least 12 hours before your flight departs. If you do not, then you do not get your special meal. A lot of passengers will tell me, Oh, my travel agent made the reservations. So what? If you or your travel agent doesn't call at least 12 hours before the flight departs, guess what? You do not get a special meal.

"What is his name again?" April asks.

"Bob Harris," I repeat.

"I don't have a vegetarian meal for Bob Harris," She says.

I look at Mr. Harris, "Mr. Harris did you hear that? She doesn't have a special meal for you. Did you or your travel agent call our catering hotline at least 12 hours in advance?"

"Yes, I did."

"Well your meal should be here, Mr. Harris."

"Could you do me a favor? If you have a vegetarian meal left over would you give it to me?"

"Sure, no problem at all." I respond and proceed to the next row.

Choppy and intermittent episodes of turbulence began to rock the plane. To that, the Captain turns on the fasten seat belt sign. I try to pour orange juice for a passenger but end up spilling some of it into my tray of ice. I notice the pagoda, a device that holds up the orange juice, water, and lemon and lime garnishes, is swaying back and forth. The passengers sitting nearby are eyeing it very carefully, hoping and praying nothing falls on them. I remember when I first started flying and the plane went through some rough, turbulent air. A couple of orange juices came tumbling off the pagoda, but luckily no one was sitting nearby.

After the three of us complete our first service, I go out again to collect the trash. Our company policy states that we shouldn't wear gloves when picking up trash but I do it anyway. You never know what you come in contact with and since we're traveling to the gay-and-anything-goes-capital of the universe, I definitely want to be on the safe side. After we complete a second service and collect more trash, I make sure the pilots get something to eat before I join Roxy in the first class galley.

She's making an ice-cream sundae.

"Who is that for?" I ask.

"It's for you if you want it," she says before adding a

cherry on top.

"You know I don't eat airplane food unless it's a salad," I respond, "you should have one left over."

"Call the cockpit," she says to me, "Rick, the first officer wanted a sundae. He's kinda cute too."

I press the button to the cockpit, "Hello Rick? Hey Skip, Roxy's coming up with an ice cream sundae for Rick."

They unlock the door and Roxy walks her tight, short dress into the cockpit. While she's in the cockpit I help myself to an unwrapped and untouched salad. After I prep my salad and add a little turkey in it from coach, I sit down on the jumpseat and try to enjoy it. Roxy walks out and joins me on the jumpseat. I pretend I'm Oprah or a talk show host and I hold the end of my fork to my mouth, "Hello, I'm Whitney Christian. Welcome to today's episode of *Jumpseat Confessions,* the show that takes an intimate look at the jacked-up lives of your airline pilots and flight attendants. Today our guest is Roxy Figueroa, a 26 year-old flight attendant from the Bronx, who is involved in a tumultuous affair with the Vice President of the airline where she is currently employed."

Roxy shoots me the finger.

"Miss Figueroa, welcome to the show. Now, tell our audience and our viewers out there all the scandalous details."

She tries to stifle a laugh, "you're so funny."

"No, you're the joke here Miss Figueroa. Let me get this correct, you're having an affair with the Vice President of the company?"

"And I'm screwing his son, too."

My jaws fall, "You slut, when did you start sleeping with his son?"

"About a month ago."

"You are too much for me."

"He irritates me sometimes because he can be just like his father, very cold and impersonal. The only time Walter,

Sr. is hot is when he's in bed. But this weekend I spent time with Walter, Jr. and I tapped into his soft, sensitive side."

"So you think you've found your soul mate in Walter, Jr.?"

"I think I've found a real person and not some tin man."

"So tell me about this Walter, Jr.?"

"You've seen him before. He's tall, dark and handsome like his father, and he's fine."

"Tell me about Walter, Jr. the person, not about his physical characteristics. What makes him soft, sensitive and personal?"

Roxy smiles the way a person smiles when they are in love, but I know it's just a phase with her. She'll meet someone else and be all over him next week.

"He played the guitar and recited a poem to me right off the top of his head as we were riding on the boat last Thursday night."

"You remember what he said?"

"Mí Boriqua, mí amor, que quiero..." She closes her eyes in hopes of trying to remember the rest.

"What does that mean?" I ask.

"Boriqua is another name for a Puerto Rican female but he began with my love, I love you more than you will ever know. Although we've just met, I feel a connection like our paths have crossed before..."

"He's got that right," I began but I remain quiet as I listen to her try to piece together the poem that Walter, Jr. quoted off the top of his head.

"Then he says something like... you are a delicate creature, a beauty to love. You are the sun, the moon, and the stars. You are everything to me."

"That's deep, Roxy." I try not to sound too facetious.

"No man has ever told me that before, Whitney."

"You're kidding, right?"

"No. I'm not. And when he told me all the wonderful

things in that poem, he made me forget about all the sexual escapades we had in the beginning and concentrate on the here and now. When I woke up the next morning and saw him lying there beside me, I could sense that he was content lying next to me and although he had a million and one things to do, I was number one on his list." She looked at me.

"Are you getting soft on me?"

"Whitney, for the first time in my life, I feel appreciation from a male."

"You didn't feel appreciation from your adoptive father?"

"Let's see, when he wasn't fucking me...he was busy convincing my mother that the other boys in the neighborhood were."

"Oh, Roxy."

"I told you about my childhood, every man I knew wanted to fuck me, Whitney."

"Tell me about it," I empathize with her on that one. The same happened to me.

"But Walter, Jr. is different and I'm seriously thinking about cutting off the relationship with his father."

"You should, Roxy, because not only will you run the risk of ruining your relationship with him, but with the entire family. Everybody loses if you keep up the relationship with Walter, Sr."

The call button from coach rings but I don't bother because Cameron or April can handle it. I try to finish my salad and take in the information I just received from Roxy. She quietly sits for a moment, thinking about what I just said.

"Thanks, Chick, I really needed to hear that." She says before getting up to check on her first class passengers.

Lucky

Scottie and I are living it up at a Luau in his parent's backyard. I enjoyed sampling poi, eating roast pig, and getting full on Mai-Tais. Scottie's Polynesian mother is gorgeous, as well as the Polynesian women who are effortlessly shaking their hula skirts. If I was a skirt chaser I'd be getting a few numbers. Some of the Polynesian men on the one hand are huge, brown-skinned, pot-bellied wonders. But there were others that looked just as good as Scottie if not better. I learned a lot about their culture just sitting and talking with his parents. It felt so good to know that no question was deemed too stupid to ask and if I had a questionable stare, Scottie's mother was there to make it crystal clear for me. He and I left around midnight. We spent the rest of the night hopping from club to club on Waikiki.

I wake up and look at my clock to see that it's two o'clock in the afternoon but it feels more like seven o'clock. My sleeping pattern is off track. I think about Brooke, but then it hits me that she isn't alive anymore and I start crying. I miss her, and right now I want to talk to her. I just want to tell her that my coming out wasn't worth her taking her life. She was a beautiful treasure and I just didn't think that she would go this far.

Quietly, without waking Scottie, I force myself to get up and go outside to take in the majestic view of the Pacific and Diamond Head. Scottie, "the big spender," didn't want us to stay at the Outrigger on Waikiki Beach where Worldwide employees get discount rates for rooms as low as $60.00 a night. Nor did he want to stay at his parents cliffside white palace on the far north end of town. He wanted to stay at the Hilton Hawaiian Village, a resort, where it costs $300.00 a night. To tell you the truth, I love it here. There's a plethora of gift shops, a few nightclubs, and my God, Wild Kingdom. I never thought I'd see penguins in Hawaii, I always thought they existed in harsh, winter environments like the North and South Poles. The place is so panache and our suite is grand, yet cozy.

"Good afternoon, or should I say, good evening" Scottie says, nearly startling me.

"Don't scare me like that," I say, holding on to my chest. For a moment there I pictured myself falling 11 stories down.

"I'm sorry, I didn't mean to scare you," he says. He notices the traces of tears, "You're thinking about Brooke again?"

"Yeah." I respond, staring at a crowd of surfers, trying to test their skills on the waves, "I came here to get away and to have a good time, but all I can think about is Brooke. She's haunting me, Scottie."

"It's just going to take some time, kid." He slaps my shoulder, "Have you ever surfed before?" he asks.

"Brothers don't surf," I reply.

"What do you mean brothers don't surf? Let's try it," he responds. "You'll never know how fun it is until you ride those waves."

"Okay, and while we're at it, let's go scuba diving and bungee jumping." I'm beginning to sound a bit facetious.

"Let's do it. I'm all for it."

"Oh, all right then, I guess it wouldn't hurt to try it at least once." I heard myself reply in defeat.

"Later. Right now I'm starving. We're getting room service?"

"No, let's go to Sam Choy's."

Within ten minutes, Scottie and I are in a white convertible Mustang rental cruising along Waikiki Boulevard, listening to DMX. Scottie loves DMX. Personally, I'd rather be cruising to the sounds of Miles Davis. I am in a jazzy mood and the clear and easy sound of *All Blues*, would put my mind at ease. Not the yelling and growling and dog barking that's so typical of DMX. Scottie is bobbing his head and mouthing each lyric word for word, "my nigga this and my nigga that." I cringe every time I hear it and wonder why some rappers think it's so cool to mouth that word with such ease.

After dinner at Sam Choy's, Scottie and I drive to this little hole in the wall where the same-gender-loving locals go to have fun and order a round of drinks. A live band called "Black Leather" is playing on stage and over to the right dancing high above everyone is this very muscular, acrobatic wonder, balancing what looks to be 170 pounds of pure muscle on his hands. He does an L-shape, a V-shape and the scissors with his lean and flexible legs. His Frappuchino-colored complexion is glistening with perspiration from what looks like hours of dancing. He pushes his weight off his hands like an Olympic gymnast on a balance beam and lands on his feet. He begins to move with grace and elegance like a ballerina with years of training.

"Check him out," I say to Scottie.

"He's good," Scottie says, not taking his eyes off the dancer's body.

I'm trying hard not to appear in the least bit jealous. However, I can't hide the expression of admiration on my face.

After entertaining me, Scottie, and everyone else, the dancer did a curtsey and rushed off stage right into a bevy of screaming females. I recognized a couple of flight attendants in the bunch. Worldwide has a base here in Honolulu and since we've been here it seems like Scottie and I are always running into someone from work. Meanwhile, the dancer is talking a mile a minute and using exaggerated expressions. I get the impression that he loves to be the center of attention.

And to some extent I can understand why. He's beautiful to look at. He seems like he's a lot of fun, and just the kind of person to lift your spirits.

Scottie and I resume our drinking at the bar and sit silently while observing the wild atmosphere. The loud house music is thumping and I can hear the dancer and the crowd of noisy girls making their way to the bar.

"Give me a vodka on the rocks, honey!" he shouts to the bartender, "I deserve one on the house!"

The bartender sneers at him like yeah right, and proceeds to prepare the drink.

"I'm serious, don't get clowned in front of these men, Butch!" The dancer apparently caught the sneer, "as much money as I spend every week on drinks I should have some stock in this joint."

"You're absolutely right," he sits the drink in front of the dancer, "you're fortunate to catch me on a good night."

"Thank you, Butch. You're so Butch," he says, and slurps loudly from his drink.

I turn to Scottie, "You think we should treat our dancer friend to another drink?"

"I think he's worthy of one," Scottie says with a smile.

"Yo Butch, get the dancer another drink. Put it on my tab!" I shout and place a $20 bill on the table.

The dancer gets up and gives Scottie and myself a hug.

"Oh family, where have y'all been all this time?"

I guess that's his way of saying thank you.

"Not in the right places, apparently," I respond.

"I'm Lucky LaCroix." He extends his hand to Scottie and myself, "And it's so nice to see family, where are you men from?"

"Houston." I spoke for the both of us.

"No shit, I'm from New Orleans."

"Are you a flight attendant? Pilot?" Scottie asks.

"I'm a flight attendant out here, I don't know for how

long. Word on the street is they might be closing the base soon," he says before taking another loud slurp.

"How long have you been flying?"

"Ten years," he responds.

As we talk, I notice how it seems everyone in the club speaks to Lucky.

"You are a popular person," Scottie says.

Lucky playfully rolls his eyes and waves his hand, "Honey, these children can't get enough of me. This place is dull and the drinks are getting watered down." He finishes the rest of his drink.

"You guys ready to go where some real excitement is?" he asks.

Scottie and I glance at each other and shrug our shoulders, "Yeah, where would you like to go?" I ask.

"Baby, there's a place on the edge of the island that's rocking all night and the drinks are so potent they make your dick curve!"

Scottie and I laugh before we follow the animated character through the crowd as he shares air kisses and chats with everyone in his path.

"These are my cousins," he responds when the eyes invade us.

When we finally make it outside to the nice, cool air, Lucky stops. "Oh shit, I need a drink for the road, you don't mind do you?" he asks with an exaggerated, yet urgent look on his face.

"Go knock yourself out," I say and turn to Scottie. He gives me a look that let's me know we're going to be in for a long night with Lucky.

Miracles Do Happen

I tie a white ribbon around Déjà's thick, black ponytail with the sounds of traditional gospel playing on my radio. Déjà sings along in her cute, eight year-old voice.

"Shake, shake, shake. Shake the devil off…in the name of Jesus, shake the devil off."

"Be still, Déjà," I say to her before she stops bobbing her head.

She obeys and stares quietly at my reflection in the mirror.

"You don't have to stop singing," I say.

"Mama, we sing that song at church."

"I like that song."

For the last month I've been attending church with Donna and Déjà. Up until that point I've been what you call, "church hopping." Sometimes I'll attend Byron and Nikki's church, other times I'll venture out on my own. Since meeting Eddie's parents at the funeral and at their invitation as well as Eddie's, I've decided this morning to attend their church services. Eddie brags at how "dynamic" his father is and how his sister, Countess, is the icing on the cake. I heard Countess sing at Brooke's funeral and the sister made the hairs on my arm stand up.

"When is Daddy going to church with us?" Déjà asks.

"I don't know."

"Gran-Gran says daddy is the devil," Déjà says, mimicking the saying made so popular in the *Waterboy* movie.

I smile at Déjà's remark, "You're too much." I pat her shoulder to let her know I'm finished and I began to work on myself. Dewayne left the bathroom a mess this morning. Hair left from shaving is visible in the face basin and on the counter top. Earlier this morning when I went to use the restroom, I sat down and my butt went straight inside the toilet, splashing cold water everywhere. When he first got out of jail, the stuff seemed cute because I hadn't had a man living with me for the past eight years. Nowadays, it's becoming a nuisance. I try not to seem so petty about it but when I wake up and see yellow phlegm floating in the toilet when it should've been flushed, that's when I draw the line. The next time I see Dewayne I'm going to let him know that I am not his maid and I am definitely not Donna.

***

Although the auditorium at St. Mark Baptist Church is filled to capacity, I spot Eddie's mother sitting on the front row when his father acknowledges her. I'm not one to sit on the front row at any church so Déjà and I grab a seat in the middle of the center section. Eddie's father makes a comment, which I didn't catch, and the congregation of over 1,000 erupts into a sea of laughter followed by a thunderous applause. Once we sit and get adjusted, I survey the section of the auditorium in front of me. The choir is massive, I'm guessing around 100, and with so many faces they seem to blend. I glance down at the church program and read over the order of service and see we're at the greeting of visitors. Pastor Kelly tells everyone to stand up and greet the people around you. Déjà and I get up and shake hands with the people around us. Two ladies compliment me on my hair and Donna Karan pantsuit. A couple of the fellows seem to undress me with their eyes and instead of a handshake, they lean forward for a hug.

After the choir sings an up-tempo song that gets most of the congregation doing the holy dance, Countess takes the microphone and proceeds to walk downstage. I remember how people at Brooke's funeral just doubled-over crying when she sang. Countess's voice was so loud, angelic and clear that she didn't need a microphone to amplify it. Today, as she did on the day of Brooke's funeral, she closed her eyes and held the microphone near her chest and clutched it in a way an opera singer clutches her hands.

As soon as she opens her mouth most of the congregation is on their feet, shouting out praises to God and lifting their hands towards the heavens. I try to hold back the tears but they fall uncontrollably down my checks and onto my hands. The lady next to me gives me a tissue and I thank her before dabbing my eyes. I look at Déjà and she's crying. I think she's crying because she sees me crying. I take my arms and wrap them around her and proceed to wipe her little tears with the tissue.

"Mama's okay, don't cry," I tell her.

She begins to sob even louder when I tell her that. She looks up at me and whispers, "I wish my daddy was here."

"Me too, Pumpkin."

I thought things would be different between Dewayne and I since his release from prison. And, actually it was for the first month or so. Then after a while the, "honeymoon" ended. I rarely saw Dewayne anymore and to be quite honest it was better when he was in prison-at least I knew where he was.

After Countess sings her song and everyone, including myself, comes down from our emotional high, Pastor Kelly gets up and sings a song in his raspy, tenor voice.

"I feel like going on..."

Those words were enough to get the congregation on its feet again, and a few of the sisters and brothers shouting out praises to God. After he sang a few bars he started on his sermon with the same title. He talked about having a closer walk with God.

"People who don't walk with God won't understand how you can smile with evil present all around you! How you can go on living for years after the doctors give you up to die..."

Pastor Kelly goes on illustrating through parables and walks from the pulpit into the audience,

"Let me show you what a closer walk with God can do for you! Stand up, Sister Christian!"

I watch as he helps a lady to her feet. With her back towards the audience it's hard to see her face, and when she turns around with a large brimmed black hat on her head it's still difficult to see.

"Church family, this sister is an example of how God works. Three months ago, Sister Christian was on crack, she was down and out living on the streets, and clinging to dear life. She came to Brother Richard, one of our street ministers, begging him to pray for her. You know what? Brother Richard's prayers, my prayers, and your prayers took her off the streets. Our prayers got her into rehab, and now look at her!"

"Hallelujah!" she shouts before taking the microphone from Pastor Kelly, "Hallelujah congregation, let everybody say Amen! God is good! God is real! He delivered me from heroin, crack cocaine, prostitution, and the depths of hell! I'm here to tell you since I found Jesus, that knowing and believing in Him has been my greatest high! Crack cocaine can't compare to him! Heroin can't compare to him! Multiple-orgasms don't even come close to the Magnificent, the Almighty God!"

I try to figure out the voice because I've heard it somewhere before. It sounded like my mother's voice. But it couldn't be her, not in church. No way!

"I've been three months clean and no turning back, I owe the Lord my undivided attention! Hallelujah! I been on the streets most of my life and I don't have a disease to my name! Hallelujah! I'm walking with God, Hallelujah, because He walked with me! Hallelujah! He talked with me! How can I turn my back when the Lord has been so good to me?" She is so overcome with emotion that she begins to jump up and down and when her black, big brimmed hat pops off and reveals her face, I realize those tears are my mother's and I scream out, startling the people around me. Before I know it, I'm shouting and kicking off my shoes. My prayers have finally been answered. I feel the hands of the women around me, trying to restrain me from falling on my face. I feel the cool, swooping sensation of a church fan, and the sound of a thousand whispers, shushing me, soothing me, letting me know that everything is going to be alright. I know it is. I've seen it with my eyes. Miracles do happen, and now that my prayers for my mother have been answered, it was time to work on Dewayne again and most of all, myself.

***

After church services I take Déjà's hand and we proceed through the crowd until we find Pastor and Sister Kelly. When I approach them they immediately reach out to embrace us.

"Pastor Kelly, I will be coming to your church from now on, I know you are a true man of God."

"We could use you Sister Whitney, you see how the Lord worked a miracle in Sister Christian's life."

"That's who I want to talk to you about, where is she?" I ask while searching for her through the crowd of people.

"If you hold on a minute you might be able to see her."

I give Pastor Kelly and Sister Kelly another hug before I make my way through the crowded church. My heart is beating 100 miles a minute. I've seen my mother clean before but this time seemed different. From where I sat it looked as if she gained a little weight and although she had a midnight blue wig on, her penny copper-colored skin had a little glow to it that I remember once when I was a little girl-before she got strung out. As I mentioned before, Mama had me when she was 15 and she was on her own pretty much after that. She quit school and since she couldn't really support me with no education and no job, I went from one relative to the next.

There was a period between my transitions when she finally landed on her feet and got a decent job. We lived in a one-bedroom apartment on MLK and some of my fondest memories were of the evenings when she came home from work and made dinner. As tired as she was, she still tried to help me with my schoolwork. Then times started getting hard in Houston around 1981 and 1982. People started getting pink slips thrown at them and unfortunately, my mother was one of them. So she sent me to live with my Aunt Maxine. I was eight years old when I realized what was going on with Mama. She found a man she thought she was in love with, but he was verbally and physically abusive to her. He talked her weak little impressionable mind into doing heroin, or as they call it on the streets, smack. She never shot it up because she hated needles, she usually snorted it because it gave her temporary relief from the reality she tried so hard to escape.

When I finally see her face to face, she notices Déjà and I, and rushes up to give us a hug.

"Look at you!" I shout, staring at her and not believing what I see.

"I know baby, it's hard to believe. I owe it all to God and Pastor and Sister Kelly."

She smiles and it looks like she has a new set of dentures. I have to pinch myself because this doesn't seem real. It seems like somebody is playing a practical joke on me. I mean, to have my mother look so decent, when I've been accustomed to seeing her dressed in any old thing. And, her eyes. They didn't look tired. Sure, they had crow's feet, but they didn't have that empty, hollow look. Her eyes sparkled just like diamonds. I couldn't stop staring at her.

"My, you look good," I said with tears streaming down my face.

"You're looking at God's handy work baby, and He don't make mistakes."

I notice her eyes wander from mine into Déjà's.

"Is this your little girl, Whitney?" she asks.

"Yes, this is Déjà. Déjà, this is my mother."

Déjà looks at my mother, who's dressed in a red and black polyester dress.

"Hi, Déjà. Believe it or not, I'm your grandmother."

Déjà doesn't say anything, which is unusual for her, but I figured her model of what a Grandmother should look like is Donna. At 55 years of age, Donna still gets around in mini-skirts and Gucci pumps. This lady standing before her is nothing like Donna, and Déjà gives her much attitude.

"Déjà, stop acting like that and give your grandmother a hug."

Reluctantly, Déjà gives my mother a quick hug and is by my side before I know it. I've never seen my child act snobbish to anyone before. I proceed to ignore it because I'm sure it will take some time for Déjà to get used to her.

"So Mama, where are you staying nowadays?" I ask.

"The church has a shelter on MLK, where I also work."

"You're working again?" I ask, not believing what I'm hearing.

"Yeah, I'm a counselor."

"Get out of here!" I shout.

"Yes baby, your mother is busy trying to get those crack-infested souls to the Lord. He's real. I'm living proof of that."

"Amen."

She leans forward and says in a low whisper, "Whitney, I've been on these streets since I was 15 years-old. Everybody on these streets knew about me. I was the biggest, most scandalous, a trashiest whore if you ever knew any. I thank God everyday that I haven't caught that HIV."

"When was your last check up?" I ask, whispering back.

"I went to the free clinic about a year ago. I think it's time for me to go back."

"Let me know so I can take you, maybe you can go some place where you get your results in two days."

She smiles, "Thank you, baby. I'll have to take you up on that offer." She leans forward to give me another hug, "Whitney, I am so proud of you baby. God is real. Ask me how I know?"

"How do you know Mama?" I ask, thinking I already know the answer.

"Because He took care of you and made you into a beautiful young lady and He made sure you were a good Mother to your little girl. You got plenty of good common sense. I know you didn't get it from my side of the family. You got book sense, because you graduated from high school and you went to TSU."

"I haven't graduated from TSU."

"You got your foot in the door, which is more than I can say for the rest of your people."

"Yeah, it was definitely the man upstairs who got me to where I am today."

"I just wished I was there for you, baby."

I thought about my childhood years growing up around her. She did the best she could when she was clean but when she wasn't, those times were hurtful and embarrassing. Most people in my position would be bitter but I'm not, I have compassion and I don't know where I got it from but it's there.

I notice Déjà fidgeting and acting like a normal eight year-old. "Mama, I'm hungry, can we go to my *other* grandmother's house to eat?"

"Not today, baby. Let's go some place else?" I wanted to take Mama somewhere special for a change.

"Gran-Gran said she was making my favorite today," Déjà says as she stares at my mother with a disgusted look on her face, "and I'm looking forward to going over there to eat."

It's obvious; Déjà's trying to be snobbish and ugly.

"What's wrong, Déjà? I wanted to take you and my mother out to eat together so you can get to know her."

"I want what Gran-Gran's cooking today, that's all."

"What is Gran-Gran cooking?" I ask.

"Macaroni and cheese."

"Is that it?" I ask. I know the real deal and I'm not going to ask her anymore. The bottom line: she's not digging my mother and for a second, I can understand where she's coming from. Déjà's not dumb, she's wondering, *if you're my grandmother, where have you been all this time?* It may take some time but I think Déjà will eventually warm up to my mother. Déjà is so much like Dewayne's side of the family. They're very proper and snobbish, especially Donna. You would think the way she acts, she was raised in some rich, big shot family but she was just like me, a girl from the bad side of the tracks who dated and eventually married into some money.

***

After I drop Déjà off at Donna and Dwight, Sr's., Mama and I go to This Is It. I get smothered chicken livers, and she gets the chitterlings. She wanted the ox-tails instead but opted not to order them because of her dentures.

"There are no virgin ears here, so talk to me Mama, how long is this going to last?" I ask after we say grace and begin to eat.

Mama takes a long sigh, "One day at a time, baby."

"Do you still get the urge?"

"Not anymore, I think the Lord is using me for good."

"The reason I'm asking you all this is I want you to get a job and maybe fly with me."

She shakes her head immediately, "Noooo. I ain't never stepped foot on anybody's plane and I don't plan to. God said *low* and *behold* I will be with you until the end..."

I laugh at her clever remark. "I'm not going to force it on you, but if you ever want a job, it's a phone call away."

"They wouldn't hire me anyway, I'm too old and fat

and I don't have my GED or diploma."

"You're right, we need to get you in some night classes."

"I keep trying but you know what always happens."

"Didn't you just have a birthday, Mama?"

"Yes, you remember. I just had my 41st birthday," she says proudly before wiping the corner of her mouth.

"Mama what is your real name?" The question just came out of me from nowhere.

"Sylvia," she says, "why did you ask me that? I thought you knew my name."

"Everybody called you Lil' Bit, so that's all I knew. Everywhere I went I was Lil' Bit's daughter."

I notice tears forming in her eyes, "You know that's a shame on my part…I just want you to know that I'm sorry for all the shame and embarrassment I put you through."

"Don't beat yourself up, nobody's perfect."

"You turned out so good, Whitney, you've done so well…" she stops eating and begins to sob loudly right there in the restaurant.

I take my hand and place it on top of hers and rub it.

"You could've followed in my footsteps. You could've not stopped and talked to me that day you saw me. You could've hated my guts, but you didn't."

I shake my head, "You know why I didn't, because deep down inside, I always knew you would eventually come to your senses and I wouldn't have to see you down and out, and prostituting yourself. I'm so glad you weren't dead before I saw it. You are alive, very much alive, and you're still young."

"Thank you, baby." She gets up to give me a tight hug, "Your love has made me better and I'm going to keep on getting better. And maybe, just maybe, even my grandbaby will start liking me." We both explode into laughter through our tears.

Crew Debriefing

I'm glad to see Eddie flying again. I missed sharing a jumpseat with him and I was about to go berserk with all the new people. Eddie appears to have everything under control, although if I were him, I would still be in shock and out on family leave. I couldn't imagine going on with life as usual after a loved one of mine had committed suicide. I haven't spoken to Eddie in over a month and I want to talk to him tonight during a crew debriefing. That's what we call it when the crewmembers gather together after a trip and discuss everything from the latest gossip at work to religion. Well... maybe not religion.

"Eddie, my man, what it look like?" I ask before giving him a huge bear hug.

"I never thought I'd be saying this to you but..."

I give him a playful nudge on the cheek, "But what?"

"I missed yo' ole crazy self."

"I missed you, too. How are you feeling?"

"I'm better." He replies, "Thanks for the card."

"Don't mention it."

Whitney steps on the plane, "The Ebony and Latina crew is back and in full effect."
She gives me an air kiss and gives Eddie a long, bear hug.

"How is my man doing?"

"Your man will be doing a lot better two-and-a-half hours from now in Chicago."

"Tell me about it."

The caterers give me a knock and I give them the thumbs up to let them know that it's okay to open the door. I check my watch and realize it's 5:15 pm and on the evening flights, the first class passengers get dinner, usually a choice of beef or fish. A short Hispanic guy greets me with a smile and proceeds to remove the old carriers and replace them with carriers full of fresh garden salads, new linen, clean China, tiramisu pie, and just as I expect, beef medallion with fresh vegetables, and salmon with roasted potatoes and rosemary lemon sauce.

"Sign here," he says.

"I usually don't sign," I take a quick look at his nametag, "José, until every meal and every piece of linen is accounted for."

He gives me a questionable look so I tell him again in Spanish.

He tells me that he doesn't have all day. I tell him to give me five seconds to count. I count and all of the meals and linen are present.

"See, that's all I needed to do." I sign my name on the catering information sheet and send José on his merry way. I never let them leave without an accurate count. Try explaining to a passenger who just paid $1,800 for a ticket why there's not a beef medallion to go with his garden salad.

I look up from icing my wine and beer and guess who's standing in the doorway? Scottie, the pilot I sample-fucked on my trip to Miami.

"Well, well, well if it isn't Miss string-em-up-and-hang-em-out-to dry."

"Do I know you?" I ask, pretending I didn't know him.

He reads through the bullshit and laughs wickedly, "You're full of it."

Whitney approaches my galley, "Hi, I'm Whitney."

"Scottie." He reaches out to shake Whitney's hand.

I hope Whitney didn't hear our earlier conversation. Some things are better kept quiet.

"Eddie is our other flight attendant in the aft galley," Whitney adds

He looks in back and waves at Eddie, who waves back.

"Scottie, can we get you something to drink?" Whitney asks.

"I'll take a bottle of water if you have an extra one to spare."

"Let me check with Roxy. Roxy do you have a bottle of water to spare?"

"No I don't, but call Eddie. Catering should be in the back with extra bottles."

She rolls her eyes at me, "I'll take one of yours and you can always get one from the back."

She helps herself to a bottle in my galley.

"Whitney, if you were anybody else you would've drawn back a nub, reaching into my galley like you own it."

Whitney waits until Scottie is out of sight.

"What is wrong with you, besides crazy?"

"I don't like people coming here, helping themselves to my bottled water when I specifically told them I didn't have any. Hell, he makes $100,000 a year. It ain't nothing for him to stop and buy himself a $2.00 bottle of water."

Whitney shakes her head before going to the back to get another bottle of water. I can't believe Scottie, of all people, is flying this trip. I'm glad it's a three-day.

***

That night, the three of us order pizza and crash out in Eddie's room. It seems we all have something to get off our chest, especially Eddie.

"Eddie, why did your wife kill herself?" I ask, not beating around the bush.

"Whitney didn't tell you?"

"Tell me what?" I ask looking at Whitney.

"Whitney, you didn't tell your girl why?" Eddie asks Whitney.

"I thought you told her." Whitney replies, with a dumbfounded look on her face.

"Tell me what? What's the big secret?"

"My wife killed herself because I told her I was gay."

"Get the fuck outta here." I look at him closely and realize that he's not joking. Whitney isn't laughing and the room is silent and still.

"Eddie, you're not gay, you certainly don't act gay and you don't look gay."

"I'm friends with Dorothy and I'm not singing in your choir."

"Eddie, I don't get it, man. I mean, I would have never guessed..."

I am flabbergasted. A man as fine is Eddie is gay. Whenever I think of gay I usually think of the flaming fag, the one who pops his fingers and whose mannerisms ooze with femininity. Not Eddie. I almost want to cry for him.

"Brooke couldn't handle the idea that I like men and instead of divorcing me, she killed herself."

I lost my appetite. I was just disgusted with the notion that Eddie makes love to other men. He was probably doing it with other men while he was married to Brooke. I think I would kill myself too if I found out my husband was gay. Imagine, Walter, Jr. or Walter, Sr. sleeping with another man.

"Hellooo." Eddie's voice brings me back from my thoughts, "I can imagine what's going on inside your head," he says.

"I'm still in shock, Eddie. I mean, you sleep with other men, you know that, right?"

He chuckles quietly to himself.

"A nice looking, fine young man like yourself should be with a woman."

He nods like he's in agreement but I'm bracing myself for some long, drawn out explanation to explain the logic behind the madness.

"I love men. I love the way they touch, taste, and smell during the heat of passion..."

"Eddie, I don't want to hear it," I say, covering my

ears. "It's men like you who are dangerous. You stick your dick in somebody's ass one day and…"

"Roxy, please. Eddie's been through enough already," Whitney says, coming to Eddie's rescue.

"No, Whitney. Let her talk."

"I have a problem with gays."

"Why? Did you have a run in with a gay man?"

"No, but…"

"But what? It's morally wrong? It's what? Unnatural?"

Eddie wouldn't let me get a word in edge wise.

"You tell me what gay is and I will tell you what gay is not."

I braced myself for this one, "Tell me, Eddie."

"It's not about sticking your penis in somebody's anus one day and turning around to place it in a vagina the next. It's who I am. I didn't choose it. It chose me. You think I woke up one morning and decided I wanted to be this? Hell no, I didn't want to be this. But I am, I have strong desires and urges to be with men, just the same as you do. The only reason I hid it was because I didn't want to hurt my family and friends because believe it or not, nobody understands you. When you are gay, you are the most misunderstood person in the world, and all you want is love and acceptance, just like all the so-called "normal" people."

Whitney and I sit and listen.

"I pretended for 11 years that I was somebody I wasn't and you know what, I suffered psychologically for it. Then one day I came to a realization. Either I kill myself or tell the truth."

"You know what, you would've been better off killing yourself," I say.

Whitney and Eddie grimace at each other.

"Roxy, I ought to go upside your head and that's on the real." Whitney says, "That's very ugly and you should apologize to Eddie."

"Naw Whitney, that's all right, she doesn't have to

apologize. I respect her honesty."

"Eddie she just told you you were better off dead."

"That's right," I say, "But instead, your wife, poor soul, she took her own life, the poor thing, I bet her whole world turned upside down when you told her you were gay."

"It did."

"You should've just pulled the trigger."

"That's all right, if my father can forgive me and still love me, what everybody else thinks means nothing." Eddie looks me directly in the eyes, "Yes, I'm gay, and if you haven't noticed already, you work in an industry that's loaded with "faggots." My advice to you, get over it."

"You're starting to talk more and more like a fag." I say.

"Get over it."

"I'm over it."

"And stay over it." Eddie rolls his eyes.

"Roxy, lay off Eddie. You want to get into some shit, let's talk about you and the two Walters. Which one are you seeing this week?"

"None of your business."

"Um, I'm surprised you haven't made arrangements with both. I hear you like riding on the D-train."

I know Whitney wasn't trying to start some shit in here. She didn't want the Bronx to come out of me.

"Well, lay off me. Hey, let's talk about your man." I say shifting gears.

"What about my man?"

"Why does he keep calling me? What's up? You can't satisfy him?"

Whitney laughs, I guess she realizes I'm bullshitting just to get under her skin. Though Dewayne does look good and if he weren't with Whitney, I would definitely ride his jock.

"The only reason he calls you is to brag about how

much I satisfy him."

"Not even close," I say.

"Or, he's calling you when we're in the heat of the moment, to let you listen in on the stuff you're missing."

Eddie jumps in, "What's up, you're seeing twins?"

Whitney answers for him, "No, she's seeing Walter Nunnely and his son."

Eddie's eyes widen, "Walter's son? Now that's what I call keeping it in the family."

"Okay, okay, you guys knock it off," I say.

"So you're seeing the son, too? Tell me Roxy, who's better?" Eddie asks.

"Why, you want one?" I say, trying to sound ugly.

"Yeah, I might teach him a lesson or two," Eddie says. He and Whitney are giggling like a bunch of schoolgirls. They both make me sick.

"The sign on Walter's ass says exit only," I respond.

"You don't know that," Eddie says.

"I know neither Walter nor his son would dream about being with a man. And furthermore, any man would be sick to leave all this for another man," I say, pointing to my voluptuous body.

"I'm sorry Roxy, but you are not all that," Eddie says, sizing me up with his eyes.

"If I weren't afraid I catch something, I'd make you change your mind right here."

"I hate to burst your bubble, but no amount of sex from you or any woman could make me change my mind."

"I guess you heard that," Whitney says, instigating.

"You are sick," I say to Eddie.

"You're sick yourself, having sex with Walter and his son. Aren't you aware that HIV is spreading more in the heterosexual community than it is in the gay community? I bet you don't use rubbers."

"If you must know, I always use protection," I lied.

"Umm hmmm." Eddie replies before taking a bite out

of his pizza, "And you talk about catching something from me?"

"So what's up? Why is everybody taking cheap shots at me today? What's up, Whitney?"

"Roxy, nobody's taking cheap shots at you. Why are you getting sensitive, that's not your style?"

"I always know that whenever you and Eddie get together, it's like you guys deliberately try to pick at me."

"Roxy, don't tell me that you take us seriously," she says.

"I don't know if you're being sarcastic or not," I say.

Again, Whitney and Eddie grimace at each other and then at me.

"Roxy, let me tell you this." Eddie begins, "And I'm only saying this because believe it or not, I am your friend. You have some issues and let me start by saying that you suffer from low self esteem, and you are very insecure."

"What?" I ask, going off the deep end. Who was he to tell me about myself when he was fucked up in the head.

"You got some balls telling me about my self-esteem or my so-called insecurity!"

"I call a spade a spade."

"Fuck you, Eddie!" I shout standing to my feet, "You don't know shit about me!"

"I may not, but I'm telling you what I've been seeing since I met you two years ago in training."

"Hey y'all knock it off, this is supposed to be a nice crew debriefing, not a therapy session, my God," Whitney says, before pouring us all a glass of "crew juice."

"I'm not thirsty," I say as I move towards the window.

"Have a drink, Eddie." Whitney offers him a glass.

"I will later."

I feel like beating Eddie's sissy-ass. I can't believe he had the nerve to tell me that I suffer from low self-esteem and I'm insecure. Every time I think about it I get angry.

"Eddie, if you think I suffer from low self-esteem give,

me an example."

"You can't be serious."

"I'm serious, give me an example of a time you thought I suffered from low self-esteem."

"Well for starters, you are sleeping with Walter Nunnely, who I understand is a married man. Why don't you cut him loose?"

A good question, I'm financially tied to Walter, Sr. because he pays the bills, and he provides me with enough cash flow to look good. I can't cut him loose because he takes care of me.

"Walter is my friend, he's kind and very generous."

"Sure he is," Eddie says, walking over to the clock radio to turn it on.

The rap song, *"It Takes Two (to make a thing go right)"* is playing on the radio.

"Heyyy, remember this song?" Eddie pops his fingers and bobs his head.

"Hey PK, what do you know about that?" Whitney asks, getting up to dance with Eddie. They pretend like they're bumping and grinding all over each other.

"Come on Roxy, you missing out on all the fun, girl!" Eddie reaches out to grab my hand.

"I don't dance with queens," I said.

"Stop being ugly and come dance with us."

I'm laughing because life and friendships are peculiar. One minute he and I are at each other's throats and the next we're dancing, bumping and grinding like old friends. It's funny how all these emotions erupt from inside us and we haven't had a single drink yet.

"How low can you go?"

The three of us try to go as low as we could possibly go until we land on the floor.

"Oh, my back!" Eddie shouts.

"My neck!" Whitney shouts back.

"My neck and my back!" The three of us shout in unison before we giggle, like school children.

"I'm 27, I'm too old for this," Eddie says, rubbing his back.

"Don't say that because I'm 25," Whitney says.

"I'm 26," I respond.

"We're getting old, guys," Eddie says, staring straight at the ceiling.

"Speak for yourself," I respond. *I haven't reached 30 yet, and I'm not about to slow down.*

"Roxy, do you go to church?" Whitney asks.

"No, it's been so long, I have to knock to get in."

"You should go to church with me sometimes."

"For what?" I ask.

"To see miracles in action."

"Whitney, I see a miracle every time I look at myself in the mirror." I respond, "I don't need to go to church for that."

"For once, could you think about someone other than yourself?"

I rise up and glance at her, "What are you trying to say?"

"I'm saying that if you come to church, you may see a miracle, hell, several miracles."

"Iyanla Vanzant is about enough church as I can stand."

"You know, Eddie's father is a very good minister and he helped me out a lot."

"How?" I ask.

"His prayers brought my mother back to me."

I rise up again to get a good look at Whitney.

"He did what?"

"His church took my mother in, got her in rehab, got her new teeth, and gave her a job as a drug counselor for the church."

"That's good news Whitney, I'm happy for you."

Whitney's mom stops using drugs, Eddie's out of the closet. Everyone is opening up a new chapter. As for myself,

I'm still stuck at the prologue. Well, maybe not that far back. But I'm stuck somewhere.

"I didn't know your mother was on drugs," Eddie says.

"She's been off and on ever since I could remember. You remember that song, "yo momma's on crack rock?" Whitney asks.

I shake my head.

"Can't say I recall it," Eddie replies.

"Well, when the song came out I was in high school, I was about 15 or 16 and everybody used to tease me, 'Hey Whitney, yo' momma's on crack rock, yo' momma's on crack, and I used to get so mad. Then one day, this boy walked up to me and told me how my mother gave him a blow job for a rock. By that time, I'd had enough so I took out a knife I had stashed away in my purse and slashed the side of his face."

Eddie and I lie speechless on our backs.

"I did that so every time he looked at himself in the mirror, that scar was a reminder that God doesn't like ugly, and you shouldn't tease people when they're in pain."

"Amen," Eddie replies.

I rise up and retrieve my cup of crew juice, which is a mixture of lemonade, strawberries, vodka, and grand marinier. Tonight seems like one of the nights where I feel like getting a lot of shit off my chest...I'm sure everyone will understand.

On the DL

I wake up this morning with a nice hangover from last night's crew debriefing. Aside from me pouring out my thoughts and feelings, it's comforting to know that I'm not alone in the so-called "dysfunctional" department. Whitney's mom, Grandma Nanna, and all her aunts combined wreaked havoc on poor Whitney. I tell you, it was enough to crush her soul; but that's the one thing I love and admire about Whitney. She's a survivor. Now Roxy, on the other hand, is a different story. She was shipped from one foster home to the next, with no stable family. Then when she finally gets a stable family, the father and brother are perverted sex maniacs. Nobody believes her because they think she's a deviant little slut and it slowly tears her down. I believe Roxy treats her wounds by engaging in casual sex. She's always having affairs with married men, lying…anything to make herself feel better. She needs to heal her wounds; I suggested she start taking heed to Iyanla Vanzant's message of self-love.

I hear Scottie. He's next to me snoring away. We're keeping our relationship on the DL and it's funny to hear some of the comments. Whitney thinks he's cute, but he's too good for Roxy. Roxy, on the other hand, thinks he's disgusting and I just haven't figured it out yet. I finally get enough strength to reach across my nightstand and pick up my phone to check my messages. The first message is from Lucky. Let me tell you a little bit about Lucky. The boy is a lot of fun, but he likes to live a little on the edge. When he's sober, he's really good people. I mean the type who will give you the shirt off his back. However, at the rate he drinks, guzzling vodka on the rocks like Evian water, it'd be a miracle if he lives beyond his 30's. Like Whitney, Roxy, and myself, Lucky dealt with obstacles in his childhood. Lucky always knew he was gay. He played with his "Auntie Jackie's dolls, he took ballet with her, he even went as far as wearing her panties. He wanted to be his "Auntie Jackie" because she was soooo pretty and she got all the attention from the cute boys. However, his grandmother, whom he lovingly calls Muh-Dear, didn't want to accept the fact that Lucky liked boys. She did everything to discourage him or scare him into thinking homosexuality was a curse. She used voodoo, took him to a therapist, beat him, even encouraged him at the tender age of 13 to have relations with an 18 year-old girl. But Lucky liked men and flaunted it like a badge of honor. He had his first sexual encounter with a prominent New Orleans government official and to this day he blissfully declares that delightful experience will forever remain dear to him. Furthermore, Lucky says that he still keeps in contact with the gentleman.

"Hello Eddie, I am so glad I met you and Scottie. Thanks for providing a listening ear. I will be in Houston visiting my Auntie before I leave for New Orleans. It would be nice if you and Scottie could meet me there. Give me a call at 808-999-0909. Ciao."

***

I sensed some tension between Roxy and Scottie. I overheard her tell him that if he didn't leave her alone she was going to file harassment charges. That's serious. I know Scottie wouldn't look twice in her direction. Also, I notice her grimace or make a face every time he talks, like the sound of his voice irritates her.

"Roxy." I take her and pull her aside, "What's going on, what do you have against the first-officer?"

"Nothing." She plays it off.

"I overheard you tell him that you were going to file harassment charges against him, what is that all about?"

"Nothing. I swear, you're hearing things, Eddie."

She thinks I'm stupid. I know what I heard. Instead of arguing with her I go to the back of the plane and set up my galley for the upcoming service.

***

I'm preparing for a full flight and like so many New York flights, you have passengers with a mile-long list of special needs. There are 10 kosher meals, and five vegetarian meals that include two Hindu/Asian meals, one ovo-lacto meal, and two strict-vegetarian meals. Now the dilemma is this: Out of 15 meals, only 12 show up. There are two passengers who claim they ordered strict-vegetarian meals, and they are pissed. The only meals I have left are kosher. Now the kosher meals consist of a sandwich and I can't really tell what type of meat is there because as a rule, kosher meals are not to be opened or tampered with, the meal itself is wrapped in cellophane. I offer carrots and peanuts to the individuals who didn't get their vegetarian meals and offer them comment cards to turn into the company. I don't blame them, I'd be pissed too after I'd paid $800 for a coach ticket and ordered a special meal, only to get peanuts and carrots. But what can I do? In this industry, you offer the passengers a choice; to eat or not to eat, it's as simple as that.

***

"Whitney, have you noticed any tension between Roxy and Scottie?" I ask, as we prepare to clean up the galley.

"Yeah, something's not right, I notice he speaks to everyone but Roxy."

"Let's face it, she's not a friendly person."

"True, but they act timid and uncomfortable around each other…you think they slept together?"

Whitney's comment catches me by surprise. "I don't think so," I respond.

"He is a very attractive guy, very quiet and reserved."

"He is nice," I reply. I'm keeping our relationship on

the DL, I don't want Whitney to know that Scottie and I are seeing each other.

Just then, Roxy pops her head through the galley curtain, "At last some rest."

She sits her big butt down on the jumpseat and crosses her legs. Her skirt is so short; I can see the bottom part of her control top pantyhose. Yes, I do know a little something, something about control top pantyhose. Brooke used to wear them all the time.

"Anybody ever tell you that your skirt is too short?" I ask, trying to ruffle her feathers.

"I wish somebody would come up to me and tell me about my skirt, they all can just go to hell."

"Why are you so rebellious?" I ask.

"Because I can be, this is a free country."

"And why are you so loud, lower your voice."

"Eddie, why don't you leave me alone, don't say another word to me."

"That'll be very easy," I say and sit down to read my *USA Today* newspaper.

"And don't sit by me either."

"I suggest you go to your galley before you get hurt back here." I say, giving her direct eye contact, "and what's really going on with you and the first-officer?"

"If I tell you, I would have to kill you."

"Tell me, then kill me. Why are y'all not speaking to each other?"

"Promise me you won't say anything."

My heart begins to beat faster than normal. I know she wasn't going to say what I thought she was going to say.

"Scottie and I inducted each other into the mile-high club."

"What?" I was on the edge of my seat.

"Scottie and I sort of fucked on a plane."

"Just recently?" I ask, now I'm furious, but I'm maintaining my cool.

"Yeah."

"How long have you known him?" I ask.

"Not long at all, as a matter of fact I met him on a flight to Miami."

I recall Scottie telling me before we left for Hawaii that he needed to check on his property in the Bahamas. He was gone for two long days. I remember because I couldn't wait for him to return so we could get on the first thing smoking to Hawaii.

"So what happened?" I ask, wanting to know the full story.

"We talked, he asked me if I was a member of the mile high club, I told him hell no, but as the flight progressed and the more I drank, Scottie began to look real good, so I invited him to join me in the restroom and..."

"And he f-ed you." I finished her sentence.

"I let him sample a little bit, I was going to give him the rest later."

I'm trying to stay calm and not appear in the least bit bothered, "So did you?"

"No, but it's so funny, I look up and he's flying this trip."

"I heard you mention sexual harassment, what did he say to you?"

"He said that he wanted to finish what he started. So I told him to fuck off and leave before I file sexual harassment charges against him."

I am trying my best to maintain my cool. I will deal with Scottie later, but right now I want to deal with Roxy. She's making it very hard to maintain a friendship.

"Roxy, I want to ask you one more question?"

"What?"

"Did you use protection?"

"Of course I did."

"Good." I get up very calmly and make my exit from the aft galley. Right now, I am shocked beyond words. Scottie is dabbing around with females too, and so close to home. Just wait until I see him.

***

When I finally have a few minutes alone with Scottie I just stare at him. I am disgusted and most of all I am hurt.

"Scottie, tell me the truth."

"The truth? About what?" Scottie asks, with a look so calm it's scary.

"Scottie, are you sleeping with women now?"

Scottie takes a moment before he answers, "What is all this stemming from?"

"Roxy," I respond.

"Roxy," he laughs and shakes his head.

"Yes, what were you thinking?" I ask.

"I wasn't," he laughs again, "I wasn't thinking at all. She was fine, and I just wanted to see if I still had the desire to be with a woman."

"So do you?"

"She was the only one."

"Why Roxy?"

"I just told you, she was fine and she was down with it."

"So with whom would you rather sleep?"

He takes time to answer, "I want both."

I shake my head, "So it's like that now?"

"Yeah."

"I can't believe you and Roxy messed around on the plane, now that's funny."

"We didn't really fuck, she let me stick it in, and stroke it a couple of times but I didn't come. She left me hanging."

I laugh so hard until my stomach starts aching.

"That shit ain't funny, she was talking about sexual harassment. Now I don't fucking play when it comes to that."

"Trust me, she won't cry wolf."

"I know."

"Dangle about $500 in front of her and you won't hear a peep. She's a paper chaser."

"You think you're talking to a dummy?"

"I'm not sure who I'm talking to."

"There was a time, Eddie," he begins, "when I thought I wanted this."

"You think you don't want this anymore?"

"Some days I do, some days I don't."

"How long have you felt this way?"

Scottie sucks in his lip, "For a long time."

I don't know what else to say. This is playing out just like a scene from a soap opera with much more drama and a plot that drags on for days at a time.

The Happiest Place On Earth

When I arrive home from my trip, Dewayne is sitting in the den watching college football on a new flat screen television.

"What's up, Pee Wee?" he says before getting up to give me a kiss.

"Hello," I glance at the television and the empty box with all the wrapping paper, "when did you get that?"

"Yesterday, do you like it?"

"It's okay," I say before taking off my jacket and stepping out of my shoes. The filth from the airplane is atrocious and a nice Calgon bath is what I need to unwind. I smell the aroma of zesty garlic.

"Ummm, smells good," I say before walking into the kitchen.

"Spaghetti with jumbo shrimp," he says while opening up the pot and letting me sample his spaghetti sauce.

I close my eyes and savor the rich garlic taste.

"It's homemade," he says.

I open my eyes, "It tastes like Ragu."

"Mama gave me the recipe."

"Thank you, Dewayne." I give him another kiss. "So what's the occasion?"

"Just because. Business is doing good."

"Congratulations."

"Thank you. So tell me, what is your schedule like for the next two weeks?"

"I have a three day trip beginning on Tuesday, and a four day trip the following week beginning Monday."

"Can you take off?"

"I'm sure I can. What's up?"

"We're taking Déjà and Diamond to Disney World."

"Great, they'll both love it."

"Nikki and Derek are coming with us, too."

"How did you convince Nikki to leave the shop?" I ask.

"Derek promised he'd take her on a shopping spree."

"And we all know how Nikki loves to go shopping."

The girl has a closet that looks like a Saks department store. Derek turned one of their bedrooms into a closet, with rows upon rows of Gucci, Prada, Donna Karan, Fendi, and Manolo Blahnik. There's also a closed in air-conditioned cedar closet built to house her ankle length furs, *Lady Di* and *Miss Thang*.

"Does Déjà and Diamond know they're going to Disney World?"

"No."

"Good, this'll be a great present for them."

"And for you too," Dewayne says, giving me a kiss while trying to unbutton the top of my uniform.

"Let me take a shower first, you know how I have to do it."

"You need some company?"

"You're supposed to be cooking."

"You've been knowing me long enough to know that I'm multi-talented," he says while kissing away at my lips, ears and neck.

"Stop, that tickles." I respond, feeling giddy and excited.

"Go and get the tub ready."

"Will you bring my dinner to the tub?" I ask, gazing ever-so-lovingly into Dewayne's bedroom eyes.

"Pee Wee, I will give you the world."

We both laugh at the semi-corny response, "You are so silly."

We kiss one more time before he gives me a smack across the behind. Before taking my bath I stop by Déjà's room. She's on the computer playing her Rugrats game.

"Déjà,"

"Mommy!" She jumps up from her computer to give me one of the warmest hugs and sweetest kisses. Other than a bath, this is what I always look forward to when I come home.

"How's my Precious Pumpkin doing?"

"Mama guess what? Diamond got a puppy today."

"She did?"

"Umm Hmm, she named it Pretty Mama."

"Pretty Mama."

"It's an ugly name, I know."

"Well, how does it look?"

"It's brown and furry and it has a little bitty nose about this big." She shows me.

"Did her father get her the puppy?"

Déjà nods her head.

"What are you doing on this computer? Don't you have homework?"

"I'm finished with my homework."

"Well, let me see it."

She then picks up a stack of papers and shows them to me.

"This is my math quiz, I got a 95 on it and it was the highest grade in the class."

"I'm checking you out, Pumpkin," I say, beaming with pride.

"I like math," she says.

"Math is the best subject to like."

"I want to be an engineer when I grow up."

I give her a kiss. "You can be anything you want to be with your good grades. Now where is your homework?"

I look up and see Dewayne standing in the doorway with a dreadful look on his face.

"Whitney, come here."

I know whenever he calls me by my first name, it isn't

good.

"What is it?"

"I need to speak with you right now."

"I'll be right back, Pumpkin."

Dewayne and I went into the next room.

"What is it?"

"Five-0 just raided the clinic and the house."

"You mean Dwight and Donna's house?"

"Yeah."

"I'll be damned."

"I want you to stay here with Déjà, I'm going downtown."

"So Dwight and Donna are in jail?"

"My whole damn family and Calloway are in jail." Calloway was Dewayne's father's right-hand man.

"Who told you? I don't remember hearing the phone ring."

"I was on the phone trying to call the clinic when Mama called me collect from jail."

"Damn, Dewayne."

"Stay here with Déjà."

I watched as he rushed out of the room, leaving a scented trail of expensive cologne behind him. The news of his family's arrest leaves me numb… but I'm not surprised. I know it's all drug-related. Although Dewayne claims he's not involved with drugs, his father and brothers are and they use his sports rehabilitation clinic as a cover up for drug trafficking.

I try to remain calm as I step into the hallway to Déjà's room; I see her standing in the doorway of her room crying.

"Pumpkin." I rush up to give her a hug.

"Mama, what's going to happen to my Granny and Pawpaw?"

"Granny and PawPaw are going to be okay, don't worry about them."

"But I don't want my Granny and PawPaw to go to

jail. Who's gonna keep me while you're gone?"

At that moment, I didn't want to think about anything but calming my baby down. She has seen and heard so much more in her eight years than some people have endured in a lifetime.

The phone rang.

"Hello."

"Whitney, did Donna call you?" Nikki asked.

"Yes, I heard what happened."

"Listen, can I drop Diamond off at your house and go downtown to try and see what's going on?"

"Yes. Has Derek called you?"

"Hold on. I think this is him calling."

I listened quietly and waited until I heard her voice again.

"Whitney, this is Derek. I'll be over with Diamond in half an hour.

***

When Nikki showed up with Diamond, I looked at Diamond's innocent face and tried my hardest not to break down. I know just like Déjà went through her infancy without Dewayne around, Diamond might be faced with the possibility of going through her teenage years and most of her adult life without her father around.

Nikki, who was dressed in a turquoise linen two-piece suit, knelt before her daughter. "Listen Diamond, you behave, okay?"

"Okay Mommy, don't worry about me."

Nikki managed to smile, but underneath I could tell her tough girl image was slowly eroding.

***

Dewayne, Nikki, and Donna came in around 2:00 am and found me, Déjà, and Diamond snuggled under the covers. I got up without disturbing the girls' sleep and met with the three of them in the living room. Donna looked so different without her make-up on but she was still dressed like she stepped out of the pages of Vogue.

"Whitney, where is your guest bathroom?" she asked.

"What's the matter?"

"I know it sounds a bit crazy but I got to get this jail-house stench off of me."

I led her to the guest bathroom and gave her a couple of my nice terry cloth towels and an unopened bar of soap.

"I'll tell you all about it when I get out, sugar." She closed the door and seconds later I heard the water spraying at full blast.

I joined Nikki and Dewayne. Poor Nikki's caramel-colored complexion was stained with streaks of tears.

"What are the charges?" I whisper.

"Derek and Junior are charged with possession."

"Pops got charged with conspiracy." Dewayne added,

"The police have him on tape saying where the pick up was to take place. It turns out that damn nurse he hired was an undercover narcotics officer. I knew it was something about her that I didn't like."

"Who, Celestine?" I ask.

"Yeah, he must've been doing a little more than business. This belonged with family. Hell, you just don't trust anybody in these streets."

"Celestine is five-O?" I just couldn't believe it.

"They confiscated 16 kilos of cocaine from the clinic," Nikki said. Her weary expression told me there was little hope in store for Pops and the boys.

"Damn," was the only word I could muster from my lips.

"Celestine had the clinic surrounded. After they took Derek and Junior in, they went to the house to raid it."

"What did Donna have to do with all this?"

"She was there when they arrested him."

"Did they charge her with anything?"

"No. They just took her in for questioning."

"What did she say?"

"Donna didn't say shit. She's talking about calling Johnny Cochran."

Dewayne added, "Momma is pissed, she came up with the same conclusion I did. There was something going on between Pops and Celestine." It seemed to me just the mere thought of it bothered him and he got up and walked towards the door.

Nikki added, "I never heard Donna curse so much in my life." Nikki was a bit amused by it.

"Five-O seized everything." Dewayne said as he opened the door, "Everything my family owned is gone."

"Pops can file a claim to get that stuff back."

"Yeah…if he was white."

"Dewayne, where are you going?" I ask.

"Out to take care of some business." And just like that he was gone. Nikki and I glanced at each other before we were both scrambling to get to the door. Outside Dewayne was turning over the engine in the car.

"Dewayne, its two o'clock in the morning. Unless you out here selling drugs you don't have a reason to be taking care of business."

"I guess that's what I have to do."

"Let me go with you. Nikki and Donna can watch the kids."

"No."

"Dewayne."

"I SAID NO! Now y'all go back inside, I can handle this on my own."

The acceleration of the car left a ringing sensation in my ears and a flood of pounding drums in my heart. Dewayne left Nikki and I standing in the driveway of our townhome. A place that until recently seemed like the happiest place on earth.

***

Déjà and Diamond didn't want to go to school this morning and understandably, Nikki and I didn't force them.

They were so happy when they realized Donna was home you'd think they won the lottery. I hadn't had any sleep since Dewayne left and I kept calling him but his cell phone was turned off. Nikki and I drove for hours looking for his silver CL 500 coupe. We even drove by Donna's house but it was taped up like a scene out of a crime thriller. Finally after three hours we called it quits.

Nikki and I must have looked like zombies to Donna. She was sitting at the dining room table in one of my nicest terry cloth robes with her face made up in shades of burgundy, not to mention a fresh coat of burgundy nail polish. She was usually a proud and tough woman but she shared some information with us that didn't set too well.

"Dwight and I kept a safe at home with everything from the boy's birth certificates to our passports and half a million dollars cash. Do you know when they raided the house they found the safe and took all that money? Until then, nobody but he and I knew where that safe was. So what does that tell you?"

"Pops was talking." Nikki added.

"You see what happens when you get caught up with..." Donna couldn't say what she wanted on account of the children being within listening distance.

"Everything we own and everything we worked for is gone." She played with her coffee mug and tried to maintain her tough girl image.

"And y'all, I'll be damned if I have to go on welfare." She whispered, "I'll slang myself before I go out like that."

"Donna, don't be ridiculous." Nikki shook her head, "Whitney and I won't let you do that."

The phone rings and I pick up by the second ring.

"Hello."

"Whitney, this is Byron. Where are Nikki and Donna?"

"Over here, why?"

"They're showing the sports clinic on television, they

just arrested Junior, Derek, Dwight and Calloway."

"We know."

"What do you mean you know, and y'all wasn't going to tell me?"

"Byron, what were you going to do? Nothing."

He sucks his teeth, "See, y'all ain't right. I'm blood and I don't appreciate you sizing me up like that. You don't know the circles I travel in. I know people, Miss Whitney."

"I'm sorry, Byron. Déjà, turn to channel 13 for Mommy. After you turn the channel you and Diamond go to my room to watch cartoons."

"How is Donna taking this?"

"She's hurt."

I caught Donna's attention as she mouthed, *who is that?*

"This is Byron, he says they're showing the raid on the news."

Nikki and Donna stood up from the table and found their respective spots on the sofa to watch the news.

"I wonder who blew the whistle?" Byron asked.

"Celestine."

"Oh, I know you're lying!" Byron shouts, ringing in my ears, "I know your ass is lying! That greasy-looking ho is responsible for this?"

"Yes, but you know what, Dwight, Sr. is just as responsible."

"How?"

"I think he and Celestine were messing around."

"Hold up!" Byron shouts, "you think so, or you know so?"

"Donna told me that when they raided the house they took $500,000 from a safe that only she and Dwight, Sr. knew about."

"So you're saying that Dwight might have told her."

"Yes."

"I don't believe this. Well, have they posted a bond?

What are the charges?" He obviously didn't hear that part in the news. "They charged Derek and Junior with possession and Dwight, Sr. with conspiracy."

"What about Calloway, what did they charge him with?"

"I'm not sure."

"Where is Dewayne?"

"He left early this morning about two. He said he had to take care of some business."

"We won't go there." Byron paused. It seemed like he was reading my mind and besides, the phones could be crawling with bugs.

"Did you want to speak to Donna or Nikki?"

"Let me speak to Nikki first."

I gave Nikki the phone and joined them on the couch. By the time I arrived to watch the story, it was over.

L.A. Nights

There are some messed up people in this world and they all prefer airplanes as their mode of transportation. Case in point, this Indian gentleman is aware that I'm working my first class cabin in a system. I can't help it if he's sitting in the last row of first class. Eventually, when the time comes, I will work my way to him. When I finally arrive, he yells at me in his strong Indian accent. "I finger you for one hour and you didn't come!"

I frown and I ask him to repeat himself. He says, "I fingered you for one hour and you didn't come!"

I try with all my might not to laugh in his face. He's really telling me that he's been trying to get my attention with the flight attendant call button and I've been ignoring him, which I have. I don't ask for very much as a flight attendant. All I ask is that you respect me and be patient. It's not like I'm going anywhere. I'm stuck in this hollow tube just like you and believe you me, I want to see you eat too, but you're going to have to work with me.

The Ebony and Latina crew are in full swing and working up a sweat. The heat inside the cabin is rising. People are asking me to turn on the AC and when I ask the flight deck crew to cool it down, the temperature drops to 30 below and people are coming out of coach to ask me for blankets in first class.

"May I help you?" I ask a lady who just walks into first class like she owns it.

"I'm looking for a blanket," she says in a British accent.

"There are blankets in coach."

"If there were blankets, dahling, do you think I would be here?"

Her little smart aleck comment catches me off guard.

"In our announcements, we say loud and clear that certain things such as use of the lavoratory, and pillows and blankets are reserved for first class and that you respect this arrangement."

"Well can you turn up the heat, it's freezing!"

I mouth and mimic her as she turns and walks to the coach cabin, where the stench of mayo and chicken salad is rampant. No coach cabin is complete without the sound of a crying baby. I can't walk three steps without people giving me their empty food trays and plastic cups.

"I'm not picking up garbage right now," I repeat to several people.

When I get near the back there is a line of people waiting to go to the restroom and they're not in a hurry to move aside when they see me coming.

Eddie and Whitney are getting ready to pick up garbage. Eddie knows it annoys the hell out of me when he gives me his bag to pick up trash but he does it anyway.

I give him the evil eye.

"Make yourself useful," he insists.

"No, you make yourself useful."

"You have any first class salads left?" Whitney asks.

"I have one, but I don't know if that guy is eating or not. He's been sleeping for the most part."

"He probably won't."

"He looks familiar too, like a rapper."

"I wouldn't be surprised."

***

After the flight, Whitney approaches me with a card. I read it and it says, "Madhouse Records Inc., Kenny "Mad Lew" Lewis, CEO."

"What is this?" I ask.

"You know that rapper with Madhouse Records, Mad

Lew?"

"That's Mad Lew?" I retrieve the card and turn it over to see a home number on the back, "Why did he give this to you?"

"He said he was impressed with the service and that if we're not doing anything tonight to give him a call and he'll have a limo pick us up."

Whitney and I look at each other like *yeah right*.

"But call him just to see what happens," Whitney says.

"I can get him to buy me something cute to wear."

"Yeah right, like he's going to swoop us up."

"Are you coming with me?" I ask Whitney.

"Are you serious?"

"I can get him to buy you something, too."

"You're talking like you know him personally," Whitney replies.

"Anything's possible," I said, knowing very well I was going.

On the van ride to the hotel, I notice Eddie not saying very much to me. He directs his conversations to Whitney, the Captain, and the first officer. If I initiate a conversation he always initiates another one as if he doesn't hear me. After we arrive at the hotel and we pay the van driver his tip, I tap Eddie and pull him aside.

"What's up, Eddie?" I ask.

"Nothing, why?" he asks.

"You're acting snobbish towards me."

He shakes his head and glances at Whitney then me, " I thought you were working on your insecurity issues. What's wrong, Boo?"

"Don't patronize me."

"I'm not patronizing you, besides you're using that word out of context anyway."

"Will you two stop it?" Whitney insists, before we all approach the desk to check in.

After settling into my room I pull out the business card with Mad Lew's name on it. His cell phone number and two-way pager are on the front. I give the cell phone number a try and to my surprise he picks up by the third ring.

"What up! What up! Holla at me!" is how he answers the phone.

"Hey, this is Roxy, the flight attendant."

"Oh snap! The phat-ass in first class."

"Yeah."

"Listen, where are you staying tonight?"

"The Sofitel across from the Beverly Center."

"My limo driver will pick you up in about an hour or two to bring you to the crib."

"What's going on, you're having a party or something?"

"Most definitely, one of my new artists is having a listening party for his CD that's about to drop in the stores next Tuesday. I want you and the other stewardess to come out, drink a little Cristal, listen to a little music, and eat a little something, something."

"Mad Lew, before we go any further, let me get something straight with you. I am not a stewardess, I am a flight attendant."

He starts laughing, "What's the difference?"

"About 25 to 30 years," I reply.

"I hear ya! I hear ya! It's all good."

"I don't know why you gave my girl a business card and not me. Why? Were you afraid of me or something?"

"Nahn, you were busy, I was going to give it to you as I walked off the plane but I didn't see you. I figured you and ole' girl were cool and y'all might want to come together."

"I don't have anything to wear."

"Don't sweat that, I will have my stylist Vikki pick you up something, you like Caché?"

"You're not serious, right?"

"You don't like Caché?"

"I wore Caché clothing in high school, I'm a grown ass woman now."

"You are that." He begans to laugh, "Hmmmphf, you remind me of Jennifer Lopez. As matter of fact you look twice as good with twice the booty."

"I want a scarf dress, just like the one she wore, only the one I want is red."

"That won't be a problem."

I like the way he thinks already, "So tell your girl Vikki to pick up a size 6 dress and a size 7 shoe, preferably a strappy red pair of Manolo Blahniks."

"What about your girl?"

"What about her?"

"Oh, it's like that now?"

"I don't know what size shoe or dress she wears."

"Find out then call me back."

I get off the phone immediately to call Whitney.

"Whitney, hey, I just talked to Mad Lew, he's throwing a listening party for one of the artists. He told me not to worry about not having anything to wear because his personal stylist is picking out something and he's having a limo pick us up and take us to the party."

"You go on, I'm going to chill here at the hotel."

"Whitney! I know you're not passing up an opportunity. Who knows, you might meet a high roller who can get you a bigger rock than the one Dewayne has on your finger."

"I just don't feel like it, I went to enough of those parties back in the day."

"Listen at you, you sound like an old geezah."

"I'm just going to go downstairs to the bar with Eddie and the guys to get a drink and come back up to the room."

"It's not like we have an early check-in tomorrow."

"You go on and have a good time and tell me about it tomorrow on the jumpseat."

"What's the matter, you seem a little down?"

"It's nothing, trust me."

"Well go on downstairs with Eddie and the guys, by the way, what seems to be his problem?"

"Here we go with that again."

"I'm serious, I think-no-I know he doesn't like me ever since I told him he was better off dead."

"Can you blame him?"

"I was just being honest, now you have to give me cool points for that."

"You're right. You are honest, brutally honest."

"If he can't understand that then fuck 'em. He's more your friend than he is mine anyway."

"Are you done?"

"And fuck you, too."

"No, that's Mad Lew's job for tonight."

"Bye, geezah."

***

Around 10:30 pm my phone rings.

"Miss Figueroa, your ride is here."

Once downstairs, I notice Whitney, Eddie, the Captain and the first officer sitting at the bar drinking. They don't notice me but I see Eddie holding everyone's attention with his conversation. Outside, the air is typical LA, nice and cool at about 65 degrees. The driver, a short Napoleon looking creature, opens the door for me.

"Good evening," he says in an unrecognizable foreign accent.

I look inside and notice a large rectangular box and a round Manolo Blahnik container with my cute new strappy red shoes in them. I am so overwhelmed and excited about my shit that I don't notice the door slamming behind me and the car suddenly taking off, causing me to lose my balance. I strip down to everything but my thong and unveil my cute red Versace scarf dress. Mad Lew has won all cool points with me. I can't believe this same guy, who literally slept most of the flight, who said about two words to me during the flight, gives his business card to Whitney and I'm sitting in the back of a Cadillac Escalade putting on a Versace dress, slipping into a pair of Manolo Blahnik shoes, drinking a bottle of Cristal, not to mention smelling two dozen roses all because of him. The shit is crazy wild if you ask me, but I'm not bugging.

After what seemed like an eternity, the Escalade pulls up into the driveway of a huge, white, three-story glass structure. I can see at least 200 people from where I stand as the chauffeur takes my hand and I step down in my shoes, that to my surprise, actually fit. There are other people arriving at the same time as me. I recognize a popular actress but I don't know her name. Next, there's another actor I recognize but I don't know his name, either. There are five huge bodyguards at the door who are frisking everyone-male, female, famous or not. The bodyguards are taking cameras and anything else that shouldn't belong, including this one chick who's wearing an outfit from last year's Gucci collection. She was quickly escorted away from the premises.

Once inside, the atmosphere oozed with celebrities and wannabees alike drinking and smoozing. There is a huge poster of this Brian McKnight look-a-like with a slamming body, I mean slamming with the chest and abs to match. The tune currently playing must be a tune of his, since this is his listening party. It's a hot tune and the dancers; some of the girls who think they're too cute to really get down, are barely moving. There are a lot of weaves present, a lot of transplants. I saw a white girl with huge Naomi Campbell lips and I know she wasn't born with them.

I search the room over looking for Mad Lew and run into men who are drooling over me like a dog with rabies in the desert. I am almost ready to go until this lady who looks like Janet Jackson's twin taps me on the shoulder. I am looking at her and thinking, *can I help you?* She reads me.

"You must be Roxy, I recognize the shoes I picked out."

"You have excellent taste, looks like something I

would have picked."

"And the dress, you like the dress?"

"I love it."

"Good, follow me."

Chick is straight forward, with no expression. I am not a lesbian but I am checking out her ass. She has an ass that commands attention. It doesn't look real. I follow her upstairs through the crowd and up another flight of stairs where a bodyguard stands. He smiles and examines us like eye candy. Without saying a word he opens the door to a room that leads to another door.

"Where are we going?" I ask.

She looks at me and without saying a word she opens the door to a room not as crowded as downstairs, but crowded in its own right. It looks like a scene right out of *Eyes Wide Shut*. Everyone has on masks and if my eyes aren't deceiving me, a couple of the servers are walking around nude.

"What the fuck is going on?" I turn around to ask the Janet Jackson look-a-like. She acts as though she doesn't hear me. This shit is wild. As we walk through the room of masked men and women, I notice Mad Lew sitting at a booth in a dark corner and right next to him sits a masked lady and the guy with the slamming body on the poster.

I strut my fine self over to the table, "You mind telling me what the fuck is going on?" I ask.

"First of all, you need to sit yo' ass down! Sunny, move so she can sit down!"

I look at Sunny, and although she has on a mask, I can tell she's pissed. "I'm supposed to move for this bitch?" she says.

"Yes, that's my future wife so get the fuck up so she can sit down. As a matter of fact, all of y'all move the fuck out of the way so we can talk in private!"

Without hesitation, everyone scatters like roaches leaving Mad Lew sitting alone staring at me with a wide smile on his dark chocolate face. I really didn't notice how big he was, but Mad Lew was mad humongous, like that big chocolate inmate dude from *The Green Mile*.

"Come here, I've been waiting for you!"

When I sit down he grabs me with his huge hands and tongue kisses me. I respond as if he's Walter, Sr. or Walter, Jr.

"Why you stepping to me like you running shit?" he asks, once we're finished.

"All of this is for your friend's listening party?"

"You never been to a party until you attend a party given by me. My shit is out there!"

"I see. Why does everyone have on masks?"

"Because I told them to."

"I suppose you told the waitresses to go nude."

"Hell yeah, everybody in here dances to my music."

"So why didn't I have a mask? Or you for that matter?"

"With faces like ours, we don't need masks." He takes my face into his hands and kisses me again. Then he tilts my head back and begins to lick up and down my neck.

"You ever made love in a room filled with people?"

"No. I haven't."

He licks his lips and stares quietly at me for a second, "Stand up and model for me!"

"I modeled for you when I walked in."

"I missed it."

A nude waitress brings a bottle of Cristal to the table and pops the top.

"You know how I like it!" he says, sneering at her.

Instead of pouring it into a glass she gives him the whole bottle. He drinks it and offers some to me. I take it and tilt the bottle to my lips. As I drink, Mad Lew is running his hands inside my dress.

"It ought to be against the law to be this fine. Get on the table, I'm having you for supper."

Hot and horny my damn self, I get on top of the table and cringe and shiver as Mad Lew pours the chilled bottle of

Cristal on my brand new dress. Then he proceeds to slurp and lap on my stuff like it's the Last Supper. I close my eyes and soak in this moment. I'm not high. I'm not drunk. Yet, I'm lying here on a table spread eagle with a total stranger between my thighs and an audience of masked people staring. I've done some bizarre shit in my life but this takes the cake.

***

L.A. nights are wild on a different level that my Boogie Down Bronx days can't even imagine. Waitresses bring in platters of cocaine for us to try. I flat out refuse, telling Mad Lew that I can't because I'm subject to a drug test.

"Fuck that, I got some shit that'll fix all that." With that he takes a one hundred dollar bill out, dips it into the cocaine and places it up to my nose.

"A sister can't fly with one wing. Try it," He insists.

I take one snort and about two seconds later my face numbs up.

"Fuck, I can't feel my nose. What the fuck is going on, I can't feel my nose."

Mad Lew and his friends find it amusing. The singer on the poster whose stage name is Diabolique snorts six lines.

"Since this is your first time I'm going to cut you some slack," Mad Lew says, before sectioning off five lines. He snorts each one before leaning back to enjoy the high.

"This is the shiznit!" Mad Lew says to Diabolique.

By now my high starts to kick in and I fall back against the wall. This is madness, the way this coke is making me feel. It's like skipping across a garden full of money on a warm spring day. It's like, it's like going to the mailbox and finding a check written out to you for one million dollars. This feeling is too good to be real, so I savor it for about three more minutes.

Picture this, me sitting at a table, totally naked, and

snorting cocaine with one of the hottest producers slash rappers in the hip-hop industry. I'm about to take another hit of coke. I'm supposed to be reporting for duty sometime today around 9:00 am. There are naked, masked women and men waltzing around the place. There are orgies going on because I can hear echoes of screaming and moaning. There's sultry music from that R & B guy Diabolique playing in the background. The Janet Jackson look-a-like chick whose name is Vikki, Mad Lew's personal stylist, is engaged in a ménage a trois on the table in the booth next to ours. Can this get any more bizarre, any freakier?

"What about the people downstairs?" I ask. My high is making me talk off the wall.

"Fuck those star struck assed people! The real deal is right here!" he shouts.

"They think I haven't arrived yet, they're waiting on me to show up downstairs." Diabolique says with a boastful smile, "It's wonderful being me."

"You on another level Di, now it's time to show me the money," Mad Lew says before locking knuckles with Diabolique.

Mad Lew lives up to his name and his large size is intimidating. I've been observing how he interacts with everyone and they cater to his every whim, just like people do for Walter, Sr. and Walter, Jr. But, Mad Lew has far more money and I suspect far more power. I overheard him tell someone that he runs a $250 million a year business. He is not only the CEO of Madhouse Records but he owns a production studio in L.A. He has a film company and a clothing line. Although he isn't the most attractive looking guy, his money and power alone makes him look like Denzel, and a bowl of cherries put together.

"You think you can handle another hit?" Mad Lew asks.

"Yes. Bring it on."

With that, he takes a scoop of coke from a nearby platter and sections the stuff into three lines.

I take the one hundred dollar bill, roll it into a small cylinder and proceed to do the three lines. The shit tickles my nose but it feels good when the numbness goes away and the high sets in.

Loose Lips Sink Ships

It is five minutes past the time the van is supposed to leave and there is still no sign of Roxy. Whitney and I called the room five or six times around 6:00, 7:00, and 8:00 am. We sent someone up to the room to check on her around 8:15 but there was no Roxy, although her things were just as she left them. Just as we're about to leave the hotel, she comes running out the door looking like death warmed over. Her hair is a mess, she has on no make-up and when she gets in the van she smells like day old liquor and sweat.

"Roxy, we've been calling you since 6:00." Whitney whispers.

"I just got in about 30 minutes ago."

Her breath smells like warm cat vomit.

"So you had a wild night?" I ask.

She looks at me like someone who has been to hell and back. She doesn't say anything.

"Roxy are you going to be okay?" the Captain asks.

"Oh yeah," she says, before taking a deep sigh.

"It's bound to happen to everybody sooner or later," the Captain says, referring to her situation. In this industry if you haven't gotten up late and had only fifteen minutes to get ready, chances are you will. Whitney and I didn't tell the guys any different. Last night they were wondering why she didn't come downstairs.

"Can you turn on the air?" Whitney asks the van driver.

"Yes, please." I reply.

Roxy smells awful and I'm positive the guys can smell it too.

***

Whitney and I drill Roxy when we finally get the chance. In spite of her condition, she manages to finish in a timely manner.

"Roxy, tell me about this party you went to last night?" I ask.

"What do you want to know?" she asks.

"Did you and Mad Lew engage in any conversation?" I ask, knowing all too well Roxy probably had her panties off the moment she saw him.

"As a matter of fact we did and you know what I found out? He was number 38 on the list of the Forbes 40 richest entertainers in America under 40. He has a condo in Malibu, a home in suburban New Jersey, and a getaway in Puerto Vallerta. He makes $250 million a year, and he has a clothing line, a production studio, and a dick that hangs down to his knees."

"That's more than what I need to know," I respond.

"So that explains why you look like a zombie, you got the bottom knocked out of you." Whitney says.

"By a 6 foot 6, 275 pound black man."

"As long as I've known you I've never seen you look this bad."

"This is the first and the last time," she says.

"I sure hope so. So were there any drugs at this party?"

She looks like the cat that ate the canary.

"Yes. Why?"

"Just a good guess, I'm sure no LA party would be complete without the drugs and the booze."

"Did you experiment with anything?" Whitney asks.

"No, I'm not crazy."

"I hope not, because if you get caught with drugs in your system that's an automatic termination and possibly some jail time."

"You don't think I know that, Whitney?"

"Alright." Whitney picks up a garbage bag and proceeds to pick up garbage in the coach cabin.

"Roxy, there's something I want to tell you and it's been on my mind for a few weeks now."

"Oh don't tell me, you're going back straight and you have a crush on me."

I roll my eyes at her, "Honey please, I told you once before no woman can make me change my mind."

"I know one night with me would make you change your mind, but I'm not going there."

"What do you mean by 'going there."

"I'm talking about flirting and sleeping around with a gay man."

Good, what an excellent segue into our conversation, "Roxy, you say you would never sleep with a gay man, right?"

"Right."

"Do you remember Scottie, the first officer who you had an encounter with on the plane?"

"Yeah, what about him?"

"Well, we've been seeing each other."

Her mouth drops open, "What do you mean, seeing each other, you mean he's gay?"

"Yes."

"Fuck no!"

Roxy covers her mouth and shakes her head in disbelief, "You and Scottie are lovers? I can't believe this."

"I'm glad you used protection because there's no telling how many other women or men he's been sleeping with."

"I can't believe this."

"Believe it. Roxy, I don't want to preach to you but I'm only saying this because I am concerned for you. Be careful who you sleep with. Now, this Mad Lew character. Did you sleep with him?"

"Yeah."

"You used protection?"

"I don't remember."

"You better remember, because HIV and AIDS are rampant in the heterosexual community. And with guys like Mad Lew, who has women by the hundreds flocking to him doing God knows what, it pays to remember, Roxy."

"I think I used protection."

"And what about the Walters, do you use protection with them?"

"No."

I knew she was lying the first time I asked a while back.

"If I were you I would get checked," I say.

"If I have it I don't want to know about it."

"Now that's ridiculous, Roxy."

"I'm going to die anyway, why die faster than slower?"

At that point a passenger peeks his head into the galley, "May I get a cup of coffee please?"

"How do you take it?" I ask.

"Black."

With that I take a pot from the warmer and pour it into a gray Worldwide Airlines cup.

"Thank you, sir," he says, and disappears behind the curtain.

"Roxy, I am really concerned about you."

"I appreciate your concern Eddie, really I do, but I can take care of myself."

"No you can't. If you could, you wouldn't be looking like this and you certainly wouldn't be smelling like you do."

"I smell like Issy Myakie."

"No, more like a smelly sockie."

We laugh.

***

I opened my door to find Lucky standing on the other side, sporting white linen and a broad smile.

"How's my handsome prince doing?" he asks, before

waltzing into the house.

"Your handsome prince feels more like an ugly toad," I respond.

"What's troubling you?"

"It's Scottie, some girl just started calling here for him."

"He needs to pick one side of the fence to stay on. He can't keep on dipping and dabbing."

Lucky gets up and pours himself a vodka on the rocks and adds a twist of lemon.

"So your man is out eating fish?" he asked. Fish, for those of you who don't know, is the term gay men give to heterosexual women.

My eyes tell him yes.

"That's a crying shame." He takes a drink. I hear the ice cubes rattling like a tune against his glass, "A low down dirty shame."

"Enough about him, I hear you're transferring."

"I'll be here next month."

"Are you commuting?"

"Yeah, I'm moving back in with Muh-Dear temporarily."

"Uh oh. How does Muh-Dear feel about that?"

"She's happy to have her baby back."

"How is your other mother doing?"

"My mother ain't got the sense God gave a goose."

I roll my eyes in agreement. I met Lucky's unforgettable mother, Ophelia LaCroix, once. "So how long are you in town, Lucky?"

"Just for today, I got to hurry home to my Boo."

"How is he doing?"

"He calls me every five minutes wondering if I made it to N'awlins. You should come with me."

"I haven't been to New Orleans in a long time, I think I may take you up on that offer."

I have four days off and New Orleans sounds like the perfect getaway, and besides I'm looking forward to meeting

Lucky's friend. He's a political figure who happens to be on the DL.

***

New Orleans has an intriguing nature about it. Once you discover what it is, you want to explore everything in depth and you don't want to miss anything. When Lucky and I pull up in the driveway of Muh-Dear's house I can smell the aroma of cayenne pepper as soon as I walk through the door. Inside, the house was spotless. Muh-Dear had expensive taste because I knew Ethan Allen furniture when I saw it and hers was top of the line. The soft canary yellow living room had a 19th century Victorian look to it. I felt like I was back in the days of slavery and this was the big house where the massa and the missus lived.

"Muh-Dear!" Lucky shouts, twisting from one room to the next, "Muh-Dear, your baby is home!"

"I'm in the kitchen!" Muh-Dear shouts.

We walk inside a bright, white-colored kitchen where a Lena Horne, sassy, café au lait queen is standing up stirring something in a big, black skillet. She has on an apron that says, "If Mama Ain't Happy-Ain't Nobody Happy." Muh-Dear is so happy to see Lucky that she gives him a long, nurturing hug.

"Boy, you don't know how happy your Muh-Dear is to see you. You look good." Her Creole dialect is as thick as the mud on the bottom of the Mississippi. It sounds like she's smoked her fair share of cigarettes.

"Muh-Dear this is my best friend, Eddie."

"Hi Eddie, I know you and Lucky are starving. Y'all sit down and let me fix you something to eat."

"Muh-Dear, what's in that skillet?"

"One of yo' fav'rites. Shrimp jambalaya," she says in her Creole dialect.

"Muh-Dear, you sure know how to take care of your baby."

She gets out three plates from the cabinet and fills

them with jambalaya, potato salad, and homemade buttered toast.

The aroma and delicious food is a welcome to my empty stomach. After I lead the blessing, the three of us proceed with eating our food and breaking the ice.

"I know your father, I watch him every Friday morning at 8:00 o'clock," Muh-Dear says to me.

"I didn't know Pa's program reached all the way to Louisiana," I say.

"Yeah, I sent him $15.00 dollars for a VHS tape of one of his sermons. He preached about the prodigal son, that's one of his better sermons."

"Why, Mama?" Lucky asks.

"Do you remember the story about the prodigal son, Lucky?"

"Yes, I remember." Lucky looks at me and rolls his eyes.

"Why are you rolling your eyes, Lucky?" Muh-Dear asks.

"Muh-Dear you saw that?" Lucky asks with a chuckle.

"You ain't funny, boy." Muh-Dear chuckles, "I'm 74 years young, I can still see, and I can still hear."

"And you can still cook, too," Lucky says with a straight face.

Muh-Dear chuckles so hard that her shoulders shake, "When you pile it on, you really pile it on, don't you boy?"

"Isn't that what you love about me, Muh-Dear?" Lucky winks.

Muh-Dear turns to me, "You see what I have to put up with?"

After eating, Muh-Dear shows me around the house; a home she's showered with love.

"This house was given to me as a gift from my son-in-law back in 19 and 65 or was it 19 and 66? Anyway, this is a picture of my son-in-law and my daughter, Dorothy, on their wedding day."

My eyes focus in on a couple, one handsome, tall gentleman who reminds me of a young Harry Belafonte and a petite and slender cocoa butter-complexioned young girl about 19 or 20. There are other wedding pictures, one of her oldest daughter, Katherine and her husband, and a picture of Lucky's mother, Ophelia, with her husband walking along the beach.

There are a lot of candles and old porcelain figurines of the Virgin Mary which leads me to believe that once upon a time she was Catholic. There was a picture of Lucky as a toddler and in front of the picture are a couple of bronzed shoes. The house is decorated like a picture right out of Better Homes and Gardens. I have to give it to Muh-Dear, her house doesn't smell like the typical senior citizen's with mothballs and medicine. It smells like Pine Sol and fresh flowers.

"I would like to meet your father" Muh-Dear says to me, "I hear he does a lot of good for the community."

"That's where he receives the bulk of his blessings."

"That's what it's all about. You know so many preachers get caught up in money. Every time you turn on the television they got they hands out begging for money. But Rev. Kelly is different and I'll tell you why. When Lucky's mother got strung out on those drugs way back in the 70's, your daddy's program helped her recover."

"That's wonderful." I reply, beaming with pride at the church's accomplishment.

"Is your mother still working with the program?" Muh-Dear asks.

"Yes, she is."

"That's a good woman."

"The church has a brand new 15,000 square foot recovery facility to house the addicts and the counselors."

"That is so wonderful. My daughter Ophelia lives in Dallas now. But whenever she gets the opportunity she comes to Houston to talk with the recovering addicts."

Lucky enters the room where Muh-Dear and I are

chatting, smelling like he just poured a whole bottle of cologne on himself.

"Muh-Dear?" he asks. Lucky is dressed to the nines in a black Armani suit and black Gucci loafers.

"What?"

"You talked to Jacqueline?"

"No, I haven't talked to her since last week. Why?"

"When I was in Houston I went by the house and she wasn't there."

"She might be in New York again."

"What's in New York?"

"Some tryout for a video."

"What video? A rap video?"

"Beats me, she just said she was trying out for a video," Muh-Dear replies.

Lucky takes out a lint brush to brush some invisible lint.

"Muh-Dear, one of these days we're going to turn on the TV and see your baby in a porno flick."

"Don't say that, boy."

"You ain't gon' know what side is which when you see her."

"Boy, quit talking that nonsense. Don't you have somewhere to go?"

"As a matter of fact we do. Come on, Eddie."

"Muh-Dear, it's been a pleasure and anytime you're in Houston let me know, I'll have my mother prepare dinner."

"How nice of you, I'm going to take you up on that offer."

Lucky gives Muh-Dear a kiss. I steal one for myself. Lucky is so blessed to have a Grandmother, I'd give anything to have a Grandmother right now.

***

Lucky's friend that's on the DL is known throughout the city of New Orleans for his "community and philanthropic service." He's handsome, sophisticated, witty, smokes cigars and wears an ascot. I understand he's married and his wife is out of town on business. Lucky helps himself to a vodka as if he's been here before.

"Where's my lime, Sookie?"

The friend looks at me a bit embarrassed by the nickname, "Lucky where do I always keep the lime? It's in the refrigerator."

"Oh, there it is, you had better have my lime, or I would've raised hell in here."

The friend, "Sookie," rolls his eyes and holds up the chitter chatter hand, "Eddie, would you care for a drink?"

"Yes, you have club soda?"

"Is Lacroix okay?"

"It's perfect."

"Stewardess." Sookie holds up his hand, revealing a nice Movado watch, "Would you get my friend a club soda with a lime please?"

"Sookie, what did I tell you about calling me that?"

"Oh, it's just a name. Lucky, get over it."

"Eddie, don't you hate it when people call you a stewardess?" Lucky asks.

"I always get mistaken for a pilot," I reply as I retrieve a glass from Lucky.

"So you don't have that problem?" Sookie adds.

"No."

"You've never been called a stewardess, ever in your life?" Lucky asks, finding it hard to believe.

"I'm serious, people mistake me for a pilot."

"How can they when you only have one stripe?" Lucky asks.

"Because I'm not prancing all around the place, flaming."

"I don't flame either, Miss Thang."

"Lucky, pour me a cognac and sit your flaming behind down."

"Sookie, don't make me hurt you. I know you're really important in these parts."

My cell phone rings. It's Scottie.

"Hello."

"Hey, where are you?"

"I'm in New Orleans with Lucky."

"For how long?"

"Not long."

"How long is not long?"

"Another day or two."

"Tell Scottie he needs to stop checking and fly his ass down here!" Lucky shouts from the bar.

"Tell Lucky I would but I'd have to wipe out my 401K just to buy him drinks."

I chuckle. "C'mon Scottie, you know that's not nice."

"You saw how much he drank in Hawaii. I hope you have deep pockets."

"What is he saying about me?" Lucky sits next to me smelling like Perfumania.

"He's wiring me some money so I can take care of your tab."

Lucky rolls his eyes. "Give me this phone. Hello." Lucky gets up with vodka and lime in hand pacing the floor, talking much noise. Sookie invites me to the game room to shoot some pool.

"So how did you meet Lucky?" Sookie asks as he sharpens his cue stick.

"In Hawaii at a bar."

"Was he drunk or sober?"

"He had to be sober to do the little acrobatic moves."

Sookie chuckles, "Yeah, Lucky's a real show stopper."

"How did you meet him?" I ask.

"He did some volunteer work with my organization and one Christmas we put on a pageant. Needless to say, Lucky stole the show and my heart."

How sweet. I hope he understands that Lucky is not my lover, nor have I looked at him in that type of manner.

He's a crazy, wild, sweet as he can be dude who's a lot of fun to be around. I consider him to be a new friend. Sookie, from what Lucky tells me, is whipped and has been since Lucky demonstrated a major talent, and I won't go into details. But I'll just say this; a man knows what a man wants and how he wants it.

Sookie is an attractive guy; I have to give it to him. Especially the way he hits the eight ball then stands back and watches the balls scatter. That's how Scottie and I got acquainted.

"So how have you and Lucky been holding up?" I ask.

"Well, considering Lucky was in Hawaii and I was here, very well."

"May I ask you a question?" I begin, before I strike.

"Sure."

"How long do you intend to keep this from your wife?" I know he and I just met but I felt I could already talk to him in that way.

Silence fills the room for a minute before Sookie answers, "She and I haven't been intimate in five years. Our marriage is for appearances only."

I guess he's not going to answer my question.

"Do you suspect your wife knows?"

"I don't know what she knows. Why do you ask?"

"Because I was like you. I was 16 years old when I knew. Yet, I kept it hidden and I got married to a female and lived in an illusion that my lifestyle was just a fad and I would get over it. I never got over it and I broke down and confessed to my wife."

"You did what?"

"I told my wife and my family about my private life. Well, my wife didn't take the news lightly. Instead of going to court to get a divorce, which I thought she was going to do, she went into the garage and started the car and never opened the door. She was too hurt and humiliated to face her family and friends and she ended her life."

Out of nowhere, I feel my lips trembling. Sookie puts his pool stick down and walks over to comfort me.

"I'm so sorry. I feel your pain," he whispers.

I am a little embarrassed, I haven't been in Sookie's company for more than an hour and I'm already pouring my heart out to him. I look into Sookie's light brown eyes and see the compassion, not to mention my own reflection.

"Is there anything I can do?" he asks.

I want to kiss his soft pink lips but I remember that this is Lucky's friend and Lucky is in the other room so I just shake my head.

"Just pray for me."

"I'm not a religious person, but I figure it's the least I can do for my new best friend."

He puts his arm on my shoulder.

Lucky sashays in with the phone in his hand, "Honey, I talked so bad to Scottie his ass hung up the phone."

"What did you say to him?" I ask.

"I told him he ain't right for leading you on."

I knew I shouldn't have told Lucky about my problems with Scottie. I forgot when a person gets a little drink in their system they want to run out and try to save the world, or better yet destroy it. Whichever was the case, I felt that when the time came I was going to be the one to tell Scottie what he had to do in order to clean up his act. I can't get angry at Lucky because I should've kept my mouth shut. I always remember what my father says, "loose lips sink ships." And you can look at it from whatever standpoint you wish.

One-Woman Mission

Dwight Sr.'s, Derek, and Junior's bond was impossible to make. They each had a million dollars over their head. Some new evidence surfaced and revealed the three were linked in the kidnapping and murder of Marco Collingsworth, the guy who blew the whistle on Dewayne.

At times, Dewayne didn't know if he was coming or going. When he finally came home I tried to understand and not jump on his case. This incident had really gotten him edgy, I hadn't seen him this distraught before about anything. I couldn't console him and he didn't want me to touch him.

"D, I know this isn't an easy situation to deal with, but please don't act like this with me."

"I'm just frustrated and angry, okay? I don't like having my back up against the wall, the shit reminds me of prison."

"How much money have you come up with?" I ask.

"About 10 percent of it."

"Here." I grabbed my engagement ring before I knew it.

"What in the hell are you doing?" Dewayne asks. His eyes are staring at me in disbelief.

"Pawn it, maybe it'll help you out some."

"Are you crazy? Put it back on. And I don't ever want to see you take it off again."

He was dead serious. So I did what I was told and slipped it back on.

"Don't even think about doing it behind my back,

either."

By this time, Donna walks in. She must've heard the conversation too because she jumps right in.

"Whitney, what is wrong with you?" she asks.

"Nothing, Donna."

"Yes it is if you're talking about pawning your engagement ring. You know you won't get half the money Dewayne spent on it."

"It was just a thought."

"And a crazy thought at that," Dewayne adds.

"When is the next hearing for Dwight and your brothers?" Donna asks, before making herself comfortable on the sofa.

"Next Tuesday. The lawyer is going to see if he can get the bond lowered."

"Who's the lawyer working on it?"

"Frazier."

"Frazier Mackie?"

"Yeah, the same guy who worked on my case."

"Can't you get somebody different like Johnny Cochran?"

"Momma, let's be real here for a minute."

I heard myself giggling, I'm sure in this situation it would cost a pretty penny to retain Johnny Cochran.

"How much is Frazier Mackie talking about?" Donna asks.

"He's asking for 20 G's."

"He better do a good job this time."

"There you go thinking negative."

"I'm not, Dewayne" She responds in a high-pitched voice.

"Yes you are thinking negative."

"All of this could've been prevented if your father hadn't gotten that woman involved in his business."

"Jealousy and envy is a mofo. That woman didn't like the idea that she had to work for a living and all you had to do was sit around all day and go shopping with your husband's so-called drug money."

Dewayne had a point. It seemed as if every black person in Houston knew about Mrs. Dwight Robinson and how she flaunted her husband's money. Some black people didn't like her because of it. Maybe Celestine saw that and set out on a one-woman mission to destroy Donna's good thing.

***

I went to work that following Monday and saw the funniest thing. You know in this industry just when you think you've seen and heard it all, there is always something bizarre happening that makes you wonder, "What in the hell was that person thinking?" Case in point, during the course of boarding I went to the back of the airplane to ask Eddie a question. Hell, I don't remember what I went back to ask him but on my way I passed by the lavatory and sitting on the pot with the door wide open was a lady who looked to be in her early 50's. Feeling slightly embarrassed, as well as shocked, I turn my head. I hear her yell.

"Excuse me, ma'am!" she shouts. "You would think as much money as Worldwide Airlines makes they would at least get doors for their restrooms."

Without saying a word and trying my best not to laugh in her face I reach up and unlatch the lock on the lavatory door so she could use it in private. Common sense evaded some people and this woman was a perfect example of that.

"Eddie, did you see that lady go into the lav?" I ask.

"No, I was too busy counting my meals, what happened?"

"You didn't hear what she just asked me?"

He paused momentarily to give me his undivided attention, "No. What happened?"

"She was using the lav with the door open because she assumed we didn't have doors."

Eddie grimaced, "How dumb."

"She said that as much money as we make we should at least get doors."

Eddie continued counting his meals and shaking his head. I remembered what I came back for and gave Eddie a list of his special meals, which wasn't very much considering we were going to Washington, DC, where people didn't seem to be finicky.

Eddie stopped counting and stared at me in a rather caring manner. "I meant to ask you this earlier, but is everything okay?"

"Yeah." I respond, trying to appear as if nothing is wrong but deep down inside, the arrests and Dewayne's handling of the arrests bothered me and it went deeper than that. Long before the arrests and for the past months I've felt that Dewayne and I were drifting apart. The connection we had before and during his time in jail just wasn't there anymore. Not since the week following his release from jail had we shared the quality time we so badly needed. But Eddie's big brother-like concern really touched me. I don't cry very easily but I was nearly moved to tears.

"I'll tell you when we get to DC," I say, before making my way through the crowd.

***

The three of us caught the subway to 16th Street and went to this jammed packed Jamaican restaurant where a live Reggae band serenaded us with the rich sounds that the island is known for. After ordering our drinks and entrees I finally break down and tell Eddie and Roxy my situation. I don't like to talk about my business but sometimes we just need to relieve the tension and tell somebody. I believe "bottled up" anger, stress and even secrets can do more harm to you emotionally and physically when you harbor them.

"So what's bothering you, Chick?" Roxy asks.

"I'm having a basement moment. Can you believe that?"

"Not you?" Roxy replies facetiously.

"Yes."

"What's going on?" Eddie asks.

"Have you guys been watching the news lately?"

"No." Roxy and Eddie shook their heads.

"My future in-laws just got busted and thrown in jail."

"For what?" Eddie asks.

"You know."

"Drugs," Eddie whispers.

I nodded, "Not to mention kidnapping and murder."

"That's serious, Chick."

"I know; they may never see the light of day again."

"Be a little more optimistic, look on the bright side. If you have money, which I'm sure Dewayne's family has a lot of, then you can beat the system. Pay the judge and the D.A. under the table and take them to lunch afterward," Roxy said with a serious expression.

"Roxy, you watch too much television," Eddie responds.

"Really Eddie, she does have a point. Look at OJ. I'm sure he was guilty as hell but he got away with it because he had a Heisman trophy." I cracked myself up because I sounded as stupid as Roxy.

"The almighty dollar rules in the courts," Roxy adds.

"Gosh. When this happened all I could think about was my baby. She's crazy about her PawPaw. If she loses him it will devastate her little world."

"Does she understand what's going on?" Roxy asks.

"Yes, she knows."

"I'll keep you in my prayers," Eddie says.

"Thank you," I respond. My eyes catch a glimpse of the waitress bringing our drinks to the table.

After she leaves the three of us toast to peace in the future. The crowd grew larger and the smell of spices and incense rang rampant through the air. I look up and see a dread-locked brother swinging his locks to the beat of the hypnotic music. I can't tell if he is inside or outside but it doesn't matter, he's digging the music and so am I.

When our entrees arrive, Eddie, Roxy and I don't say very much. I sprinkle some hot sauce on my curry chicken and watch as Roxy picks through her rice and lima beans. Out of the corner of my eye I feel someone staring at me. I make direct eye contact and notice a honey-complexioned, dread-locked brother locking eyes with mine. He nodded as if to say how are you and I acknowledged him before diverting my eyes back to my plate.

"So how are things going with you, Roxy?" Eddie asks.

"There's never a dull moment in my life. Mad Lew's flying me to New York to see him at the Garden next Friday. You guys want to come?"

"I would take you up on the offer but considering my circumstances it's best I keep my behind at home," I reply.

"Live a little, Miss Slam Clicker."

"I would like to come with you too but I got a little business to tend to as well," Eddie adds.

"Are you still seeing that Scottie guy?" Roxy asks.

"Yeah, as a matter of fact I am."

I notice an awkward moment of silence between the two.

"How is everything with you and Scottie?" she asks.

"Questionable. You know he's been known to slip on occasion."

Roxy gives Eddie a long lingering stare before rolling her eyes.

"What's that all about?"

"Scottie and I kind of messed around a little. Of course that was before I found out he was seeing Eddie," she explains.

"When did this happen?"

"A while back. To tell you the truth, I forgot all about

it." She nibbles at a lima bean.

"A small world." I can't help but chuckle. Roxy reminds me of the promiscuous girl from *Sex in the City,* you know the one. Samantha is her name. Samantha screwed around so many times she got lost somewhere in the double digits.

"How did this surface?"

"Scottie is a pilot with us. As a matter of fact he's flown with us. Do you remember the handsome black first officer who flew with us on the Chicago trip?"

"He's gay?" I ask, remembering the guy as if it were yesterday.

"As I said earlier, he doesn't know what he wants."

"He's dangerous, Eddie." I reply, "And you, Miss Thing, have you gotten checked?"

"No, I haven't."

"Get checked, please, and if you don't have it thank God He spared your life."

"Okay, Mommy."

"Don't 'okay Mommy' me, and have you slept with this rapper?"

"Yes, Mommy."

"You are going to learn sooner or later."

"If sex wasn't supposed to be good for you why in the hell did God make it?"

"Oh, Lord." I hear Eddie mumble.

"Oh, now you're getting philosophical," I respond.

"Yes, I like sex and before you jump to conclusions you didn't ask me if I used a condom."

"I'm sorry, forgive me, but did you use a condom?"

She rolls her eyes at me before getting the attention of the waitress, "I'm finished, can you get this?" She points to her plate.

"In a minute." The waitress replies.

"Make sure she gets this, I'm going to the restroom." Roxy gets up with her purse and shuffles her way through the crowd, getting the attention of both men and women.

"Let's say a prayer for the girl while she's gone," I say to Eddie.

He chuckles, "I'm glad you're feeling better."

"Thank you."

"Your situation and my situation can only get better."

The waitress stops in front of our table to pick up Roxy's platter. She barely touched her food.

"Was dere some'ting wrong with t'is?" she asks in a Jamaican accent.

"No, I think she's finished," I reply.

"Can I get you any'ting to drink?"

"I'll take another Red Stripe. How about you, Eddie?"

"I'll take another one, why not?"

When the waitress leaves I glance across the room and lock eyes with the dread-locked brother sitting three tables over to my left. He smiles, showing a perfect row of teeth. I look at the band playing in the corner near the door and the guy with the dreads was still swaying his locks to the music.

"Check out the guy dancing by the window, is he inside or outside?"

"I think he's outside," Eddie replies.

"That's funny."

"Check out the guy to your left wearing the black shirt," Eddie says.

"You've been checking him out, too?" I ask.

"He's been looking since we got here."

"Is he checking me out or checking you out?"

"I think he's checking you out but you never know nowadays."

"You're so silly."

Roxy comes back singing and playing with her hair.

"So what did I miss?" she asks, in a different voice.

"All the gossip about you," I reply.

She shoots me a birdie, "So let's go, this place is getting dull. Let's go Salsa, you guys Salsa?"

"I like to Salsa. Come on, Eddie."

As we walk outside the club we notice the guy with the dancing locks. He's either high or really into the music.

No Stopping Me

"Son of a bitch," I whispered to myself when I looked through the peephole and saw Walter, Sr. standing on the other side of the door. As usual, his timing was always bad.

"Walter," I say when I open the door.

"Don't 'Walter' me." He closes the door and walks inside the house smelling like a bottle of expensive cologne, "When were you going to tell me about you and my son?"

"I was going to tell you, but..."

"But what? You wanted to see just how long you could keep playing these games?"

"I didn't want anybody to get hurt."

"You better hope like hell he doesn't find out about us." Walter studies my expression and my wardrobe for a moment, "Where are you going?"

"To Connecticut to visit some old friends." I lied.

"How long?"

"A couple of days."

"What time does your flight leave?"

"An hour and a half from now." I wasn't on stand-by either, because Mad Lew had a first class plane ticket waiting for me and Walter was holding me up.

"I'll gladly step out of the equation and let you and my son continue."

"When did he finally tell you about me?"

"Yesterday."

"How did my name come up?"

"He told me he had someone special in his life.
I asked him what did that special someone do for a living. Then he said your first name. Then he mentioned the Bronx

and that you were Puerto Rican and a flight attendant. It didn't take a rocket scientist to figure out it was you."

"Walter. Look, I don't mean to sound hasty but I got a plane to catch."

"It can wait."

I was trying to stay calm but I was fuming underneath the surface.

"Now, as I was saying, I have no problem with you and my son. Just don't let him know about us."

"You think I'm stupid, Walter?" I say, still holding on to my luggage.

"No. I think you're a very sexy and intelligent girl who stops at nothing to get what she wants."

"You're right about that," I say before opening the door and pulling my bag behind me.

Walter grabs my arm.

"Hey, Walter look, I told you I had a flight to catch, so don't stop me."

"And I told you it can wait." He takes my luggage, closes the door and leads me into the living room to the sofa.

"I'm really not in the mood for this, Walter," I reply, turning my head to avoid his kisses.

"You don't seem to have a problem when Junior does it, do you?"

He tightens his grip on my arms and lays me down on the sofa.

"Walter, please." He reaches underneath my skirt to remove my panties and finds nothing but the thick coarseness of my vaginal hair.

"Why don't you have on underwear?" he asks, poking inside of me with his finger.

"Walter, please..." I tighten up and cross my legs around his arm.

"You always were a kinky little something, I'm not sure if I want you around my son."

I had just about enough of Walter and we fought and

tussled until I was on the floor and he was on top of me with my hands pinned against the floor.

"Walter, stop it I mean it. Stop it!"

He finally let up and sat on the sofa, breathing like he had just ran a race. I ran to the mirror to straighten out my hair and my outfit.

"Are you coming behind me, or are you staying here?" I ask, before grabbing my roller bag and pocket book.

"Why don't you go on and enjoy your two days with your friends."

"Bye, Walter," I say, before walking out the door. When I start the engine I realize my car is on empty.

"Shit! Fuck!" I get out of the car and walk inside.

"Walter, I need some money." I cut the bullshit and shoot right to the hip.

He reaches into his pocket and pulls out a roll of 100's. He peels back five of them and gives them to me.

"You have any 20's?" I ask, "I need to fill up my car and I doubt seriously if they take 100's."

"I exchange my 100 dollar bill for five 20's." For dramatic effort I lean over and give him a kiss on the cheek and run to my car like a kid ready to enter the gates at Disney World.

***

Mad Lew had me staying in this crazy large suite at the Marriott Marquis near Times Square. I opened my windows to a 180-degree view of Manhattan's architectural wonders. You don't get a view this magnificent in the Bronx or in Hartsford. I put a message in Mad Lew's two-way and wait for him to reply. The concert starts in two hours and I needed a new outfit, preferably a nice unit fresh off the racks of Gucci. I also put a message in Vikki's two-way. I ordered a bottle of Moet and a movie and charged it to the room, then sat on the ledge of the window in my purple satin Victoria Secret negligee and sipped on my champagne. Outside my 20th story window, Manhattan buzzed with the roaring sounds of taxis, fire engines, buses and other vehicles trying to meander their way through the throngs of pedestrians, mainly tourists who weren't in any hurry to make it to their destinations.

Finally the phone rang. I pick up. It's Vikki.

"Hello, Vikki. This is Roxy."

"Hi Roxy! What can I do for you?"

"I want to know what Mad Lew's wearing tonight."

"Some Mad wear and probably some Phat Farm or FUBU, why?"

"Vikki, I really like your taste in clothing and I was wondering if you could pick up something for me, preferably something from Gucci."

I hear a sigh on the other end, "Mad Lew never told me anything."

"Why not? He knew I was coming to town."

"Roxy, I don't want to burst your bubble but I don't move unless I'm advanced something up front."

"That's cool so don't even sweat it. Where's Mad Lew?" I wanted to tell him about Vikki's advance.

"At rehearsals right now."

"Are you there with him? Can you get him on the phone?"

"Roxy, the man has a show in two hours. After he's finished rehearsals, he hibernates and no one, not even myself, is allowed to go anywhere near him."

For some reason I wasn't buying that but I didn't want to spoil my own good mood. I'll just go downstairs and find something nice at the hotel and charge it to the room.

"Peace out, Vikki."

"Later."

***

I was looking fierce at the concert all dressed in red. It wasn't Gucci but what the hell! I was wearing it and getting access backstage to the real action. "Damn, Shorty!" I heard a voice shout behind me followed by a couple other voices instigating the booty. The crowd grew louder as I neared the area where the performers gathered before they walked onstage. Brick-wall bodyguards stood by nonchalantly and unmoved as rappers smoked L's and fed their adrenaline with bullshit talk and champagne. The crowd cheered and rapped along with the current performer who was none other than Mad Lew. He was the shit. Everyone seemed engulfed by his stage presence. During some performances all he had to do was turn the mic toward the crowd and they would finish his lyrics. As I stood there watching him, I wondered what it felt like to be him and listen to people mouth the words to rhymes you created. I turned and walked into the area where there were platters of seafood, small bottles of water, and cans of beer. I could mainly see Heineken and 40-ounce bottles of Old English. Who in the hell drinks that shit?

***

When I finally spotted Mad Lew he was surrounded by an entourage of bodyguards and other rappers. I saw them going into a room followed by another group of guys who had a group of women, I counted five.

As I make my way to the door a bodyguard stops me.

"This is private."

"Kenny is expecting me."

"I can't help that."

"That's fucked up."

"That's the reason you're not in there right now. Your ass can't keep your mouth shut."

Suddenly the door opens and out walks Mad Lew, holding hands with a female.

"Kenny!" I shout, calling him by his first name to let Ms. Thing know I was on the up and up. He looks at me and nods his head as though he had never seen me before.

I step to him, totally oblivious of the woman standing next to him still holding his hand.

"What'ssup? When did you get here?" he asks.

"Just in time," I respond.

"Who is this?" The woman standing next to him asks.

Mad Lew turns to the woman. "Look, Shorty it's been real. Enjoy the rest of the show."

"Unh, Unh. Hell no! I'm not about to be anybody's sloppy seconds or side show." She releases her hand from his and walks off ranting and raving down the corridor with nappy blonde extensions in her hair.

"Who was that?" I ask.

"She wanted my autograph."

"Do I look shallow to you? Do I give you that impression?"

"Come on, let's go, and one more thing."

"What?"

"Don't ever call me Kenny."

"Whatever."

"I haven't given you permission to call me Kenny yet."

"Yet? I take it I'm moving up in the ranks."

"If you act right."

As we walked hand in hand down the corridor, groupies left and right were trying to get Mad Lew's attention. When they saw me, looking ever so stunning in red, they stepped back. The comments I heard went a little like this:

"Who is that bitch with Mad Lew?"

"Jennifer Lopez-wannabe bitch."

"They can never be satisfied with a sister."

"Are those Manolo Blahnik?"

"Fake ass booty."

Outside, near the limo, the crowd of females grew wilder as Mad Lew's bodyguards had to shield us from panties, bras, and anything else aimed at getting Mad Lew's attention. These females stopped at nothing. Once we settled down inside the limo one female managed to plant her naked breasts against the glass, making a squeaky sound before being thrown back by a bodyguard.

"These ho's are wild!" Mad Lew shouted to one of his two bodyguards who joined us in the limo.

"You see my performance, baby, wasn't it off the hizzzzoook?"

"Yeah, it was off the hook."

"I like this," he says referring to my outfit, "Where did you get it?"

"At the hotel."

"At the hotel? Why didn't you call Vikki?"

"I did."

"What did she say?"

"She has to have her cheddar up front before she goes shopping."

Mad Lew studies me for a moment. "That ho said that to you? Wait until I see her ass, as much cheddar as I give her she ought to bend over hand and foot for my black ass. What's that ho's number!"

I spat out the numbers as Mad Lew keyed them in on his cell phone. As he waited for her to answer the phone he turned and eyed me again.

"You are the baddest bitch on the planet, I ain't never... Hello! Vikki...where are you...listen up, you talked to my girl Roxy...she told me some shit that I didn't care to hear from you...she wanted you to find her an outfit for the concert...why didn't you?"

Mad Lew listened as she gave him her explanation, "From now on, when she asks you to do something your ass better do it...no fucking excuses, I pay your ass too much money for you to disrespect me and my lady. You better be lucky I'm in a good mood tonight because I was close to issuing your ass some walking papers...Fuck with my lady again and your ass'll be flipping burgers." He hung up.

He had me feeling sorry for the girl but the feeling didn't last very long. I like the way Mad Lew had everybody at his beck and call. Money and power gave you the authority to think you didn't need people and they always needed you. You had the power to turn out the lights and keep them off for as long as you wanted. Your access to excessive money and power, not to mention fame, made you untouchable and unscathed. Sure you may have a few run-ins with the law and lots of player haters but give them a little hush-hush and watch how they respond.

"Where are we going tonight?" I ask.

"Wherever you want to go. But first I need to make a couple of fifteen-minute appearances."

The bodyguards cleared the way for us as we bypassed the line of ordinary party people and walked down the red carpet, through the velvet rope and upstairs to the VIP room. A waitress greeted Mad Lew with a bottle of Cristal with a long straw inside. Some of the VIP's ranged from mega music producers, a model-turned-actress-turned-activist, a plethora of rappers, and a legend in his own right known for his androgynous persona. They all showed Mad Lew much love and I sat and listened as they talkedabout upcoming collaborations, new talent, the talent they already had, and even some talent that needed improvement. Being in the room and conversing with some of the entertainers I grew up listening to on the radio would have blown away the mind of an average person, but not me. I held my own. A couple of the ladies complimented me on my red dress and asked how long had Mad Lew and me been dating. I told them the truth, not long at all. The two just looked at each other like they shared an inside joke. I know Mad Lew has a wandering eye and I know he probably freaks with every girl, in every city, every chance he gets. I knew that going in. That's why it didn't surprise me to see him with that girl at the concert. I don't trip and I won't trip, just acknowledge me when I'm in your presence and everything will flow like gravy.

We left that club and went to another club that was jammed packed and had more star struck fans than the first. The crowd, both men and women, got rowdy when they saw

Mad Lew, myself and his entourage. The DJ started playing his song, which happened to be the #1 hip-hop song in the nation. Stations everywhere rocked "The Good Life," Which happened to be the title of his fifth CD. The song had an original beat and it wasn't sampled from an old R&B or pop track. It was the brainchild of Papì y Juan, two of the hottest producers in the hip-hop industry. When people in the club hear the opening beat of the drum followed by the DJ's scratch and Mad Lew's massive voice they jump to their feet and grab somebody to dance with on the floor.

A tall, voluptuous chick with Asian features and large breasts caught Mad Lew's attention. I saw her put her finger into her mouth and down her neck and to the opening of her cleavage. If I wasn't mistaken, I think part of her nipple was showing.

"Oh, shit!" Mad Lew covered his mouth. I noticed a platinum Rolex and large diamond bracelet on his hand. He looked at his bodyguards and a few more guys from his camp who noticed the girl as well. I gave him a look and he looked at me, finally realizing I was there.

"I don't care what you do as long as you don't do it in front of me!" I shouted over the loud music and all the yelling from the DJ.

"Quit tripping. I'm not trying to disrespect you!" he shouted back.

We found a booth near the corner of the room in the VIP section. Girls from all over were coming up trying to get Mad Lew's autograph.

"Let me enjoy the rest of the evening with my girl," he said to a homely looking girl who had on shoes similar to those worn by Herman Munster. Mad Lew noticed them too and made a joke about them.

I noticed a couple of athletes mingling in the place. This one in particular who happened to play with a New York team spotted us and he slapped high-fives and talked much shit to Mad Lew and his boys. No one said anything to me and Mad Lew didn't introduce me, either. I noticed right away that he was inconsistent or "sometimey," as I hear some people down South say. I noticed the athlete staring at me on the sly as he talked to Mad Lew. He was kind of cute, but I don't dig light-skinned guys, especially one who looks just as good as me.

We left that club around 4:30 in the morning and went back to my suite at the Marriott Marquis where Mad Lew, Diabolique, and the rest of the camp partied until about 8:00 am.

Too Much Like Right

As always, church was crowded on Sunday with the ushers having to put chairs in the aisles and Pops warning people they were in violation of the fire code if they didn't clear the doorways. Whitney, her daughter, and her mother were present but Whitney's mind was in a place far away from the church. Her eyes were filled with tears the whole time although the songs were very uplifting and lively. After church I offered her and her mother an invitation to brunch but she told me she had other plans, which I understood.

When I arrived home the house was empty. It was Scottie's day off but there was no telling where he might be. I was in the mood for a golf game but I knew Pops couldn't make it. He has a funeral to officiate this afternoon and the family was expecting him and Moms to show up afterwards for dinner. I got on the phone and called Lucky but got his answering service. I called my brother-in-law, Kenny Ray, who is also an avid golfer as well as my nephews, KJ and Corey. Great, I thought. It's been a while since I played a game of golf with my brother-in-law. The last time we shot 18 holes he had just learned how to play and he wasn't bad for a beginner.

"Watch out, Tiger Woods!" I shout when KJ shot the ball out past the ninth hole.

My nephew had such a nice form and his swing actually looked identical to Tiger Woods'. Corey didn't want to be outdone so he stepped up and shot with the same form and if I'm not mistaken, his ball went into the hole.

"Yes!" He shouted to his brother and father, "A hole in one, Tiger Woods better watch out for me!" He strutted or better yet showed off in front of the two.

"Just luck, pure luck," big Kenny said as he took his turn to swing.

After the golf game I went home and Scottie was there.

"What's up?" I ask.

"I'm thinking about selling the house and moving to the Bahamas."

"Why?"

"I'd like to have more days off and the commute from Nassau to Newark is a lot easier than Houston to Newark."

"You think so?"

"Oh yeah."

"When did you decide this?"

"A month or so ago."

"Where does that leave us?" I ask.

"That's what I want to talk to you about."

I braced myself for the unimaginable.

"I think it's best that we remain friends."

"Are you running away from me? Because you can't run away from who you really are, Scottie."

"I understand that Eddie, but look at us. We have nothing in common. What we have is really physical. Listen... I'm not trying to run away from who I am."

"Then what exactly is it you're trying to do?"

"To not feel that I'm obligated to a commitment."

"Commitment." I shrugged my shoulders, "I don't see any rings on your fingers or mine."

"I understand that you love me and care about me and I feel bad that you lost your wife as a result of us, but I'm unhappy and you're unhappy and I've lost all my passion in trying to save this relationship."

It hurt me to hear that Scottie felt that way but there was no use in staying in a relationship where there's no mutual attraction so I packed all of my clothes that night. I gave Scottie a goodbye kiss and went gently into a darkened night.

***

I finally caught up with Lucky and had one last cry for Scottie before moving in with him. We talked all night about our lifestyle and how hard it is to find a good, faithful companion. It's too much like right, as I heard my father once say, to have everything go so perfectly. Nothing's perfect, no matter how much I want to perfect things in this runaway freight train called life.

Lucky and I went out to *Club Incognito* where all the masculine homos hung out. Lucky found this one cute Columbian guy named Santiago and I found a cute brother named Richard. Any woman would fall head over heels in love with this guy Richard and not know that he was gay. His smile just warmed my heart. In the few minutes that we talked I found out he was an attorney but he wouldn't name the firm he was affiliated with, which lets me know that he's still on the downlow.

"Let's go!" I heard myself tell him. He followed me home. The next morning I woke up in bed alone with the sun shining in my eyes. I smelled bacon and before long, Lucky was entering the room with a tray of breakfast.

"My man left before I got up, what about yours?" he asked.

"He did the same."

"Ain't that funny, trade don't wanna hang around for breakfast. That's okay."

He smeared cream cheese on top of a bagel and offered it to me.

"Thank you." I took a bite, "Richard wasn't that bad."

"Child who you telling, Santiago had me screaming in five octaves. You'd have thought I was Leotyne Price at the Metropolitan Opera."

"He had you doing the victory dance?"

"Oh yes, honey!"

"You are silly," I say before biting into my bagel once more.

"So what are your plans for today?" Lucky asks with a mouth full of bacon.

"I don't know. I feel like jumping on a plane and going to Cozumel."

"I hear that place is excellent for deep sea diving and snorkeling. I'd go with you."

"How many days do you have off?" I ask.

"I have four days off."

"Are you still on reserve?"

"Nope, I've been flying for 10 years."

"So that means you're a Senior Mama."

"Watch it now."

"Why don't you like me calling you a Senior Mama?"

"Do I look like some of those senior Mama's you see floating around Worldwide?"

"No."

"That's right, you don't see me walking around with bags under my eyes and a pot belly like some of those girls."

"Don't they look horrible?"

"Yesss, baby this one dinosaur based in LA had two cosmetic surgeries and she still doesn't look any better."

I laugh, "What does she look like?"

"If you really must know, this heffa's face looks like an L.A. road map. One wrinkled looked like the 405 freeway, the other one looked like I-10."

"Lucky, everyone wasn't blessed to have flawless looking skin like yours."

"You got that right."

"You ought to be ashamed."

"Don't hate me because I'm beautiful."

"I've got nothing but love for you, ole' fella." I lean over and give my friend a hug, "How old are you by the way?"

"You never ask a girl her age." He playfully rolls his

eyes at me.

"For real, how old are you? You look good for your age."

"Honey, I look good at any age." Lucky examined a piece of scrambled egg on his fork before eating it.

"When is your birthday?"

"February 15th."

"So you're an Aquarius."

"As a matter of fact I am."

"Aquarius. Every time I hear the word I think about that song by the Fifth Dimension."

Lucky chewed quietly for a moment.

"A penny for your thoughts?" I ask.

"I'm just thinking about my father," He replies in a somber tone.

"What about your father?" I ask.

"I wish I had gotten the chance to know him."

"What happened?"

"I think I told you he died before I was born. He was killed in a car accident."

"What made you think about your father?"

"My birthday. He died the day before I was born."

"Does your mother have any pictures of him?"

"No photos. But she does have some sketches and paintings of him."

"Lucky, that's sad and right now I don't want to be sad."

"I'm sorry, dear."

After we finish our breakfast, Lucky and I go the Galleria to do some shopping. Lucky buys a new pair of Gucci shoes and a pair of slacks. I bet you're wondering how can he afford that on his salary? Lucky's been flying for ten years and he makes $45.00 an hour. He flies internationally, so he gets an extra dollar for that, not to mention he's a French interpreter and he gets an extra two dollars on top of that. He flies over 90 hours a month. He showed me his paycheck one month and I must say $4,500 goes a long way when you don't have a car note and all you have to pay for rent is $800.00.

Dewayne

My mother came home with me after church and fixed me something I hadn't had in a long time; a home-cooked meal. I sliced tomatoes, cucumbers and onions for a salad as she prepared black-eyed peas, candied yams, meatloaf and a hot pan of Jiffy cornbread. I vaguely remember the times before she got strung out on drugs when she came home from work and God knows where she got the energy-but she would cook a good, hot meal. I'm not talking about hot dogs and chips, I'm talking about macaroni and cheese, chili beans and a pan of Jiffy cornbread with a tall glass of red Kool-aid. I went to bed satisfied and never hungry.

"Thank you, Mama," I said when she sat the steaming hot plate in front of my face.

She took my hand and we said grace, "*Dear Lord.*" She began, "*I thank you for another Sunday. I thank you for allowing me the opportunity to spend it with my beautiful daughter. I thank you for this wonderful food we're about to receive and I pray that it will nourish our bodies and spirits I ask these and all other blessings in Jesus' name, Amen.*"

"Amen," I reply before digging in.

Mama and I don't say anything for the next two minutes. One taste of the meatloaf and I realize Mama hasn't lost her touch.

"This is good, Mama."

"Thank you."

"This reminds me of the times you used to come home from work and cook dinner."

She chews slowly and nods her head. Every day she looks more attractive. I remember the beauty of her face.

Today she has on a canary yellow blazer, a white blouse, and a navy skirt. Her hair is flipped on the ends and she even has on makeup.

"I got some good news," she says.

I wait until I swallow my drink before I ask, "What is it?"

"I got a job, a real job."

"That's good Mama, what is it?"

"A door greeter at Wal Mart."

"That's excellent, Mama."

"It's a start."

"It's better than nothing."

"I'm so proud of myself, I always knew I could do anything."

"Yes, you can."

Our conversation is interrupted when Dewayne enters the room with a bewildered, empty look in his eyes and I am reminded once more that misery is just below the happy surface.

"Hi, Dewayne."

"Hi," he replies, opening up the refrigerator and pouring himself a glass of Kool-aid.

"Dewayne, you remember my Mama?" I ask. I'm pretty sure he remembers her.

Dewayne sees my mother looking healthy and beautiful and doesn't believe his eyes.

"Lil' Bit?" he's shocked.

"Yes, believe it. I am saved by the grace of God."

"Good for you, Lil Bit! I'm proud of you."

"I'm proud of myself. I'm six months clean and counting."

"No turning back?" Dewayne asks.

"No turning back," my mother replies.

Dewayne opens the top to the black-eyed peas and peeks inside.

"Fix yourself a plate and join us at the table."

"I'm not hungry right now but I will later on."

After he left Mama says, "He doesn't look right, Whitney."

"Probably worried how he's going to make bail money for his daddy and brothers."

"He's not selling, is he?" she asks.

"Dewayne sells real estate now."

"That's what he told you?" Mama asks.

"Yeah, I heard him talking to a few people about home loans and refinancing and what not."

"He's just a plain old realtor?"

"Yes, but he mentioned something about real estate investing as well."

Mama placed a forkful of black-eyed peas into her mouth.

"The poor thing looks like he hadn't slept in days."

"He did look tired, like he was out of it."

Mama just shook her head and we ate quietly for the rest of the time. Afterwards, I prepared a plate for Dewayne and sat it on top of the stove. When I walked into the kitchen an hour later it was still sitting on the stove where I had left it. I didn't hear him leave. Now he had me really worried. I called Donna, who was now living with Nikki, and asked if he was over there. She told me he wasn't and asked if anything was wrong. I told her about Dewayne and how he looked. She also said she noticed how tired and bewildered he looked and asked him not to worry about the situation with his brothers and father. That was easier said than done.

Mama and I camped out on the sofa and watched a marathon of shows on the Lifetime network. I noticed every show had the same story line. Woman versus man, man has control over woman, woman seeks help, woman triumphs over man. Around 7:00 that evening Donna shows up with Déjà.

"Have you met my mother?" I ask.

"No, I haven't," she says. I thought she was going to introduce herself but she didn't.

"Donna, Sylvia. Sylvia, Donna." I finally said.

The two exchanged lukewarm greetings, which make me wonder if their paths had somehow crossed before. Déjà isn't much better with her greeting. It isn't three minutes before she's asking me if she can spend the night with Donna.

"You have to go to school tomorrow," I say.

"Let her spend the night, I brought her by so she could get her things."

"Go get your things and let me see them before you leave, okay?"

"Okay! I get to spend the night with Gran Gran again!"

She looks at my mother and runs out of the room, which leads me to believe that sing-a-song comment was directed at her.

"I don't have a daughter anymore," I say to Donna.

"She loves it over there. I got her a computer."

"But she has a computer here Donna, and Diamond has a computer." What I really wanted to say was how can you afford a computer when you need to budget to get your husband and children out of jail?

"Don't mention it. I wanted to get her a computer for the house, she likes it because it has a CD-ROM and she just loves to play those interactive learning games."

"What else did you get her?" I ask Donna. She spends so much money on Déjà and Diamond that it's unreal.

"I got her these cute little shoes with the roller wheels on the bottom."

"Roller shoes?"

"Yes, she loves them."

"Donna, please don't buy anything else for that child, she has enough."

"I'm not hearing you. I am that child's grandmother and that's what Grandmothers are supposed to do."

She cuts her eyes at Mama before answering the cell phone that's ringing in her larger-than-life Louis Vuitton bag.

"This is Mrs. Robinson," she answers.

I glance at Mama. Her legs are crossed and her foot is twitching as she concentrates really hard on watching television. She asks me, "where's your bathroom?"

"Down the hall, last door on your right."

As the door to the bathroom closes, Déjà enters the room with her overnight bag and backpack for school.

"Let me see what you have in here." I open up Déjà's overnight bag to take a look inside.

She had a couple of blouses and a cute little navy pleated skirt with white leotards.

"I taught you well, I'm glad to see you didn't get anything that was too little. You have some underwear?"

"Mama where's my pink blouse?"

"You wore that last week, remember?"

"Oh yeah, I like that pink blouse."

"It needs to be washed."

Déjà zipped up her suitcase and sat on the couch waiting for Donna.

"And why are you acting so anti-social to my mother?"

Déjà shrugged her shoulders. "I don't know."

"That's not an excuse. I always taught you to speak and respect your elders. Now, I don't want it to happen again. Do you understand?"

She mumbled something.

"What? I can't hear you."

"I said, Yes ma'am."

"That's what I thought you said."

Donna stopped her conversation, "Why are you fussing at that child?"

"It just occurred to me that Déjà is learning everything but manners and if that's going to be a problem then she needs to stay here and get a refresher course."

"I don't have a problem with Déjà. As far as I'm concerned, she is very polite to her elders."

"I don't know if you noticed but she came in here and walked right by my mother and didn't speak."

"She didn't mean it, Whitney."

"Don't let it happen again." I said to Déjà, "Now give me a kiss."

She gave me a quick peck on the cheek, "I love you."

"I love you, too."

"What time do you go to work tomorrow?" Donna asks.

"Around 9."

"Where are you going?"

"Cleveland and Toronto, I'll be back by Wednesday."

"Dwight and the boys'll have another hearing on that day to see if they can lower the bond."

"Donna, call me as soon as you get home. I want to talk to you about your son."

"My child looks different."

I nodded sharply and Donna knew I didn't want to talk about Dewayne in front of Déjà.

When they left, Mama emerged from the bathroom.

"Donna Robinson still walking around here like her stuff don't stank."

"You know her?"

"Not well, I knew of her. Even before she met Dwight she always carried herself like she was important, even though she was living six deep in a two-bedroom shotgun shack in Kashmere Gardens."

I picked up the phone to call Dewayne's cell phone but after three rings his answering machine picked up. I then paged him and waited for him to answer but he didn't call back. After I dropped off Mama, I went home. I made it inside just in time to answer the phone. It was Donna on the line.

***

When my alarm went off at 7:00, I woke up. It took me a moment to I realize I was in my own bed. I always get that strange feeling when I'm on the road, I forget what city I'm in and what day it is. Of course, I should be alone on the road. However, right now is different. Dewayne isn't next to me. I paged him again and called his cell phone. I called Nikki and Byron and they haven't seen him. By then my stomach was boiling with anxiety and I was close to tasting warm vomit. After I got dressed I didn't bother to eat breakfast because I didn't have an appetite. I paged Dewayne again and waited. When I opened my jewelry box to get my watch and engagement ring, they weren't there and neither was my diamond tennis bracelet. I searched frantically through the box, emptying it and still nothing. I searched my bathroom and medicine cabinet, but nothing.

"Oh no," I heard myself moan. I don't think Mama could have taken my things. Oh God, I don't think she could have relapsed and stolen my jewelry. She looked alright; but maybe she was fooling me? I felt my hands shaking and before long I was on my knees looking underneath the bed. I looked outside in the car and in the kitchen. I paged Dewayne again and called his cell phone number ten times. I got in my car and drove to the apartment where Mama lived and knocked on her door. Much to my surprise, she wasn't there. I knocked on the neighbor's door and out appeared a woman whose eyes searched my uniform.

"Have you seen Sylvia?"

"You mean Lil' Bit? She left out this morning."

"Do you know where she went?"

"She looked like she had on a Wal Mart smock."

"Where is the nearest Wal Mart?"

"In Meyerland."

I drove to the Wal Mart in Meyerland. Keep in mind, I have thirty minutes before my check in at work and the drive is an hour away. I searched Wal Mart high and low for her and didn't see her. As I drove back to her apartment I got on the phone and called crew scheduling. I told them I was sorry for giving them a short notice but I was seriously ill and on my way to the hospital. The traffic on 610 near the Astrodome had stopped completely and I began weaving my way through the stop and go traffic like a mouse weaving through a maze. When I got to her apartment I was out of luck. She wasn't there. I left there and went to the church. I found her there lecturing to other addicts about the ills of drugs. She had an alarming look on her face when I entered and she immediately stopped. "Excuse me everyone." Her eyes searched mine for answers, "Hey Sweetie, is everything all right?"

"No it's not, some jewelry is missing from my box."

"You don't think I took it, do you?"

"Did you?"

She looked at the five people sitting in the classroom staring back at her, "No Sweetie. Where is Dewayne, did he come home?"

I was too upset to answer her.

"Everybody take a 15 minute break," she said to the small crowd gathered in the tiny, intimate classroom.

"Whitney, I'm going to tell you this and you're probably not going to believe me. But Dewayne has taken your jewelry, honey. Remember the way he looked when he walked into the house yesterday? I know that look, that faraway empty look."

"Mama what are you trying to say?"

"Dewayne is bugged out on that stuff. Trust me, I know what I'm talking about, Whitney."

I shook my head not wanting to believe that Dewayne could take my jewelry. When I suggested it earlier he was dead set against it and for him to take it without consulting me first seemed unreal.

Alone

I'm finally getting the opportunity to meet Mrs. Walter Nunnley, Walter, Sr.'s wife and Walter, Jr.'s mother. Walter, Jr. called me up out of the blue and asked if I wanted to have dinner with him and his mother. He's trying to get serious but now that I'm seeing Mad Lew, I don't see anything developing between us. When we did a quickie and took a shower together, I didn't get excited like I normally would before Mad Lew. I remember the times when he would kiss my big toe; I would get a prickling and crawling sensation up my spine but this time I didn't. On the ride over, he kept looking at me and smiling like a school child.

"What's going on? You've been doing an awful lot of smiling."

"I don't know… it must be that voodoo that you do."

"I can't help it, I'm a phenomenal woman! When Maya Angelou wrote that poem she had me in mind."

"You're silly."

"So I finally get to met your mother and your father."

"My father is out of town, which is probably a good thing. If he saw you he'd probably flirt with you."

"Tell me, is your father just like you? Charming, good looking, a ladies man?"

"I wouldn't be surprised if he was still raking in the ladies. A man like him travels so much, I'm sure he gets lonely."

I wonder if loneliness drove him to me?

"Does that bother you?" I ask.

It seemed like minutes went by before Walter, Jr. answered, "It used to. When I was little I used to hear him and my mother arguing all the time about women. A couple of his women were bold because they'd leave things behind for my mother to find.

"You mean your father would bring these women into the house?"

"No. They'd leave their lipstick and panties in the car."

"Now, your father needed to be caught."

"You ever dated a married man before?" Walter asks me out of the blue.

"Yeah," I replied. "Why?"

"Did he have children?"

I wonder if he knew about his father and I? Or was he being cool about it? Naaah, he couldn't know, wouldn't possibly know.

"Yeah, he had children."

"How long did it last?"

"Two years."

"Why did it stop?"

"I met someone else. Somebody with no commitments and no responsibilities."

"That's funny, you make it sound as if the person was irresponsible and incapable of a commitment." Then he looked at me, "You're not talking about me, are you?"

"No." I had to think of a quick lie. "I was with this guy just before I met you."

We rode in silence and I realized we were in Kemah. *So this is where Walter, Sr. keeps Mrs. Nunnley.* The homes reminded me a bit of the homes in Miami, extravagant and large, with nice St. Augustine lawns, palm trees, and the prerequisite circular driveways. The only difference between Miami and Kemah was the water. The waters in Miami were so blue and inviting. The waters in Kemah were gray and murky. I wouldn't stick my big toe in them, let alone swim in them. Now here I was standing in the circular foyer of the house and in front of me stands a woman who looked as if she should grace the cover of Vogue magazine. Her skin was smooth as dark chocolate, just like a Hershey bar. You couldn't tell where her skin ended and the hair began. Her hair was like gossamer and it hung like silk past her shoulders. Veronica Hunter Nunnley stood at least 5 feet 10 inches with the elegance and demeanor of a royal African Queen.

"Pleasure to finally meet you," she says in a loud and very clear West Indian accent. She's wearing a nice, light scent that I didn't recognize but smells quite expensive. Her eyes were warm and inviting and somewhat familiar. She welcomed me in like we were old friends.

We sat together in a plush white living room overlooking the Bay. A Hispanic maid brought in a tray of chamomile tea and scones and placed the delicate display of China on the table in front of us.

"You are beautiful. Your son wasn't kidding when he described you to me," I said.

"Thank you," She replied with a nod. "Roxy, you are a flight attendant?"

"Yes, I am. I'm glad you didn't say stewardess."

After sipping daintily from her tea she replied, "Oh, why?"

"It makes me think you haven't flown since 1975."

"Of course, there are equal opportunities now for men. I remember when you had to be a certain height and a certain weight to be considered for the job."

"You talk from experience."

"Yes, I was a stewardess in 19...I don't want to give my age away, but let's say when I became pregnant with Walter I had to quit my job," she said with a smile.

"Is that where you met your husband?"

"Yes, he was the first black pilot at Worldwide Airlines."

"I didn't know that," I replied before taking a sip of the chamomile tea.

"Son, where does your father keep the family photos?"

"Mother, I haven't lived in this house in ten years, I

don't know."

"Excuse me, Roxy." When she tapped my knee I noticed a diamond about the size of a dime on her right hand.

After she left Walter, Jr. sat next to me and kissed me tenderly on the lips. His eyes were transfixed into mine and he looked as though he had found the special someone to make his life complete. I hate to burst his bubble, but it's not happening. This relationship is not happening anymore. When Veronica came back she had a couple of photo albums in hand. The three of us sat and talked and I listened as they reminisced over pictures. I saw a different side of Walter, Sr. When I saw their wedding pictures I saw two people happily in love, with a promising future ahead of them. The photos captured the pureness and excitement of their youth. I saw Walter, Sr.'s big afro and Veronica hadn't changed; even as a young woman she displayed style, grace and class. I saw pictures of Walter, Jr. playing with his mother on the beach and pictures of the Nunnley's celebrating Christmas. I saw pictures of Walter and Veronica holding hands and pictures of them with Walter, Jr. and a newborn baby.

"You have a little sister?" I asked, staring at the baby wrapped in a pink blanket.

Walter, Jr. stared at his mother like the two shared a secret that I had intruded upon.

"I had a little sister, but she drowned. She was only five years-old."

"I'm sorry." Sweat began to tickle my arms and drench my palms.

Veronica closed her eyes and shook her head slowly, "she was a beautiful baby."

I saw for myself a picture of Walter, Sr. with the little girl upon his shoulders and another picture of Walter, Sr. kissing his daughter on her cheek as she lay asleep.

"These are lovely pictures," I say. I felt envious of Walter, Jr. and his growing up in a normal family. I also felt a sense of sadness because the little girl died so tragically. I'm sure Walter, Sr. misses her to this day and I'm still amazed that I didn't get to know this side of him. But I often wondered what was on his mind when he stared into my eyes and when I asked him what thoughts he harbored, he would just say nothing. I wondered if he thought of his daughter. If she had lived, would she be in the arms of a man old enough to be her father? My thoughts are interrupted when Walter, Jr. invites me to join him and his mother in the dining area for dinner.

"Roxy, what do your parents do?" Veronica asks.

"I was adopted so I don't really know my real parents. As far as my adoptive parents, my mother was a psychologist and my father was a judge."

"Do you have siblings?" she asks, with her hand rested on her cute little chin.

"I have an adopted brother." *Son of a bitch,* I thought. I hated my brother, the perverted motherfucker. He couldn't keep his hands to himself, he and my father. My adopted brother digitally penetrated me the first night I came in from the foster home, telling my Moms how he wanted to tuck me in and say goodnight.

"Are you close to your brother and parents?" Veronica asks.

"No," I reply and glance at Walter, Jr., who nods his head to an imaginary beat.

Veronica ponders my answer and I guess whether or not she'll let the buck stop there or keep going.

By that time the maid brought out the entrée consisting of chicken Kiev with wild rice and string beans. She offered a Reisling, to which I gladly accepted.

"You sound so bitter," Veronica said, eyeing the flute as the maid filled it with the wine.

"Because I am. I went from a foster setting with very little love into a home with no love at all. My parents were successful but they had issues, deep-seated issues and let's just say when the lights went out, my father accidentally stumbled into my room."

"That's awful, Roxy. I'm sorry to hear that." She said it with the utmost sincerity.

I felt Walter, Jr.'s hand reach for mine. *He's so sweet, it's too bad he's not the man I want anymore.* And furthermore, I should be ashamed sitting here in the Nunnley home. What kind of woman sits at the table with the wife and son of the man she had an affair with? Huh. This isn't right. I lose my appetite.

"Are you okay?" Veronica asks. "Forgive me for being so inquisitive."

"It's quite okay. Where's your bathroom?" I ask.

"Walter, honey can you show her to the bathroom please?"

"Sure."

Perfect, this will be my cue to tell Walter how I really feel and make my exit, catch a cab, and go home.

"What's the matter, sweetie?" Walter asks, holding my hand ever so gently.

"Umm, I'm not feeling good."

"Is it the chicken?" he asks jokingly.

"No, Walter it's me. I'm not feeling too well."

"Well, you certainly don't look like it."

"Trust me, I feel awful."

"My mother didn't intimidate you, did she?"

"No, she didn't. As a matter of fact, your mother is beautiful. I can't see how your father could stay gone from her for so long."

"Makes you wonder?"

"Walter, there's something I think you should know."

Walter's ebony eyes danced back and forth between my eyes as he waited for me to begin.

"Walter, I've been seeing someone else and when I saw you tonight I thought I could quell those feelings but I couldn't, I can't."

Walter cast a downward stare at the polished marble floors.

"I'm sorry for any inconvenience I may have caused but I really feel awful, Walter."

Walter didn't say anything.

"Say something."

"I don't know what to say, Roxy."

"Um, tell your mother that the food was wonderful and I really enjoyed her conversation but…"

"You're leaving."

"I have to Walter. I can't stay here, I just feel terrible." I heard myself stumbling over my words.

"Wait a minute, I'll take you home."

"No, don't bother, I'll call a cab."

"Roxy listen, just let me tell my mother and I'll drive you home."

When he returned, his mother was with him. She had a concerned look in her eyes.

"Roxy, I apologize if I offended you."

"No, Mrs. Nunnley you didn't offend me, I'm just not feeling good."

"What's the matter, you have an upset stomach? A headache?" *It was more like an attack of the guilts.*

"No, I've been feeling a little lightheaded lately."

She gave me a look that I read so well.

"No. I'm not pregnant."

She smiled and tapped my hand with hers.

"I'm going to take her home, Mother," Walter said before giving his mother a kiss.

"You must bring her around again," Mrs. Nunnley said. I thought I was going to throw up with guilt. She was so sweet.

In the driveway of my home, the soft, soothing sounds of Maxwell played softly from Walter, Jr.'s car speakers.

"So you've found someone who makes your heart flutter more than me?" he asks.

"Just as much," I reply.

"Does he treat you right?"

"Yes, he does."

"He had better."

"Thank you, Walter," I say before giving him a kiss on the cheek.

"What is that for?"

"For being such a gentleman."

I guess Walter, Jr. gets his kindness from his mother. I didn't want to go to bed alone that night. I needed someone to hold me and that's just what Walter, Jr. did. He held me until the wee hours of the morning.

The Sun Is Always Shining

I'm not flying with Whitney and Roxy this time, instead I'm flying with another Houston-based crew and they are very wild. I say that because Houston-based flight attendants have reputations for being uptight and stuffy. However, this crew was a different story. We all hit it off immediately in the terminal and the chemistry we shared made me really look forward to working with these guys. Nicholas, the flight service manager, has been flying for 5 years. Melissa, the junior in the bunch, has only a year.

"So how do you like being based in Houston?" Melissa asks.

"I like it, it's home."

"I used to be based here in Newark but my family is from Houston and besides it's a lot cheaper to live there than it is here."

"You're right."

"Some of my classmates and I had a room at the Swan. Can you believe we were paying $1,200 bucks a month for one room?"

"I was based here for one month and I lived at the Swan."

"So you know what I'm talking about."

"Oh, absolutely."

"I was apprehensive about transferring to Houston at first, I hear that's where they send the tattle-tellers from all the other bases."

"No way."

"Yes, a couple of girls from my class had to transfer because they turned in a Senior Mama who took a bottle of wine off the plane."

"Really?"

"They started getting nasty letters in their v-files from other flight attendants."

"No way."

"The same thing happened to this guy who turned in another flight attendant because she read a newspaper while sitting in the passenger seat."

"I bet he got a slew of nasty letters, too."

"Yes, and a transfer to Houston."

After Jim, the Captain, and Dave, the first officer, introduced themselves to us and Jim gave us a crew briefing it was time for the passengers to board. Newark flight 200 was bound for Cancun, Mexico and I was anticipating the madness because, yes, Newark passengers were the most unfriendly, rude, and obnoxious group of people you'd ever encounter on a flight. The madness began with catering, which didn't have enough milk to go with the cereal.

"Where's the rest of the milk?" I ask a grumpy old man pushing the 300 pound beverage cart.

"If you have a problem, talk it over with my supervisor," he replied in a harsh foreign accent I didn't quite recognize.

"Sir, that won't be necessary. All I need is milk."

He says something to the other guy who's helping him before he finally tells me,

"Call catering hotline."

"Thank you." The catering in Newark is just as bad as the passengers. Not one person working speaks clear English and if you don't check behind them before you take off, you will regret it later. Case in point, on a morning flight to Fort Lauderdale, granted there were only 55 people on the flight, but they gave me only one carton of orange juice. Another time on a trans-continental flight from Newark to L.A. they gave me seven bags of ice and the flight was full. You should've seen us rationing out the ice.

During boarding I stand and watch as the people slowly walk on one by one, then two by two, then four by four until there are people as far as the naked eye can see. White people, tall people, skinny people, and fat people ringing their call buttons to see if you can find them a seat belt extension. I hear people ringing their buttons and motioning for us to help them because someone is in their seat. I hear babies crying. I see a little Asian Hindu boy about 2 years-old reaching up to play with the flight attendant call button and when he sees me shaking my head he thinks twice before doing it again. I see people trying to stuff oversized bags in the overhead bins and Melissa telling them to take something out or have it gate checked.

That silly Frank Sinatra boarding music is playing throughout the cabin and only gets louder when you stand in the galley. I've been flying for 3 years now and I'm tired of hearing the same music over and over from Frank Sinatra, the Beatles, and those sing-along songs like, "Our house is a very, very, very fine house with two cats in the yard..."

As we take-off down the runway at a speed reaching 180 miles per hour, I sit on my jumpseat, and recant one of the most exciting exhilarating experiences; the take-off. The first time I took-off on a plane I was 5 years-old and I was flying with my parents and sister to California. I can remember that feeling when the plane lifted off the ground and I saw the tops of the tallest trees and the tops of buildings for the first time. I saw the cars and people getting smaller and smaller and I remembered the sinking of my heart the first time the plane made a slow bank to the right. I thought it was going to tilt over and we were all going to crash to the ground and die, but that wasn't the case, because I saw the clouds. I saw funny-shaped clouds that were so close you wished you could reach out and grab them. I remember it was overcast that day and the plane shook and rocked us a bit but soon we rose above the clouds until we were cruising at 30,000 feet and I saw the sun. Wow, it was a welcoming sight for a frightened little boy like myself. I was happy to see the sun because it guided us all the way to LAX. At 5 years-old, I realized that no matter what's going on below the clouds, the sun is always shining above the clouds.

Melissa and I switched positions on the jumpseat because I always like to look at the New York City skyline. From my window, I saw the Newark skyline and cars flowing through the city like blood pumping through the arteries of a living body. When the plane banked left I saw the great skyline of New York City; the Empire State Building, the Chrysler building and the giant Twin Towers. Then I look closely and I see a plane that's flying awfully low, I mean so low that it's... Ah shit, it just hit the side of one of the Towers!

"Melissa look, a plane just hit one of the Twin Towers!"

"Yeah, right."

"I'm serious, look!"

She leaned over to take a look, "I can't see it."

"Trust me, it hit one of the Towers."

"That's horrible," she looked out the window again.

I heard someone ring a call button. Since we were under 10,000 feet and still climbing at an angle, we couldn't answer their buttons right away. Then a second bell rang, then a third one. Nicholas got on the PA and gave his greeting to the passengers. When the plane soared above 10,000 feet I got up to answer the call buttons.

"Is there something I can help you with?" I ask.

"I just saw a plane hit one of the World Trade Center towers, I swear, I'm not crazy!"

"Just stay calm. Just remain calm."

I went to answer the next call button.

"Sir, I saw a plane hit one the Twin Towers."

"Just remain calm, you're the second person who told me."

The third person told me the same thing. By then I knew I wasn't seeing things. This was really happening.

When I went to check on Nicholas. He had this ghost-like expression on his face.

"The Captain just got word from Newark operations that a plane just hit one of the Towers," Nicholas said.

"I saw it too! And, a few of the passengers saw it," I respond.

We attempt to do a service but twenty five minutes later we got word from the flight deck that a second plane just hit the second World Trade Center tower. This was no ordinary accident. Melissa started crying. I was on the verge of crying. A few of the passengers were crying. Then we got word that a plane went down at the Pentagon and another went down somewhere in Pennsylvania. Our plane circled in the air for about 30 minutes, dumping fuel before we got permission from air traffic control to divert back to Newark. When we landed I turned on my cell phone and immediately got a page that I have seven messages waiting on me. I listened to the first message and it was from my parents.

"Eddie, this is your mother and father, call us and let us know that you are alright. This is horrible Eddie, please call us."

The next message was from my sister, Countess, and my brother-in-law, Kenny Ray.

"Eddie, this is Countess and Kenny Ray. What in the world is going on up there? Two planes just crashed into the World Trade Center towers. Oh my God, it's awful. Call us and let us know that you are okay? We love you and we're praying for you."

The third message was from Lucky.

"Eddie, heffer you better call me! Call me right now. I'm in New Orleans. Call me at Muh-Dear's, 504-987-1212. Bye."

The fourth message was from Whitney.

"Eddie, this is Whitney, I'm at home. Please give me a call at 713-520-7777, and let me know that you are okay! This is horrible, Eddie, this is so horrible." She sounded like she was crying, "Call me, Eddie. Bye."

The next three messages were from my parents, my sister and Scottie. I got on the phone and called my parents. They were relieved to hear my voice.

"Eddie, can you come home?" My father asked.

"I don't think I can right now, I think all the airports are closed."

"Well, can you rent a car and come home?"

"I could but I have to stay with my crew."

"But if the airports are closed, there are no planes going out."

"Pops, I just have to play everything by ear. Where's Mom?"

"She's right here, hold on I'll let you talk to her."

"Hello, Eddie?"

"Hi, Mom."

"Eddie, Son it's so good to hear your voice, our phone has been ringing off the wall this morning and I was beginning to get a little worried. But, you know your father. Being the wise and great man he is he told me that if I pray then I wouldn't have to worry. And, if I worry, why bother praying." I chuckled, my old Pops was one with words.

"Son, it's scary. What is this world coming to?"

"A new war Mother, and I get the feeling that this war is never-ending."

As we talked, I could hear the background noise of news announcers. Giving their up-to-the minute accounts of the events surrounding the disaster. I still can't believe I saw the plane as it hit the building. I saw the tragedy as it happened. I became a mixed up bottle of emotions. I thought about all those innocent people and when I finally got a moment to myself, I cried from the pit of my soul. I hadn't cried like that since Brooke's death.

***

I called Scottie who answered by the third ring.

"Where are you, man?"

"In Newark, where are you?"

"In Houston."

"Are you on a trip?"

"Yeah, I'm just finishing up a four-day."

"I'm stuck here at the Holiday Inn North. I tell you, this place is a madhouse today."

"It's madness everywhere. There are about a thousand pilots in this crew room watching this. They keep showing it over and over. I tell you, it looks like something straight out of "Independence Day."

"I said the same thing," I reply.

"Osama bin Laden is behind this."

"He was the mastermind behind the World Trade Center explosion in '93."

"These Muslims are crazy. Allah wouldn't advocate the killing of innocent people and children."

"You know what these fools believe? They believe when they die they go straight to heaven and live large with 72 virgins."

"You're right."

"These weak-minded fools actually believe that."

As Scottie and I talk, my call waiting button beeps.

"Hold on Scottie, I got another call coming through."

I click over and listen at Lucky boohoo like a baby.

"Thank God, praise the Lord! You are alright! Praise God!"

"Yes, Lucky. I'm okay."

"Oh, Hallelujah!"

"I know." I listened as he shouted praises to God and cursed me in the same breath, "Bitch, why didn't you call me right away! All I could think about was your ass on one of those planes."

"Lucky, I don't fly for United and I don't fly for American."

"But a plane originated out of Newark."

"You're kidding."

"Turn on the television and look at this shit! Those damn Muslims are out of control!"

"Lucky, can I call you back? I got Scottie holding on the other line."

"Scottie? Where is he?"

"In Houston."

"I know this ain't the time to be bringing up old shit, but tell him he needs to get his house in order."

"I will, Lucky. I'll call you back."

"Don't forget."

"I won't."

I click over, "Hello. Scottie?"

"I'm still here."

"That was Lucky."

"Good, he's okay."

"Yes, as long as he's drunk and talking noise."

"He's a trip, but um…I just called to tell you that I was a little concerned, although we're not together anymore, you still have a special place in my heart."

"Thanks, Scottie. Where are you staying tonight?"

"At the Marriott if it's not already booked."

"I don't know how long this'll last but you can always call my parents, you still have the number."

"Thanks, Eddie."

"I still love you, Scottie."

"Me too. You stay tough and don't let this get you down, you keep flying."

"I will."

The silence that followed lingered on for a moment or two before I got on the phone to call Whitney.

When Disaster Strikes

When I see Dewayne, I immediately get on his ass about my missing jewelry and not returning my calls. His eyes looked empty and cold. His hair needed cutting and his five o'clock shadow looked more like an eight o'clock shadow.

"What the fuck is going on with you?" I asked.

"I'm stressing like a mofo."

"Where is my jewelry, Dewayne?"

"I took it and pawned it, I needed the money for Pops and 'nem."

"I suggested doing that a long time ago and you were dead set against it. Now you go behind my back and take it, and stay gone for two days. I don't understand it, Dewayne!"

"I'm sorry, Pee Wee. I'ma get it back."

"Squash the jewelry. Why did you stay gone for two days?"

"I was in these streets. You know I'm back hustling."

I closed my eyes and shook my head recalling what he told me the night of the arrest. "What happened to the real estate business?"

"It's slow money, Pee Wee. I gave it up a long time ago"

"So you're back to selling drugs?"

"Yeah."

"Whatever happened to *'Pee Wee, I'm not going to sell drugs anymore. I'm going square when I get out,' huh?*"

"I lied."

"You've been doing a lot of that lately."

"I know it and I'm sorry."

"Yes, you are. You are a sorry-assed liar, Dewayne." I looked at him closely; his lips looked burned, "Are you smoking it now?"

He couldn't look at me when he responded and walked away from me mumbling, "You straight tripping."

"Look at me when I'm talking to you, Dewayne."

"You tripping!" he shouted reaching for the door-knob.

I grab the back of his shirt and he spun around, glaring at me.

"Why can't you look at me when I'm talking to you?"

"Because you accuse me of smoking. How in the hell am I supposed to make money if I'm smoking the shit, Pee Wee? Listen at how you sound."

"Don't act all innocent with me Dewayne, I know what time it is."

"I'm gone."

"If you leave this house, don't come back and don't come around your daughter."

"I'm coming back and you can't stop me from seeing my daughter."

"You are out of control, Dewayne."

"I'm tired of hearing this. I'm going to Mama's."

"From now on you tell Donna if she wants to see Déjà, she's gotta come over here. Do you hear me?"

"That's messed up, Whitney!" His voice picked up some base and the coldness in his eyes melted away like ice on a hot sidewalk.

"It's too bad, Dewayne, that you took a turn for the worse."

"Wait a minute. Let's back the fuck up. You act like you got all this shit from winning the lottery. Everything you own, from the rings, the tennis bracelet, right down to the bed you sleep in was bought with money made from drug sales. When I was on lock down, Pops and the boys took good care of you. You wasn't tripping when they got you this house. As a matter of fact, come to think of it, your ass should be packing. This is my motherfucking house!"

"You are right, I need to get as far away from here as possible." I couldn't agree with him more.

"Now that you got a job with the airline you think you better than me now? How soon you forget you used to hustle with me on these streets!"

I didn't say anything. That was one week in my life I wished I could forget. I hated Dewayne for bringing it up. I remembered how I raked in 2 G's in one week, selling $20 bags. Crack fiends offered to do all sorts of things to get one. I really wanted to forget about it because I remember seeing Mama strung out and when she saw me on the street she told me that she wouldn't call the police if I gave her a $20 bag. How awful is that? My own mother was blackmailing me for crack? I told her she'd have to turn me in because I wasn't giving her a damn thing. I laid low for about a month after that and I told myself that if she weren't my mother she'd be dead. God, that was awful. I still get teary-eyed when I think about it. But I still didn't wake up because I started enjoying the lifestyle. I had Gucci and Louis Vuitton clothing in my closets, a candy-apple red Mustang 5.0 convertible on my 16th birthday, expensive jewelry, trips to Vegas to see the Tyson fights, and cash for days. That was a dream come true to a girl like me.

"I'm waking up, Dewayne, and I should've done this a long time ago. But, I'm cutting you lose. I can't deal with this anymore."

"I see how you are. I see the shit crystal clear now. When disaster strikes, your ass make a b-line to the nearest exit. You ain't shit, Whitney!"

"Dewayne, I know for a fact you are smoking crack because I could've made a b-line to the nearest exit when you went to prison, but I stayed with you. I waited on your ass for nearly ten years. All your so-called friends and even your brothers, yes, both of your brothers, were trying to push up to me. They were telling me how I was wasting my time waiting on you. So, for you to say that I leave when disaster strikes lets me know exactly where your head is these days- up your fucking ass!"

I tried to slam the door, but Dewayne caught it and slammed it against the wall like a mad man and came for me, his face was moist with sweat and his eyebrows furrowed in anger. He grabbed my tiny arm and threw me against the couch. He realized what he was doing and caught himself.

"Look, Pee Wee, I'm sorry."

"Oh, I'm Pee Wee now." I reply, half laughing, half crying.

"This ain't no time for fun and games."

"Who's playing, Dewayne? You are the one messing up. You can't even admit to me that you have a problem."

"I don't have a problem."

I shake my head and listen as the phone rings once, then twice, then three times, before I answer it.

"Hello."

"Whitney, turn on the TV girl. A plane just crashed into the World Trade Center." Nikki's voice is going a mile a minute.

"Say what?"

"Girl, go turn on the television and look!"

I grab the remote to turn on the flat screen TV. In spite of Dewayne's current situation, we still had it in tact. I'm sure if Dewayne had some help it would have been the first thing to go. The thing costs $6,000.

My eyes began to focus on the screen at a live shot of the Twin Towers. One is already on fire and I look closely and see a plane crashing into the second building. I turn up the volume. The footage is taken from a video camera so it's unedited, raw footage and someone is swearing on national television.

"Oh my God, Roxy and Eddie." I grab my chest feeling my heart, "I got to call them."

"Are they in New York?"

"Yes."

"Well, three-way them."

I call Eddie. "Come on Eddie, pick up. Pick up the phone." I feel the tears gushing from my eyes. By the fifth ring his voice comes on the answering machine.

"Eddie this is Whitney. Please give me a call at 713-520-7777 and let me know that you are okay! This is horrible, Eddie, this is so horrible. Call me Eddie. Bye." I let out a huge sob. Dewayne sits on the couch beside me and takes me into his arms. I didn't want him touching me.

"Move, can't you see I'm on the phone?" I give him the most vicious evil-eyed look.

He stares back with this sad, puppy dog look in his eyes.

"Who is that?" Nikki asks.

"Who do you think?"

"Oh, he finally decided to come home?"

"Yeah, girl."

"I know you can't talk right now but put Dewayne on the phone."

I give the phone to Dewayne, "It's Nikki."

When he grabs the phone, I get up to find my cell phone in my purse that's hidden under the dirty clothes in the garage. I call Roxy. She left for New York yesterday to visit Mad Lew.

I call and wait for her to answer but she doesn't, so I end up leaving a message on her phone as well. I hear Dewayne yelling at Nikki and I see him slam the phone on the couch and storm out of the place.

"Dewayne!"

He starts up the car and without looking in my direction, backs out of the driveway and drives away down the street like a contestant in the Indy 500.

"What did you say to Dewayne?" I asked Nikki.

"I told that son of a bitch he needed to get off that

crack and get his head straight."

"Who told you about it?"

"Byron told me. I was wondering when you were going to say something."

"That's not the shit you go around broadcasting, Nikki."

"Derek and Pops and Dwight, Jr. are hurt. I told Derek about Dewayne and he broke down crying."

"When is the next hearing?" I ask.

"Next week. Frazier says it looks good and the judge may lower the bonds."

"I'm moving out of this house, Nikki. I was wondering if I could move in with you and Diamond?"

"Yeah, even with Donna here we have a lot of room. Since Derek's been locked up, these bills have been stacking up."

"We can help each other out." I respond, looking at the horrible images of people jumping from the burning buildings and people running for their lives in horror as a rush of debris engulfs the streets.

"My God!" I cried watching in disbelief as they showed the Pentagon and a field covered in smoke and debris outside of Pittsburgh, Pennsylvania.

"Hold on, Byron is trying to call me." Nikki says before putting me on hold.

I turn the channel and every station is talking about the incident, even the Home Shopping Network interrupted its programming.

I heard my other line beeping. It's Eddie.

"Hello, Eddie. You are alright. Thank God."

"Believe me, I've been calling you but the lines were tied up."

"This world is going crazy, Eddie. Hold on, I got someone on the other line. Hello Nikki, are you still there?"

"Yeah."

"I have Eddie on the other line, I'll call you back.

Hello, Eddie?"

"I'm here."

"So how did you find out about it?"

"Whitney, if I tell you, you wouldn't believe it."

I listened as he told me how he watched the first plane hit the building from his jumpseat.

"How could you see it from the inboard seat?"

"This time I was sitting outboard. I told the flight attendant sitting next to me that I wanted to catch a glimpse of the city, so we switched."

"What did you think when you saw that?"

"I thought that plane was flying too low but when it hit the side of the building and exploded I thought I was dreaming. Then, a few other passengers saw it and I realized I wasn't."

"I'm worried about Roxy."

"I am, too. The phone lines here are messed up and she might not be able to call."

As we talked, Eddie kept getting calls to his cell phone from people wondering if he was okay.

"I got calls from cousins I hadn't heard from in ages," he says.

"My mother hasn't called me," I say, looking at the caller ID.

"Is she still doing her work for the church?" Eddie asks.

"Yes, she even got a job at Wal Mart and her own little apartment."

"That's good, Whitney."

"Dewayne's not doing so good these days."

"What's with him?"

"He's sucking that glass penis."

"Not Dewayne!" Eddie sounded sincerely shocked, "What are you going to do?"

"What am I supposed to do? Dewayne is out of control."

"But that's your man. It's up to you to get him in line."

"I'm not his mother, Eddie."

"It doesn't matter. This man is going to be your husband one day, or isn't he?"

"No way, Eddie. Dewayne needs to get himself together first."

"What happened? You called off the engagement?"

"Might as well. He pawned the engagement ring."

"Honey, hush."

"I kid you not."

"Whitney, I'm sorry."

"I'm leaving him. It's just that plain and simple. I should have left him a long time ago."

"If there's anything I can do, let me know. How is the situation with Dewayne's father and brothers?"

"Hopefully, the lawyer can convince the judge to lower their bonds."

"My Pops is having a special healing service this Friday. If you're not doing anything come out and whatever troubles you have, leave them at the altar."

"Oh Eddie, I wish it were that simple."

"What? Are you having doubts?"

"Sometimes I wonder, Lord, what have I done to deserve all this chaos?"

"Don't question God because it could be a lot worse."

"You're right," I say, turning my attention to the people covered in ash, "It could be worse."

"Remember how you prayed for me when I lost Brooke?"

"Yeah."

"Let's pray."

After we pray, I think about Roxy.

"Have you talked to Roxy? Where is that girl, she needs to call me."

"What's the number?" Eddie asks.

"832-555-0909."

"I'll try to call her and if I get through I'll tell her to call you."

"Thank you, Eddie."

"Don't mention it."

I call Dewayne's cell phone and pager and he doesn't call back. That's it. I'm washing my hands with it. I turned on the radio and Magic 102 is talking about the disaster, 97.9 the Box is talking about it. I feel so bad for those people. And I shed more tears. I cry for those poor flight attendants and their families, not to mention their friends and co-workers. I was overjoyed to hear Eddie's voice, but others weren't as fortunate.

I called Roxy's number and got her voice mail and the message that her mailbox was full.

"Damn, where is that girl?"

I tried not to think bad thoughts; I really wanted to think positive.

The City – 9/10/01

Monday morning after Walter, Jr. left, I took the first thing smoking to the City. Although I've had good times with Walter, Jr., Mad Lew was much more exciting and I couldn't wait to see what we were getting into. He left a message on my phone that I checked the moment Walter, Jr. left the house, saying that he wanted to use my voice for a couple of songs on his upcoming CD. I can't sing a lick, so why would he want to use my voice?

I called him just before I got on the plane and asked him why he wanted to use my voice.

"I'll tell you when you get here," he said.

"Why is it such a secret?"

"You ask too many questions."

"Why didn't you book me in first class?"

"You the flight attendant, don't you get first class perks?"

"I fly standby."

"My bad, I'll make sure you get first on the way back to Houston, a'ight?"

"And don't forget." Now he knows better. This is my first and last time flying standby anywhere.

Upon arrival I noticed the driver standing at the bottom of the escalator with my name scribbled on a card.

"Good. You're on time," I say to him.

"Hello," he says, with a friendly nod.

"Take me to Times Square, what's your name?"

"Ramon."

"Ramon, where you from?"

"South Bronx."

"No shit, me too. You look familiar."

"You do, too." He took my bags and put them in the trunk of the black Lincoln Navigator and opened the door to help me inside.

"So you work for Mad Lew?" I ask once he closed the door and we pull away from the curb.

"Yeah."

I get on the phone and called Mad Lew's cell number and get his voice mail. That annoying, "Yo! Yo! Holla at me!"

"Yo Lew, this is Roxy. I'm just leaving LaGuardia airport. It's about 12:45 and I'm on my way to the studio. Have someone listen out for me! Bye."

"How was your flight?"

"Horrible. They had me in coach and I hate coach."

Ramon thought my comment was so funny, "It couldn't be any worse than riding the bus," he said.

"Actually a bus is much better, at least you're not crammed in like sardines."

"Oh yeah?"

"Have you flown commercially lately?"

"No, not lately."

"Unless you're flying first class, don't bother. The food stinks and good service depends on the mood of the flight attendant."

"The last time I flew, I rode in one of those small planes. Similar to the one that girl got killed in."

"Oh yeah, I hate those," I said, thinking about Aaliyah's plane crash in the Bahamas.

***

As I look out my window I remember why I love this city so much, there is so much energy. When I was 17, this same energy lured me away from the confines of my screwed-up home in Connecticut and back to my roots in the Bronx. The YMCA was my new home at night because I combed the City during the day looking for work. That's how I found out about Georgian Airways, I stumbled across a flyer at NYU. I wasn't going to school but I remembered a lot of cute and smart guys went there. Atlanta had it's own energy but it wasn't like the City, especially my neighborhood in the South Bronx. When I lived in Connecticut I ventured to the City on the weekends. On Saturday mornings I took the early train with my small, black leather backpack purse. I had clean underwear, deodorant, money I stole from my parents and a fake I.D. in case I needed to get in the clubs. I lost touch with Ana and Carmen, the only friends I had before I moved to Atlanta. But when the three of us got together we made sure there wasn't a part of the city we missed. I miss those girls. Last I heard, Ana got caught up with a drug dealer who got her hooked on the shit and Carmen was in Rikers Island barely clinging to life with AIDS and a grand larceny case.

Now I remembered why Ramon looked so familiar-he used to drive the BX35 bus. Ana, Carmen and I rode his bus countless times, but he looks so different now. Dude gained about 20 pounds and he shaved off his hair plus he had a goatee working.

"Hey, didn't you used to drive the BX35?"

"Yeah."

"That's why you look so familiar. How did you get turned on to this gig?"

"A buddy of mine who works as a bodyguard told me about it."

"Who, Ernesto?" I asked, referring to one of Mad Lew's bodyguards.

"Yeah, how'd you know?"

"Next to Big Pun and Fat Joe, Ernesto is the largest Puerto Rican I've ever seen."

"They call us the twin towers."

I didn't comment. They weren't as tall as they were wide.

***

When I walked inside the studio, Mad Lew was behind the glass wearing a pair of headphones, rapping to a slow melodious beat. It sounded like old school music. I recognized Papì and Juan at the controls bobbing their heads and another dude, who looked more like a character out of Austin Powers, standing next to another set of controls bobbing his head as well. I sat my bag down on a sofa nearby and watched as Mad Lew spat out lyrics about making love on a cloud and going 300 miles per hour. The more I listened, I realized he was talking about making love on an airplane. Then I heard a woman's voice singing low and breathy like Toni Braxton saying, "Heaven must feel like this, it must feel like this."

I must admit I was digging the tune myself. The song reminded me of lazy Sunday afternoons spent sitting on the stoop outside Ana's apartment. Papì, still bobbing his head, got up and starting playing with a nearby keyboard putting drum beats here and there. Before long I was bobbing and weaving my head, I liked the way Mad Lew had me grooving. The boy could rap his ass off and he wasn't always talking about sex or killing niggas. Mad Lew was conscious when he wanted to be. I listened to all of his CD's and each one improved with the next. He was always outdoing himself and for some rappers, that's kind of hard to do.

After the song, Mad Lew took off the headphones and walked out, "That's a wrap, fellas."

"Wrap my ass!" Juan shouted.

I watched as the three of them talked shit with each other. They were totally oblivious of me sitting on the sofa taking in every joke, every remark, until I laughed at a comment my baby Lew made to the Austin Powers guy about updating his image.

"Ah shit! It's on now!" Mad Lew shouted before walking over to scoop me off my feet. I wrapped my arms and legs around him and kissed him, not holding back, and he didn't either. We kissed until I felt him walking me outside to the balcony. He smelled so good to me, and the cotton soft shirt he had on felt like a cloud in my fingers.

"I like that song, are you dedicating it to me?"

"How'd you guess?"

"'Cause I make you feel like heaven."

"That among other things." He looked at my outfit, "I like this. I'm firing Vikki and hiring you to coordinate my shit."

"Hell yeah! When can I start?"

He laughed at my go-get-her attitude. Shit, the more I think about it, the more I want to quit my job. Who needs $26.50 an hour when you got a man making $250 million a year? Why fly standby when you can fly first and you know me, that's the only way I go.

***

"You want me to do what?" I asked. I was standing in the studio with a microphone in front of my face, wearing a pair of headphones.

"I want you to pretend you're on a plane making an announcement to the passengers, you know the shit you stewardesses do!" Papì shouted at me through the headphones.

"Flight attendant," I corrected him. "And could you not scream so loud!" I swear, my eardrums were ringing.

"Well, whatever. I want to you to sound sexy and say you're with Air Ecstasy or Air Erotica."

I giggled and glanced at Mad Lew who was nearby talking on the phone and smoking an L.

"Okay." I waited for my cue from Papì and began, "Ladies and Gentlemen, you've just boarded Air Ecstacy," I said in my sexiest voice.

They stopped me again, "Okay, this time I want you to say your name is Heaven. And I want you to say Heaven really, really sexy."

I did what I was told and for the next hour I moaned and talked sexy. Around 6:00 the song was finally complete and I was deadbeat tired, I didn't want to hear it. This shit isn't easy and with producers like Papì and Juan you almost want to say forget it. Let somebody else to do it. But that's what makes them mega-producers. They work with you until you can show them that your best is all that you bring to the table. Throughout the day other people started popping up into the studio, one of them was Mad Lew's manager, Pat Schneider. Another famous producer known for his heart-wrenching ballads stopped by and chilled with the crew. He wanted Mad Lew to rap on the re-mix of his song that happens to be number one on the R&B charts. They put on what I now call the "Hell" song for the producer to listen to. When my low, breathy voice came booming across the loud surround sound speakers he looked at Papì and Juan and asked with this incredible look on his face, "Who is that?"

"The young lady sitting behind you," Papì says, spinning around in his chair.

After being in my presence for more than 20 minutes, he finally acknowledges me. That's how the rich and famous treat you. They don't acknowledge you or have anything to say to you unless they can somehow or another find a way to use you to bring a dollar to their pockets.

"What you think about that there?"

"Wicked," he says, staring at me, "and I mean that in a good way." He began to bob his head as the base line came in along with Papì's hypnotic drumbeats.

"Ohio Players. "Heaven Must Be Like This." He stuck out his clenched fist and gave Papì and Juan daps. "I love your voice. Just enough New Yorker without overdoing it, you feelin' me?"

"Yeah." *It'll cost you big bank if you want to use it. Have your people call my people.*

By 9:00 pm I was ready to go but Mad Lew told me he was spending the night at the studio. He had to have the album completed, so I left. I used the $1,500 he gave me to get a room at the Marriott Marquis. I called Whitney and told her about my day but this chick was out of it. She had too much going on in her life to hear about mine so I squashed the conversation after five minutes. I hung up the phone a little messed up about her situation. I'm usually the one having hard times but it's different when the shoe is on the other foot, especially when you're used to seeing that person with everything together. I turned on the television and ordered a movie and room service. I spent the evening thinking about the shopping I was going to do tomorrow.

***

My cell phone rang and I thought I was dreaming but I picked up.

"Hello?"

"Get dressed, I'm coming to scoop you up," Mad Lew's massive voice instructed me on the other end. I looked at the clock beside the bed and it was 5:45 am.

"Where are you?"

"On my way out of the studio."

"Alright, give me a few minutes to get dressed and check out."

By 7:00 am we were on our way to West Orange, New Jersey to Mad Lew's house. They had all but two songs left to do in the studio but Lew told me they would finish them in Atlanta later in the week. Right now he wanted to take a hot bubble bath and make love on top of his new, imported Egyptian cotton sheets. We did just that and the moment I felt him explode inside of me, I knew any day now I would be calling Worldwide Airlines to tell them just what they could do with their wings.

Trouble Doesn't Last Always

By Thursday I was going crazy. If it weren't for my cell phone I would have committed a terrorist attack myself. My crew was cool and fun but there are only so many card games you can play and so many stories you can hear from both pilots and flight attendants alike about other flight attendants' and pilots' faults. The Holiday Inn North was more like an Inn for every airline crew in the industry. American and United crews were there. I felt so awful for those crewmembers, they probably had friends flying on those planes. Continental, Northwest, US Airways and Delta made their temporary homes there as well. Everyone was talking about the tragic events. One pilot said he would've taken a nosedive before he allowed the terrorists to storm into the flight deck. As tragic as it was, I was getting tired of hearing it and I couldn't wait to go home.

Friday morning on the way to the airport I looked out across the New York skyline and saw a billow of smoke where the Twin Towers once stood and I couldn't hold back the tears any longer. I thought I cried them all away but here they were and everyone was staring back with compassionate and pensive stares. Melissa took my hand and squeezed it. I heard her sniffle. The airport was opened for the first time since Tuesday. It was very quiet and eerie. There were a few passengers but the majority of the crowd consisted of airline employees trying to get home or working a flight. Once on the plane, I grabbed my first class seat and called my mother to tell her that I was finally coming home. She promised she'd have a home-cooked meal and I couldn't wait.

When I pulled into the driveway around 4:30, the

aroma of fresh-baked bread along with the nose-tickling scent of Cajun spices invited me in before I opened the door.

"Mom, I'm home."

I walked into the kitchen where I found Mom along with Countess.

"Hallelujah, and praise the Lord," Mom said, before she and I embraced, "my baby is home."

"Yes, I am." I gave my sister a hug. When she hugged me she used her size to squeeze me.

"Your nephews were so worried about you, they were going to stay home from school but I told them your flight didn't get in until 2:15."

"Where are they?"

"I believe they're in the den."

"Ummm, what's cooking?"

"I have some black-eyed peas, sweet potatoes, your favorite green beans with a little Cajun spice and Cornish hens with Mama's homemade rolls."

"I smelled the rolls when I got out the car."

"Sit down so Mama can feed you."

"What's for dessert?"

"Sock-it-to-me cake."

"I love you, Ma."

"And I love you, too." She kissed me on the forehead.

My nephews, KJ and Corey joined us in the kitchen. My nephews were such handsome young men. Looking at them, then looking at my sister and my mother, all happy to see me alive and well brought on another round of tears. During supper I shared with them my stories gathered from three days trapped at the Holiday Inn North. For the first time in the history of aviation the airports were closed on Tuesday afternoon, Wednesday, Thursday, and limited flights were scheduled to go out on Friday. The crew scheduling lines were busy with flight attendants and pilots alike calling in to get an update on the schedules. What used to take less than a minute to get through took at least 30 minutes.

"Uncle Eddie, you think you'll want to keep flying?" KJ asked.

"Yes." I reply without reservation, "I like my job and I'm not going to let some terrorists scare me away."

The boys shook their heads. "Couldn't be me," Corey said.

On Tuesday I asked Lucky to come over and have dinner and he joined us just as we were eating dessert. We were as happy as two sissies could be when we saw each other.

"I brought you a little something, something." He opened a round metal container full of pecan pralines. "Muh-Dear made them especially for you."

"You tell Muh-Dear I said thank you."

"Try one, Mrs. Kelly."

Mama grabbed a tiny piece.

"You too, Countess, don't be bashful."

"No thank you, Lucky. I just had some of Mama's sock-it-to-me cake."

"Okay, but you don't know what you're missing."

He sat them down on the table in front of her. Before long, the boys were digging in. It didn't take long before Countess was digging in, too.

***

That night Daddy had everyone's ears with another rousing sermon. Then Countess added the icing on the cake with her soul-stirring rendition of an old time gospel favorite, "Trouble Doesn't Last Always." Weeping may endureth for a night, keep the faith and it will be all right. I thought about Brooke and all the things that had been going on in my life for the last two years. I still miss her and I was shocked when my parents said her mother called to see if I was okay. Then my life came full circle when I saw Broderick Hines all grown up and in a frail looking state. Poor thing looked as if he was on his last leg but there he was clapping and singing like it took all the strength he could muster.

Broderick couldn't be any more than 28 but he looked like a man in his late 40's all gray and humped over. I thought back to that night years ago and the lean, muscular track athlete in the car with me. I am more grateful because God has been good to me. I still have my health and strength and although I've had tragedy and grief to deal with, I am grateful that I no longer have to depend on antidepressants to get me through the day. I stopped taking those the moment I broke up with Scottie. I now have a new sense of direction and some peace of mind for a change. This 9-1-1 tragedy, as I refer to it, brought a lot of things into perspective. Number one: you can't take anything for granted. Don't take for granted your friends, don't take your family for granted. Don't even take for granted your enemies. Number two: don't underestimate your importance to anyone's life. I never knew how many people cared about me until I got the seventh phone call and every single one of them let me know just how much they cared about me and loved me.

When Pops invited the congregation to come to the altar he asked for a simple wish; for everyone who understood him to leave all troubles and burdens at the altar and he began to pray. Then he allowed each member of the congregation a quiet moment to converse with God. Now some of the sisters couldn't keep quiet, they were praising God out loud.

"Thank you Lord!"

"If I had 10,000 tongues I couldn't thank you enough!"

Later that night I caught up with Whitney and after we embraced for what seemed like an eternity I asked her how she felt?

"A little better," she said with a tired sigh.

I put my arm around her and we took a walk along the trail at Hermann Park.

"Talk to me," I began.

"Dewayne is history."

"That's it?"

"Yes. I can't deal with his problems anymore, Eddie."

In spite of her situation she still looked her best. Whitney had her silky hair pulled back into a ponytail that bounced like a tassel when she walked.

"So you're giving up on him?"

"Eddie, sometimes the hardest thing is the best thing, you know?"

"Yes, I do." I couldn't forget about Scottie. I guess I had some nerve urging her to work it out with her man when I didn't do the same with mine.

"When your heart says it's enough, it matters not what the rest of you thinks. Am I making sense, Eddie?"

"I hear you."

"It's like ending a chapter and starting a new one."

"I know what you mean. I know exactly what you mean. I saw the guy who I guess, 'turned me out' tonight at church."

Whitney stared at me for a moment before asking, "did you say hello to him?"

"No."

"Why not?"

"I don't know."

"How did he look?"

"Awful. I assume the lifestyle finally caught up with him because he looked old, frail and skinny."

Whitney and I trudged quietly along.

"I'm worried about Roxy, I think I told you she didn't call me until Wednesday."

"What's with her and this Mad Lew character?"

"She thinks they're an item."

"Well, if she likes it then I love it and that's all I have to say about that," I say, repeating the line I heard Forrest Gump say several times throughout the movie.

"I'm happy for her, too."

My cell phone rang and I didn't have to look at the ID

to know who it was.

"Lucky, what is it?"

"Did I interrupt something?"

"No, I'm with Whitney. What are you doing?"

"Sitting here about to mix up a nice concoction. Ask Whitney if she likes Piña Coladas?"

"Lucky wants to know if you like Piña Coladas?"

"Tell him only if he leaves out the liquor."

"Only if you leave out the liquor, Lucky."

"Tell her if she wants a pineapple slush she needs to stop by Sonic."

"You're so silly."

"What did he say?"

"He said if you want a pineapple slush be sure to stop by the Sonic Drive-In."

"Tell him I'll be sure to do just that."

"Lucky, we're on our way."

We ended the night sharing everything on our minds, and yes, we talked about the events surrounding September 11th.

Left At The Altar

Saturday morning I called crew scheduling. They didn't have a trip for me today but they had one for me first thing Sunday morning. I don't usually fly on Sundays, but because I had such a good time on Friday night at church, I made an exception. It's been a little over a week since I last saw Dewayne but I spoke briefly to him on the phone. I can't deal with him anymore. I waited for him to get out of the physical prison. I'm not so sure I can hang around and wait for him to escape from the mental prison. From this day forward, I'm not going to waste my time dealing with people who don't want to help themselves and that includes my mother. If I'm wrong for thinking this way, may God forgive me because Dewayne's problems, his family's problems, and my problems got left at the altar on Friday night.

I opened my closet and took my blouses, cotton shirts and pants and began to fold them neatly inside a box marked miscellaneous. When I had everything in my bedroom closet packed away in boxes, I started into Déjà's room. Moments later when I cleaned off my bookcase I came across a video of my flight class, along with an 8 x10 picture of the group. There were 33 faces smiling back at me. When the tragic events of September 11th occurred, I got on the phone and called as many as I could. We shared a few tears but for the most part I was fortunate to get in contact with 15 of my classmates.

I put on the tape and laughed so hard I had tears in my eyes. We thought we were really doing something when we performed our mock evacuations. I laughed at the way were we all so attentive during the First Aid portion of training. I remember it like yesterday; everyone was on edge, hoping and praying to earn an 85 or better on each test. Three classmates stumbled and flunked out and one classmate got all the way to finals and froze. We all cried when she left but were happy to know that she was returning a week later to do it all again. Was flight attendant training hard? Hell yeah. Would I do it all over again? Hell no. You couldn't make me do it if you paid me. Before I got this job I used to think a flight attendant did nothing more than look cute and pass out peanuts. But after one day in initial training I knew there was much more to it than asking the passengers if they want peanuts. Flight attendants are lifesavers, ministers, psychiatrists, babysitters, midwives, paramedics, bottle warmers, and hell-raisers. I could go on forever because that's just the tip of the iceberg. We have to know airplanes inside and out, from the type of doors all the way down to the engine-type and oh yeah, there are Rolls Royce engines on the 757 and General Electric engines on most of the 737s.

Tears cloud my eyes as the video comes to an emotional end. Our smiling faces signal the beginning of a long, easy road because yes, this is the easiest and the best job in the world. Where else but here can you spend one night lounging on the beach in Cancun and hitting the slopes in Park City the next? We never imagined that an event as horrific as September 11th would test our love for this industry. Eddie told me the silence and the emptiness and the paranoia rang rampant when he got on the plane Friday. If one person got up to use the restroom, all eyes were on them. He said simple things we take for granted like getting up to stretch prompted suspicious stares. This industry will never be the same. Our lives as we know them will never be the same. But, I put America's problems on the altar and I put my faith in God. Although there were talks of a "second wave" of attacks, I wasn't going to let that scare me.

When Sunday came around I got on a flight that had ten people on the whole plane, I'm talking about a five-person crew and five passengers, who all sat in first class. Our crew briefing was different, with the Captain having zero tolerance. Any action that aroused suspicion was grounds for expulsion. We made up a code word in order to get into the flight deck because the terrorists knew the other one, which I might add, hadn't been updated in the last 14 years. Our first destination was Phoenix, then back to Houston and tonight we'd end up in Norfolk, Virginia for two days and play everything by ear.

***

I got a bolt of energy the next morning and went downstairs to the workout facility to unleash it. The air that morning was crisp and cold. After warming up for five minutes, I was on the treadmill in my cute little Nike outfit running as fast as my long legs could take me. In my mind, I was running to New York to rescue as many people as I could from underneath the debris. Then I walked across water to Afghanistan, Pakistan, and Iraq and hell hath no fury like mine as I wiped out all the terrorists. I took no prisoners in my conquest. Tears came to my eyes because I wished it were that easy. Revenge is always easy to seek out but my experience last Friday night taught me those battles were better left up to God to fight. My legs were sore but I kept on running until my chest began to burn inside and sweat started trickling down my spine like rain drops.

Just as I was leaving, Jack, our Captain, was walking inside.

"Hi Jack."

"You can't leave just yet," he said.

"I must, I've been at this for an hour now."

"Okay, but don't forget lunch downstairs at noon."

"I won't forget," I said, drying my forehead and running up the six flights of stairs instead of taking the elevator.

***

I was surprised but the entire crew met downstairs for lunch. We walked next door to the shopping center to a steakhouse with a view of the Norfolk Harbor. I ordered soup and salad and enjoyed the afternoon with my crew. Jack, our Captain, was a 20-year veteran and a commuter from Denver. Victor, the first officer, was a handsome chestnut-colored brother and a commuter from Dallas. He and the Captain didn't see eye-to-eye on a few things politically but they coexisted like true professionals. The other flight attendants, Leslie and Tina, are senior to me. This is Leslie's 12th year and Tina's 8th.

Of course, the lunch topic concerned the events that happened last Tuesday. Jack, our Captain, lost all cool points with me when he said, "shoot them all and sort out the rest later."

"You've got to be kidding?" I reply.

"No. I'm not." He replies sternly, "They used innocent people as targets. It's time-out for tactics. It's an all out war and if Bush and his boys don't put an end to it, this country will never see the light of day."

"They're just jealous of the freedoms we have," Tina adds, as she butters a piece of her honey wheat roll.

Throughout the conversations, Victor and I give each other knowing looks. For example; when Tina, Leslie, and Jack talk about the freedoms we have in America, I can't help but think of how black people make up 12% of the regular population and over 50% of the prison population. We listen and listen and I add a little input here and there. Victor gives his opinion and whenever he opens his mouth, Jack always comes back with a rebuttal but Victor ultimately ends up with the last word and a comment that just blows us girls away.

I find it very funny and this has happened only one other time, but whenever there is an attractive looking brother and an attractive looking sister on a trip, someone is always trying to play matchmaker. Leslie and Tina kept nudging me and making eyes at me.

"He's cute," Leslie keeps repeating, and he is. Victor

has a smile that brightens up an already bright room but right now I'm not trying to get involved. I have the interests of my daughter to be contented with. And, as far as Dewayne is concerned, it is over.

"You two make a cute couple."

"I'm sure we do. We're both attractive people," I say, speaking for Victor.

"Well turn the attraction to each other," Leslie says as she curls her tongue over her lips.

Victor and I laugh and give each other those knowing stares. I'm sure every time he flies with an attractive black female flight attendant somebody is always trying to match him up. He has no rings and black male pilots are a dime a dozen anyway at Worldwide.

After lunch we all take a ride on the steamboat ferry and travel across the Harbor to the small town of Portsmouth, Virginia. Small boutiques, book and antique shops make up the majority of this predominately black town.

"I could live in a small town like this," Victor says as we stroll quietly along the narrow streets.

"It's nice and quaint, I bet you can sleep with the windows up at night and not worry about a thing."

"I bet. It seems like this place is light years away from the confusion and pandemonium in D.C. and New York."

The clicking of our shoes against the cobblestone and the chirping of birds overhead, coupled with the wisp of the wind, seemed as if it agreed with us. I wish I could cut out this moment and keep it on the mantle of my fireplace. There we were, the five of us, walking down the street and stopping to admire everything from an oversized chair all the way down to a grave marker of a baby girl in a small, well-kept cemetery. This town has a lot of history and on my days off I'm going to bring my daughter back to see this place.

Las Vegas Style

It didn't take very long before everyone was back to normal. That first week after everything happened you couldn't pay some people to get on an airplane. Myself included. On the day it happened, Mad Lew and I were at home knocking over furniture and leaving scratch marks on his baby grand piano. When we finally turned on the TV, we had been high after smoking weed and we started tripping.

"What the fuck is that?" I remember Mad Lew frowning at the television. "that looks real…wait a minute…that is real…what in the fuck is going on?"

When Mad Lew turned on his two cell phones, his pager, and two-way, he had close to 20 messages on each. When I finally found my cell phone I saw where Whitney had left five messages. When I called her back she cried like she lost her best friend. Poor thing. I couldn't wait to see her and give her a big chick hug to let her know that I was okay.

But back to what I was saying about the passengers. The first week following the attacks, people were so nice it was unreal. I mean the empty planes and the politeness were too much for this Bronx girl to bear and the moment I got on the plane this morning I literally grabbed this woman and gave her a hug when she insisted I hang up her coat in the first class closet even though she was sitting in coach.

"Yes, yes, yes!" I screamed.

She and the people around her including Whitney thought I was nuts.

"Why did you do that?" Whitney asks, her eyes demanding an explanation.

"Because she was a bitch and guess what? I like that!"

Whitney shook her head in disbelief and proceeded to take my drink orders for predeparture. It was good to see her and she looked happy although things weren't so good at home. Her ex, Dewayne, was on the street full time and Whitney lost her apartment. She told me she didn't renew her lease but I know better, she probably couldn't pay the rent. Dewayne's father and his brothers were still in jail and the money that she used to get from them during Dewayne's incarceration was down to pennies, shit, probably nothing, to tell the truth.

On the other hand, things looked good for me. I finally got the hell out of Texas and out of the townhome Walter, Sr. had me in and moved into Mad Lew's place. The transition was simple because I'm always looking for the best opportunity. When I gave Walter, Sr. the keys, he told me that I was a special person and he was glad that I was moving on but sad that he wouldn't be able to see me anymore. He looked like he was hungry for one last piece of the Latina Mamacita. I gave him the keys to the house and the car and a simple peck on the cheek.

"So you found another man with money?" he asked, cynically.

Hell yeah! So what if I wasn't with him anymore? He didn't have to know everything.

"I'm just moving on, I want a new change of scenery."

For some reason, I felt he didn't believe a word I was saying.

***

There was an hour left before the start of the New Year and I couldn't wait. Neither could Eddie and Whitney, who were rushing me to get dressed so we could go to Caesar's Palace.

"Why are you so slow?" Eddie asks.

"Why are you so fast?" I replied. "Damn!"

I didn't bother to go into the other room to change

clothes. I stripped down to my underwear in front of Eddie and Whitney. Whitney's seen me partially nude before and Eddie thinks he has the same thing I have, mentally.

"Roxy, have you gained weight?" Whitney asked, looking at my stomach.

The silence that followed and my blushing gave it away.

"Oh no," she said, her eyes dancing back and forth between my eyes and my stomach.

"Oh yes."

"Who's is it?" she asks.

"Kenny's."

"You mean Mad Lew?"

"Yes."

"Oh look at her, she's just gloating," Eddie adds.

"How far along are you?" Whitney asks.

"Three months."

"And you weren't going to say anything to us about it?" Whitney asks.

"I just didn't want to feel like I was rubbing it in your face. You know, with all the stuff going on with you and Dewayne."

"Rubbing it in my face? No, you weren't rubbing it in my face." She glanced at Eddie.

"Well I'm due in June and I want you to be my baby's Godmother. Eddie, I want you to be the baby's..."

"Fairy Godmother?" Eddie replied, before I could get it out.

"Yes, you can be the Fairy Godmother."

"You are so silly," Whitney began.

"And Whitney, I'll try not to rub it in your face." Eddie tapped her on the shoulder and blinked his eyes in an exaggerated fashion.

"So Roxy, how did Mad Lew react when you told him?"

"He was happy. He kept rubbing and talking to my

stomach. He's excited because it's his first child."

"That you know of, right?" Eddie asked.

I gave him the bird.

When I looked at myself in the mirror, I was flawless. I wasn't out to here, but I could tell and others that knew me well could tell that I was pregnant. My breasts were getting bigger. As a matter of fact my cleavage was so ample, my breasts actually jiggled when I walked and I was wearing a bra. My ass was already rotund and the hip-huggers I was wearing made it stand out and salute.

"You know when I have this baby I'm quitting Worldwide," I said, gathering the surprise reactions from the two.

Whitney nodded her head and gave me this knowing smile.

"What?" I replied, like I didn't know what was on her mind.

"Don't act innocent."

"I'm serious, why are you smiling?"

"Your behind knew what you were doing when you got pregnant."

"Let's just say I saw an opportunity and took advantage of it."

Eddie and Whitney let out a huge guffaw. They were rolling on the bed for a minute.

Then Eddie stood up, "I have to give it to you Roxy; you really seized an opportunity and I wish you a happy and healthy pregnancy. By the way, do you know what you're having?"

"I don't want to know, all I want is for this baby to be healthy." I rubbed my stomach.

"Come on, Mommy." Whitney grabbed my hand, "let's bring in the New Year Las Vegas style."

***

When we walked inside Caesar's Palace the place was ringing and dinging with jovial gamblers emptying buckets of coins into the nickel, quarter, and dollar slot machines. The place sounded like a bell factory. I can't imagine working in a place like this, I would go crazy hearing bells. The high rollers were at the black jack table with a small crowd of spectators behind them and a few people were gathered around the roulette table.

"Are y'all drinkin' tonight?" I ask.

"I don't know," Whitney responded.

"I may settle for a virgin daquiri, myself," Eddie added.

"What do you mean you don't know?" I asked Whitney before giving her and Eddie the gold access passes Mad Lew's manager had given me.

"You know me, I always have to feel like I'm in control."

"One drink isn't going to hurt."

We got on an elevator and I pressed the button for the 30th floor. Mad Lew was throwing a New Year's Eve party for a small crowd of 250. Security was frisking us down as soon as we got off the elevator. They didn't care if we had access badges.

"You know who I am," I said to the guy who must've been about 7 feet tall.

I flashed my badge with Mad Lew's face and his manager's name. Whitney and Eddie followed my lead.

He stood aside and opened his tree trunks called arms and allowed us to go inside the double doors leading to the suite. Mad Lew had the entire 30th floor leased out, not to mention a list of Who's Who performing tonight.

When we walked inside the crowded suite the guests were already counting down from seven. I searched the room over for Mad Lew because I wanted to be by his side by the time it got to one. Instead, when twelve o'clock came, I found myself embracing the only two people I called friends. As far as I was concerned they were more like family, I couldn't ask for a better group of people.

"You guys have a seat, I'm going to see if I can find Mad Lew!" I shouted over the band's funky rendition of Auld Lang Syne. I danced my way through the crowd until I heard a rich familiar voice that sounded like music resonating through my ears, "RAISE YOUR HANDS IN THE AIR, AND WAVE THEM LIKE YOU JUST DON'T CARE, AND IF '02 IS YO' YEAR TO GET YOUR FREAK ON, EVERYBODY SAY OH YEAH!"

Of course both male and screeching female voices shouted in unison, "OH YEAH!"

Mad Lew's massive physique was on the small stage with a bottle of Cristal in one hand and a cigar in the other. I made myself visible and it didn't take long before he was off the stage and in my arms.

"Happy New Year!" he shouted.

"Happy New Year back to you!" I shouted.

"Where are your friends?" he asked.

"They're here but they found a spot to sit down."

"I reserved a spot for you and your friends over here," he said, pointing to an area that was roped off. "Just chill there for now. Are we hungry?" he asked, rubbing my stomach.

"Yes. We are." I smiled back at him.

"Sit down and I'll have someone take care of that."

Whitney and Eddie joined me at the table and minutes later we downed shrimp cocktails for appetizers. Whitney was full on the shrimp and the Perrier while Eddie and I pigged out on prime rib and veggies.

"I can't remember the last time I saw you eat this much," Eddie told me.

"I'm pregnant, dammit. What do you expect?" I stuck a forkful of mashed potatoes in my mouth.

"I remember we used to pig out at Luby's in initial training," Whitney said, with this reminiscent shine in her eyes.

"Oh yeah, I didn't know what a chicken fried steak

was until I met you guys," I said, with the same reminiscent shine in my eyes. I can still taste the creamy gravy.

"Eddie, remember when your mother made us a pot of seafood gumbo?" I asked. Since becoming pregnant I have become fixated on food. Not junk food, but the good shit.

"I'll get her to make another one especially for you," he said, reading my mind.

"Thank you Fairy Godmother." I gave him a peck on the cheek and rubbed away the plum-colored lip marks I left on his jaw.

The entertainment was incredible. There was a fire-eater who entertained us along with a quartet of male R & B singers from Mad Lew's label who dazzled us with hit after hit from their platinum debut CD.

"Jerry, the lead singer, is cute and he's available," I told Whitney. She seemed blasé and not very interested in him and told us that she had been seeing this guy who was a pilot with Worldwide.

Eddie's eyes widened.

"No, it's not Scottie," Whitney clarified it quickly.

"Is he white?" I asked.

"No, he's a brother."

"He's not married is he?" I asked.

"No."

"Is he gay?" Eddie added.

"Hell no." Whitney rolls her eyes.

"How long have you been seeing him?" I ask.

"Three months."

"Oh," I leaned forward. I wanted to find out more about this pilot, "So is he a lot of fun?"

"Yeah, for our first date we took our kids to Celebration Station."

"Why?" I asked.

"I wanted our children to meet one another. I wanted to meet his 10 year-old daughter and he wanted to meet my child, so we spent an afternoon playing put-put golf, riding go-carts and eating pizza."

I rested my hand on my chin, "So you think you guys are serious?"

"I think so."

"Good, anybody is better than that crackhead Dewayne."

Whitney remained silent. I took it as a cue to move on to a different subject. "So Eddie, what's happening in your life?"

"I'm on the market." I noticed his doe like eyes staring in a dream-like state at the guys on stage.

"Come on you guys, lets dance." I took their hands and we danced to the quartet's version of the classic, Ain't No Stopping Us Now. And there wasn't. I was glad to be celebrating 2002 with my friends and oh yeah, I couldn't forget my *babydaddy*.

About the Author

T. Wendy Williams is the author of *I Laugh to Keep from Crying* as well as a flight attendant. She is a native of Huntsville, Texas and a 1996 graduate of Sam Houston State University. She is also the president and founder of Nia Publishing. Ms. Williams currently resides in Houston, Texas where she is at work on her third novel.

You can order your copy of **Confessions from the Jumpseat** to share with your family and friends. To order, send your check or money order for $12.00 plus shipping and handling payable **to T. Wendy Williams**:

P. O. Box 228
5315-D FM 1960 West
Houston, TX 77069-4410

832-541-4989
twendywilliams@yahoo.com

Name______________________________________

Address____________________________________

City____________________State__________Zip________

Number of Books:______________X $12.00 = $_________.

Texas Residents add 8.25% sales tax ($.99ea) $_________.

Shipping:__________X $2.00 per book $_________.

TOTAL $_________.

Please allow 4 to 6 weeks for delivery